STREET ROD

STREET ROD

By Henry Gregor Felsen

RANDOM HOUSE • NEW YORK

Seventeenth Printing

Copyright 1953 by Henry Gregor Felsen

All rights reserved under International and
Pan-American Copyright Conventions

Published in New York by Random House, Inc.
and simultaneously in Toronto, Canada by
Random House of Canada Ltd.

Library of Congress Catalog Card Number: 53-5030

Manufactured in the U. S. A.

To my fellow members of the
Iowa Timing Association

This manuscript is being mailed from Des Moines on Friday afternoon, January 16, 1953. By the time it reaches its destination in New York on Monday morning, a grim percentage calls for two teen-agers to die in auto accidents in Iowa, for half a dozen to be injured, and a score to be arrested.

Galley proofs of the manuscript will be mailed back to me in three months. In that time another fifty-one boys and girls under twenty-one are scheduled to die by the automobile in Iowa, 150 to be injured, and several hundred to be arrested.

If the printing schedule permits, this book will be published sometime in July. Between the time it is mailed today as a manuscript, and read by the first purchaser as a book, perhaps 150 young people will have died in this state by the automobile, close to 500 been injured and maimed, and a thousand or more arrested, fined, jailed, or deprived of their licenses.

Is there an answer, a way to reduce the toll of young lives that a motorized civilization collects as the price of transportation?

There is no answer, no way to stop the accidents.

There are answers, and there are ways. Some of them are written about here.

H. G. F.

STREET ROD

1

Ricky Madison, sixteen, sat at the Dellville Drug soda fountain, slowly sipping a warm Coke through a straw. His elbows rested on the counter, his palms supporting—and hiding—his thin brown face.

The others stood behind him carrying their swimming suits wrapped in towels, looking impatiently at the curve of his lean back.

"Come on, Rick," Link Aller ordered harshly. "We ain't got all day."

Ricky kept his head bent over the Coke, his brown eyes focused on the last tiny piece of ice in the glass. He spoke without lifting his mouth from the straw. "I told you I wasn't going."

"Why not?"

"I *told* you. I don't want to go."

"Aaaaaa . . ." Link lifted his fist as though to hit

Ricky in disgust, but merely pushed his straight black hair back from his narrow, sullen face.

Chub Turner punched Ricky's arm playfully. He was a round-faced, pink-cheeked fat boy. "Don't be crazy," he coaxed. "Everybody wants to go swimming on a hot day like this. It's human nature."

"You guys can go," Ricky said without turning. "You don't need me."

"We know that, big shot," Link said, his dark face showing his annoyance. "We're just asking, that's all."

"I know you're asking," Ricky said, doing his best to sound insulting. "You've asked about ten times and I've said no about eleven times. What do you keep bothering me for?"

"Oh . . . bull!" Chub said tiredly, looking for something to kick. "Here we go through the same old routine again."

Chub began pacing up and down. Link stood staring at Ricky's back as though he wanted to attack him. Jerry Long, a well-knit, handsome boy with wavy red-dish-brown hair, stood by the door talking to the four girls who were going. Big Sherm Lucas was the only one who took no part in the argument. As usual his husky body was perched on a counter stool as he lost himself in following the plot of a comic-book story. The girls looked bored.

"We don't have to ask you," Link said to Ricky's back. "We're just trying to do you a favor."

"Any time I want any favors from you," Ricky said, "I'll ask."

"For crying out loud, Rick," Chub complained. "Us

4

guys have always stuck together. What do you want to bust things up for now?"

Ricky sipped at his Coke without answering. The more they argued with him, the worse he felt.

Jerry left the girls and went to Ricky's side. "Ride with me, Rick," he said quietly.

Ricky spun around on the stool, his brown eyes hot with anger. "I don't want to ride with *anybody!*" he yelled. "Can't you get that through your thick heads? Why don't you leave me alone? If I want to go swimming I can get there by myself!"

The fellows were silent. They knew what was wrong with Ricky, but there wasn't anything they could do to help. They understood, and they didn't mind.

Ricky looked toward the girls. Everyone had asked him to go swimming but Sharon Bruce. The one person he would have said yes to. She stood by the door dressed in white shorts and a white T-shirt, carrying a white towel. Her arms and legs were tanned dusky by the sun, her hair was light brown, her wide eyes gray-green. There was a sprinkle of light freckles across the tip of her small straight nose, her teeth were white and even, her lower lip soft and full. Ricky would do anything for her she asked. But she never asked. The way she acted, it was as though he didn't exist. She looked over him, around him, through him. But never at him. It drove him wild.

"Rick," Link Aller said slowly, wanting his words to hurt, "if you want a car of your own so bad, why don't you buy one?"

"You know why . . ." Ricky began in an aggrieved tone.

"Nuts," Link said. "We've heard that excuse a million times."

"My folks won't . . ." Ricky said defensively, trying to keep up his argument.

"Do what I did," Link challenged, moving closer to Ricky. "When I wanted a car I just said I was going to have one. My old man said I couldn't have it. So I told him if I couldn't have one at home, I'd leave home, find a job and buy one anyway. He didn't want me to leave, so I got the car. It takes guts, that's all."

"I've got guts," Ricky muttered. "But it's different than you think."

"Yeah," Link said. "I'm me and you're you, that's the difference. I never let my old man push me around, that's all. You could leave home and get a job if you had to. All you've got to do is stand up for your rights, and you'd have your way. Try it once. Come on, guys."

Link walked out and the others followed. Jerry paused at Ricky's side a moment, as though to ask Ricky once more to ride along, but the look on Ricky's face made him change his mind. "See you later, Rick," he said, and went on.

"Yeah," Ricky answered bitterly. "Sure."

The screen door banged closed after them. Ricky turned and put his head in his hands, listening. He heard the car doors slam, and then, one by one the motors started. He knew them by heart. They all carried straight pipes, but there was a difference in the way each motor sounded, a difference that was under the deep, powerful roar. He listened, riding with them as they backed away from the curb, turned, and thundered away toward the lake without him.

Now he was sorry he hadn't gone. He wanted to swim, why had he refused? It wasn't the first time he'd sat around and made them coax him, but it was the first time he hadn't given in. He'd never give in again. Even if it meant he didn't have any friends. He'd hung around with Link and Chub and Jerry and Sherm since they'd been in kindergarten, but there was no sense kidding himself. It was different now. They had their own rods, and he—had his bike.

No, if he couldn't keep up with them as an equal, he wasn't going to hang around with them, that was all. Always needing charity, and depending on somebody else for transportation. That wasn't any way to be.

Ricky got up and went to the magazine rack, looking for something new to read. He was a slender boy, with a thin face, brown eyes, and straight brown hair. He wore a pair of run-over moccasins, denim pants faded almost white at the knees, and a yellow seersucker sports shirt. He was getting tall, and hadn't learned to carry his height straight up. His favorite position was a half-slouch, with his thumbs hooked in his wide leather belt.

He found what he wanted and carried it back to where he had been sitting. It was a magazine about sports cars. Ricky's heart almost burst with longing as he looked at the lucky people who posed in their Jag-

7

uars, Cunninghams, Nash Healeys, Lancias, Allards and Ferraris.

He looked closely at every picture, and read every word about specifications and performance data, although he already knew most of the information by heart. And as he went from car to car, he carried in his mind a picture of the dream car that he would build some day. A car that incorporated all the best features of all the cars. He'd have everything right, and under one hood. The most beautiful car in the world.

It would have sweeping fender lines, and white leather, and an instrument panel that held every instrument he needed to record every detail of his motor's performance as he drove.

Someday, with his own hands he would design and build that car. A car that would shame anything Detroit ever turned out, that would make other custom jobs look sick. Someday he'd make up for being the only one of the guys who didn't have his own car. Someday he'd show them all.

The screen door at the front of the drug store squeaked as it was pulled open. Ricky looked up quickly, with hope in his heart that they had come back for him, yet ready to refuse again. But hope died as he recognized the familiar bulk coming through the doorway. It was only Arnie VanZuuk, the fat old man who had been Dellville's police force for thirty years.

Fat, good-natured Arnie, with his tremendous belly, his square face, and the clear blue eyes that looked out through ridiculously tiny rimless glasses. Arnie in his usual uniform. Shiny blue pants, a gray shirt open at the neck and soaked dark with sweat, a blue police cap that perched on top of his head, and, almost hidden by the overhang of his huge belly, his belt and gun.

Arnie waddled across the floor and leaned against the counter next to Ricky, blowing and snorting like a hippo just coming up for air. He wiped his face with a red bandana. "Hot," he said hoarsely. There was no complaint in his voice. He said it like news.

"It's good weather for corn," Ricky said, suddenly angry. "That's all you hear every time it gets too hot for people. Good for the corn. You'd think there wasn't anybody else in Iowa but farmers."

Arnie reached across the counter, got a glass, and filled it with carbonated water. He drank slowly, put down his glass and exhaled heavily, a faint spray coming from his lips.

"You're the only one in town," Arnie said.

"You're telling *me?*"

"Everybody gone to swim?"

Ricky nodded, thinking about the lake, seeing the others splashing around in the water. Jerry on the diving board, showing off his body control. Chub asking everybody to time how long he could stay under water, and getting mad because he was fat and floated to the surface. Sherm taking it easy, dreaming in the water with his eyes half-closed as he floated on his back.

The girls would be having fun too, making a ritual of anointing one another with sun-tan oil, giggling as they declined help from the boys. Then lying in the sun with the tops of their bathing suits rolled down as far as they dared. And when they went in the water the boys would be after them, grabbing them by the legs and pulling them under. Link Aller not knowing when to quit, grabbing too hard, hurting, until somebody got mad at him. But they would all be friends again on the way home.

"Lucky young people," Arnie sighed. "You don't go to swim?"

"No car," Ricky said.

"You could ride with the others."

Ricky looked at the floor. "A guy can't be a car suck all the time."

"It shouldn't be hard on a day like this," Arnie said, chuckling.

"One of these days," Ricky said grimly, "I'm geting me a car of my own. I've got the money."

Arnie took off his police cap and wiped his forehead. "Your papa will let you have a car? I don't think so, Ricky."

The moment the words were out Arnie felt like kicking himself. He saw Ricky wince, and the stubborn, defiant look that came into his eyes.

"Maybe I won't ask him," Ricky said, thinking of what Link had said, and how the others had agreed by the way they had looked. "I've got the money. I can leave home and get a job if I have to. I'm not a kid any more."

"You take my advice," Arnie said, hitching up his pants. "Save your money, stay home, and be some more a car suck. Later you can buy something good, not some piece of junk."

10

Ricky didn't answer, and Arnie walked out of the store, dreading the burning sun that awaited him.

Your papa won't let you. Arnie knew it, the guys knew it . . . *everybody* knew it. Other guys could own cars when they were sixteen. Other guys could be independent and go places when they wanted to. Other guys didn't have to stand around and hope they'd be asked to go along. Other guys had . . . guts.

Ricky turned back to his magazine. Ever since he could remember he had been crazy about cars. Even when he was a little kid he liked to sit and look at them and listen to the sound of their motors, and dream about the day when he would be driving his own car, speeding down the highway, passing everybody.

And now he was old enough to own a car, and all the other kids he hung around had cars, and he—he was still dreaming, and a car suck. Not any more though. He'd never step in a car again in his life until he had his own. He had the money, and he knew where there was a rod it could buy. All it took was his father's permission. Or . . . guts.

The siren at the fire station blew the long note of noon. Ricky got up and put his magazine away, and went outside, squinting as the bright sun hit against his eyes. Outside he paused, thumbs in his belt, for a slow look around.

At this hour of twelve the town was almost deserted. It was no time for farmers to be shopping,

11

women were home getting lunches ready, and just a few men were getting into their cars to drive home. Ricky watched them enviously. *If I only had a car.*

Dellville was built around a square. It wasn't a big square, but it had a bandstand that needed painting, grass, several large trees, and, in the shade of the trees, some benches. When Ricky looked at the square he saw the same old men on the benches he always saw there in good weather. It was as though the old men had been ordered, manufactured, and delivered as part of the bench. Each old man had his place, and would no sooner think of moving to another bench than he would think of trading his old pipe for a package of perfumed cigarettes.

Around the square were the usual stores. The drug store, the hardware store, the dime store, the combination city hall and jail, the clothing store, the movie house. On a corner, the small red bank where his father worked. The feed store, a grocery store. An empty store that had been used for a recreation center until it died because nobody wanted to hang around in an old store room with nothing to do but play checkers and cards. Filling stations. Stores. Awnings hanging limply in the heat. Even the barber shop empty, and the barber dozing in his own chair.

If I only had a car!

If he had a car he could escape. He could open the door and slide behind the wheel, turn the ignition key, punch the starter. There would be the throaty music of straight pipes—*he* wouldn't be caught with a conventional muffler—a smooth shift into reverse, back-ward motion into the center of the street.

And then!

Then a snap-shift into low, a heavy foot on the gas pedal. Tires screeching as he came around straight, almost on his hub caps, and headed down the street. Duals blasting and tires screeching, leaving rubber on the bricks. People swinging around to look at the sleek rod that was streaking down the street, chopping a corner like a track racer, flattening out, digging its nose down as he headed toward open country. Then the winding white highway, picking up speed as he moved in and out of turns, roaring, speeding, streaking, burning up the road as he hit peak rpm on his way to . . .

To where?

He relaxed the tense grip of his fingers on his belt. He kept his thumbs hooked to keep his hands from falling dispiritedly at his sides.

To where? It didn't have to be to anywhere. Just to ride around and be free and equal and *know* he could go anywhere. That's what counted. Not to be a kid any more. To be one of the guys who could get to wherever he was going under his own power, and not have to stand around waiting to see who'd ask him to ride along. To be equal, that was where.

The front door of the bank opened and Ricky saw his father come out on his way home to lunch. Ricky started toward him, meeting him halfway and, turning, fell in step with his father.

"Sure is hot, isn't it, Son?" Mr. Madison greeted Ricky.

"Sure is, Dad."

They walked along the bright hot street, anxious to get away from the square to the side streets, where Dellville's big trees would give them shade. Mr. Madison stepped along briskly, nodding to almost everyone they met. As cashier of the bank he knew everybody in and around Dellville, and he knew as much about their affairs as the local doctor. Sometimes more.

He was a slightly built man, not quite as tall as Ricky, with thinning hair and a sharp, but friendly, face. He dressed neatly, carrying the exactness of his work into his private habits. Even on this hot day he wore a tan summer suit, white shirt and tie. He looked fresh and unwrinkled, his white shoes were clean, his light summer hat unsmudged.

"I hope Mom has a cool lunch today," Mr. Madison said as they crossed a street. He touched Ricky's arm lightly and protectively, as though to guide him across safely. "I'm in the mood for a good salad. Try to straighten up, Son. Your posture isn't at all good."

"I'll try, Dad," Ricky said, slouching along, his moccasins dragging.

"Doing anything interesting today?" Ricky's father asked.

"Not much."

Ricky's father glanced at him quickly as he caught the dullness of Ricky's response. He noticed the sullen, beaten look on Ricky's face, and the flat look in his eyes.

"Nothing bad happened, I hope."

"Nothing."

They walked on a bit in silence. "Sure is hot," Mr. Madison said again. "I'd think you'd be swimming on a day like this. I saw your friends driving out toward the lake. Didn't you want to go along?"

"Sure I wanted to," Ricky said. "Who wouldn't?"

"Why didn't you go? You didn't have a fight with them or anything, did you?"

"No. There wasn't any fight. They asked me to go along."

"I'm glad they did. Why didn't you go?"

Ricky lifted his head for a moment and then looked down again. "I didn't have any way to get there."

"But they . . . Now look here, Ricky, there's no sense going into a tantrum because you can't have a car. That's all you're doing, acting like this."

"Why can't I have a car?" Ricky burst out. "I'm old enough to get a license. Gee whiz, if the state thinks I'm big enough to drive, why can't I have a car?"

"We've gone over that before. First of all, you don't need a car. Secondly, you're saving your money for college. And thirdly, I don't think you should have a car. It's too dangerous. When boys your age buy old cars and soup them up, somebody gets killed sooner or later. I think too much of you to let you kill yourself in some foolish, needless accident."

"But I'll be careful!"

"Even if you are, others are careless. At your age, you don't understand what caution really is. You *can't* be careful enough. I know that."

"Other guys my age have cars," Ricky said. "I can be just as careful as they can."

"That's what I'm afraid of," his father said. "No, Ricky, I'm not impressed by what other guys do. If other guys jump off a roof is that any reason why I should let you do it?"

Ricky lifted his hand and pushed back his hair. He was shaking. "You're just not being fair, that's all," he stammered. "Not fair. You won't let me have a car, but you think it's all right to ride with the other guys in *their* cars."

"To be frank, Ricky, I don't approve of the others having cars either. But . . ."

"But they *have* them! They *have* them. And you yourself said I should have gone with them! You just don't think I'm as good as they are or something! You don't know what it's like to be called a car suck!"

"Let's not have a public argument," Mr. Madison said, glancing around. "There's no reason why we can't settle this quietly. Who called you a car suck?"

"Nobody to my face," Ricky said. "But that's what everybody calls a guy like me. A guy who always has to suck for a ride and can't get around in his own car."

"If the boys feel that way, you aren't forced to associate with them."

"No, I guess not," Ricky said bitterly. "I can give up all my friends and go play in the sand pile with the rest of the little kids."

"You don't have to be sarcastic, Ricky. I'm just trying to help you look at the problem reasonably."

16

"It's not a question of reason," Ricky said. "Either you're one of the guys or you're not. That's all."

"I think we're both a little too hot and too hungry to discuss the question," Ricky's father said as they neared home. "We'll talk about it some other time."

They walked on quietly until they turned in at the big white house with the spacious lawn where they lived. It was a high square house, with a big front and back porch, a double garage behind the house, and an outdoor fireplace that Ricky had helped his father build. A white fence enclosed house and yard.

"You've done a nice job of mowing," Mr. Madison said. "We'll have to get out with the 2,4-D and get at those dandelions. We could keep them under control if the neighbors would cooperate."

"I'll get at them," Ricky said. "I don't have anything else to do."

"I said we'd talk it over later," Mr. Madison said. "Whatever we decide, it won't help if you go around with a long face feeling sorry for yourself. You're not the *only* boy in the world who doesn't own a car."

Ricky didn't answer, but went in the house and went upstairs to wash.

"I wonder if he thinks I'm old enough to turn on the water by myself," Ricky said savagely as he twisted the faucets. The water came out with a rush, hitting the curved bottom of the lavatory and splashing on the floor. Ricky turned off the flow and washed his hands with a vicious, fighting action. Then he dried them and went out, ignoring the water splashed on the floor.

17

Ricky took his place at the table in the dining room and looked critically at the lunch his mother had prepared. There was a big salad full of lettuce, sliced tomatoes, sliced hard-boiled eggs, celery and young onions. A bowl of creamed soup was at his place. There were crackers, bread and butter, and a tall glass of milk.

"Don't we have any meat?" Ricky called out at his mother.

"This is an excellent lunch, Ricky," his father said. "It has everything you need in the way of vitamins and all that. You don't need meat on a day like this."

"Well." Ricky sat with his hands in his lap, staring at the food with distaste. "That's something else I can do without. It doesn't look like I need *anything* I want."

"Ricky, you're acting like an eight-year-old."

Ricky's mother came in from the kitchen. She was wearing a white blouse and a full yellow skirt with a peasant design around the hem. She had brown eyes like Ricky's, brown hair cut short, and a smooth, clear skin. She looked young even to Ricky.

"What's the argument about?" she asked brightly, sitting at the table.

Ricky's father tried to make light of the situation. "Ricky wants a hot rod for lunch," he said, smiling at Ricky.

Ricky didn't smile back. Nor did he make any attempt to eat.

"Cars . . . again? . . ." Ricky's mother buttered a

18

cracker. "I thought we had that settled long ago. No car for two years, when you're eighteen."

Ricky sat staring at his soup. Well, Link Aller *had* put it up to him. *Link* had delivered an ultimatum. Link had . . . guts. All the other guys had managed it somehow. Why couldn't he?

"I want my car now," Ricky said, his mouth dry. "I don't want to wait two years."

"You'll have to," his mother said. "Please pass the salad, Ricky. And drink your milk."

This was it. This was the time. Ricky kept staring at his soup, listening to his own words as though hearing a stranger speaking.

"I'm not going to be treated like a little kid any more," he said, squeezing his hands together under the table. "I want a car. If I can't have one I'll . . ."

"You'll what, Ricky? And pass the salt, please."

He said it slowly. "I'll leave home. I can get a job and support myself. I'll buy my own car and be my own boss."

He waited for the explosion, but none came. He looked up. His parents were calmly eating. It made him furious. They considered him so much of a kid they didn't take anything he said seriously. He pushed back his chair, scraping the floor.

"What kind of a job are you taking?" his father asked.

"Any kind!"

"How does it pay? It won't be easy, supporting yourself and a car, you know."

19

"You're making fun of me!" Ricky said hotly. Other parents didn't sit around eating when something like this happened. They shouted back and ordered and got mad and finally gave in. That's the way it had been with the other guys. Other parents didn't make a joke out of it.

"We're not making fun of you," Ricky's father said. "We're trying to help you. If you feel you can't live here any longer, we can't keep you here. But you're still our son, and we're still concerned with your welfare. If you strike out for yourself, we want you to know where you're going. Right, Mother?"

"Right. Where do you intend looking for work?"

"I don't know yet," Ricky said sullenly.

"What kind of work can you do?" his father asked.

"I'll do anything," Ricky answered.

"That's rather vague. How will you live until you get a job?"

"I've got my fifty dollars."

"That will go pretty fast. And once you have to support yourself, you won't have much left to buy a car with, will you?"

"I don't know," Ricky said, feeling cornered. "I don't know. I'll find a way."

"If you stay home," his mother said, "you'll have a car in two years. That might be sooner than you could buy one if you lived by yourself. Think of it that way."

"Suppose you get a job and a car," his father said. "Then what? Your life is just beginning, you know. Are you going to make that your goal in life . . . any

20

kind of a job and any kind of an old car? What about your future? About college?"

"We're not trying to stop you, dear," Ricky's mother said, leaning over to pat his hand. "We just want you to be realistic. If you decide to leave home, we want to be sure you're aware of the problems you'll face, and that you'll be prepared to meet them."

Ricky stared at them helplessly. They did it so easily, so effectively. They didn't storm or rant or fight with him. They smiled and acted helpful and interested, and when they were through "helping" him he was licked. It had always happened that way; it was that way now. His revolt had fizzled out, his threat to leave home had been sweet-talked to death. They'd shown him up for what he really was, a big, gutless kid!

"Eat your lunch, Ricky," his mother said gently.

He looked at her, hating the love and tenderness he saw in her eyes. "I'm not hungry," he muttered. "I don't want anything. I'd like to be excused."

He got up and put his chair back in its place at the table and walked away, head down, thumbs hooked in his belt, his moccasions dragging.

"Try to straighten up, Ricky," his father called after him. "Your posture is getting terrible."

The front door slammed Ricky's answer.

For a moment after Ricky left his parents were silent. Then his mother sighed and spoke. "I think we handled that rather well, don't you?"

"About as well as it could be handled," Ricky's father said. "He was spoiling for an argument. I guess the trick is to agree with those wild schemes until he sees for himself how fantastic they are."

Mrs. Madison went into the living room and returned carrying a large book. She put it on the table next to her plate and leafed through it. "This psychology book has certainly earned its keep in this house," she said. "It says here the important thing to remember is to never argue with children. Once you let them get you in an argument you descend to their level, and you lose all authority."

"Those people certainly have it all down to a science," Mr. Madison said, nodding toward the book. "It takes a lot of guesswork out of being a parent."

"The way he sat there and pouted," Mrs. Madison said, looking through the book. "I think you would call that a symptom of regression as goal-motivated behavior. Wouldn't you say so?"

"It could be," Ricky's father said. "Still and all, though, Ricky has a point."

"What's that?"

"Well," Mr. Madison said, toying with a spoon, "we forbid him to have a car, but we allow him to ride with his friends, who aren't any older than he is. It's as though we trust them, but not him."

"I don't trust them at all," Mrs. Madison said. "I wish he'd stop riding around with them."

"Shall we forbid him to? If we don't, it makes us look like hypocrites in his eyes."

Ricky's mother shook her head. "We can't expect him to give up the friends he's had all his life, even if we don't approve of everything they do."

"He's giving them up. They wanted him to go swimming with them today, but he wouldn't go. He told me he was through being a car suck."

"A *what?*"

"A car suck," Mr. Madison said, grinning. "That's the boy who has to mooch rides from his friends if he wants to go where they're going. Ricky said if he had to be that, he wouldn't go any more."

"He'll change his mind," Ricky's mother said.

"Not Ricky. You know how stubborn he can be if he really works at it."

Mrs. Madison glanced at her book. "Schweinkopf says it's emotionally damaging for a child to feel that he isn't a part of his group. If Ricky feels that way, it could have a bad effect on his mental attitude toward life."

"That's the way he feels," Madison said.

"If he only had different friends, with different ideals and interests. . . ." Mrs. Madison began.

"He said he could play in the sand pile with the kindergarten kids."

"What *are* we supposed to do?"

"I don't know," Ricky's father said. "I'm afraid he'll be hurt or killed if he starts driving around in a hot rod. On the other hand, he is riding with other boys. Or was. If we don't let him have his car, he'll quit being a part of his group. They'll grow away from him, and there's nothing to take their place. There might be if we lived in a city, but this is Dellville. I know cars are dangerous, but I don't want Ricky going around feeling he's inferior to the others."

"He's not inferior. If he'd only realize that he's blown this car thing up way beyond its real importance. . . ."

They looked at each other across the table, feeling the same helplessness Ricky had known a few minutes before.

"It's so dangerous," Ricky's mother said. "He might be hurt . . . or killed."

"That's the chance we take every time he leaves the house," Mr. Madison said. "We held off getting his bike for the same reason, remember?"

"A bike is different. It isn't so dangerous."

"We didn't think so when he first wanted one. We felt the same way we feel about the car now."

"We can't protect him from everything," Ricky's mother said, half to herself. "Over-protection is bad too. But we haven't over-protected him. We've always let him do anything he wanted to . . . within reason."

Mr. Madison took a small notebook from his pocket. "I think I have the answer," he said, putting on his glasses. "I think we can compromise. We want Ricky to feel that he's a member of his group, but we also want him to avoid the dangers. Here's what we'll do: We'll let him buy a car, but we'll retain the right to deprive him of it if he is careless.

"I'll write down a set of rules governing his behavior with the car, and we'll put it up to him. He can have the car if he obeys the rules. If he violates the rules, he loses his driving privileges. The way I see it, this will give him something to work for. Pride of ownership,

24

and pride of being trusted. He won't want to lose the car once he has it."

"I suppose you're right," Ricky's mother said reluctantly. "But I'm so afraid. . . ."

"We'll talk to him about it tonight," Mr. Madison said. "Ricky's a boy of his word. If he says he'll be careful, he will be. . . . And as long as we have final control of the car, we can take it away if he betrays our trust. It will work out all right."

"I wish I believed *that*," Ricky's mother said as she began to clear away the dishes.

When Ricky left the house and turned toward town he knew what he was going to do. He didn't dare put it in words, or allow himself to think it out step by step. But he *knew*.

Consciously he was boiling over with rage at the way he had been treated. If they'd only yelled at him, or argued, or fought it out! No, they'd just made light of him. Made believe they were interested in his welfare. He knew all about that phony *interest*. They'd used that trick ever since he could remember when they wanted to deny him something. They'd done it with the bike, and a million other things he'd wanted to do.

Every time he wanted to do something they had to go through that old routine about his *welfare*, and what was best for *it*. It sure was funny that it always turned out the best thing for his welfare was what *they* liked. As though his welfare was something they kept in a safe or something. They never seemed to

25

understand that maybe what he wanted was just as important as his *welfare*.

They thought they had him licked again, too. He could tell that by the way they acted. They thought that they had him all figured out. Maybe they were in for a surprise!

Ricky loped along with his fists clenched, the rebellion in him growing with every step.

Maybe the only way to let his parents know that he was grown up was to *prove* it. Other guys did, somehow. Other guys weren't treated the same at sixteen as they were at six. He didn't have to leave home to show his independence, either. There was another way. He could just stay home and have his car too!

"What would they say?" Ricky demanded of himself in a fierce whisper. "Suppose I just drove home in my car and said it was mine and I was going to keep it? *What could they say?* Couldn't say anything. It's my money. I could run it. They couldn't take it away. They wouldn't kick me out, either. They'd just have to accept it, that's all. Then they'd know I had a mind of my own! They wouldn't think it was funny if I talked about leaving home then, I bet!"

He was back in the square, and he slowed his pace.

What was he waiting for? He had the money. He knew where there was a car he could buy. If Link wanted the car and had the money *he'd* buy it. So would Chub, or Sherm, or Jerry. They weren't scared. Why should *he* be afraid? If he wasn't just a kid and a mama's boy, he'd buy that car any time he wanted to.

26

Well . . . he wanted to. Right now!

Across the square Arnie VanZuuk came out of the police station and walked slowly toward the Town Cafe. Arnie's husky voice and Dutch accent sounded in Ricky's mind. "Your papa will let you have a car? I don't think so, Ricky."

Ricky licked his lips, feeling a strange tension. Once he got his car and was on his own, just let *anybody* try to tell him what he could or couldn't do. Just let anybody try!

He was moving toward the bank, thumbs hooked in his belt, eyes narrowed against the sun. He knew why he was going toward it, but he tried not to admit it to himself. If the knowledge formed into words, he might turn back. He'd be licked again.

He went up the three stone steps slowly, uncertainly, almost hoping something would happen to stop him. He was sweating, but it wasn't from the heat.

Now he was inside, moving toward the teller's window. Moving slowly, as in a dream, his stomach in a knot.

Annie Myers, the assistant cashier, was eating her lunch at a table near the vault door. He stood at the teller's window, watching her. The bank was merely one big room, divided by a partition not more than five feet high. Everything, everyone, was always in plain sight.

Annie heard him and looked around. She was a small woman of about sixty, with a pale face and bushy hair that had faded from red to a light orange.

"Your father's already gone," she said without waiting to hear what Ricky had to say.

If she had asked what he wanted, he was ready to back down by asking for his father. Now he could only go on.

"I know," he said. He stood with his hands resting on the little shelf at the window, looking anxiously at Annie.

"Do you want something?" There was an unconcealed note of annoyance in Annie's voice. She didn't like to be disturbed during her lunch. Sometimes she made bank customers stand and wait until she was through eating before she would start to wait on them.

"I . . . I want to draw out some money," Ricky said, still staring at Annie.

Even then he wasn't sure he'd actually said it out loud. Knowing what his action meant, he looked at Annie pleadingly, hoping she would refuse his request, so he could leave and call it quits. He was really afraid now. He wanted to turn back.

"Does your father know you're taking this money out?"

Annie's sharp voice, her speaking as to a small child, angered him. This was too much.

"I'm not asking for my father's money," Ricky blurted, his voice loud and belligerent, beyond his control. "I'm asking for mine. It's in my name, ain't it? I put it in by myself, so I guess I can draw it out by myself."

Annie was disconcerted. She knew Ricky never did

anything important without his father's assistance. His anger frightened her.

"You needn't think you can stand there and shout at me," she said shrilly. "Even if your father is my boss. I don't have to take this kind of behavior from you or any other boy. I've a mind to call your father right now and tell him. . . ."

"You just keep away from that phone and give me my money," Ricky ordered. The harsh, tough voice that was coming out of his mouth sounded strange and frightening.

The annoyance in Annie's eyes gave way to a quick look of fear. She had read about the crazy things that boys did. And it was always the nice ones who suddenly went berserk.

Ricky saw the fear, and in turn was even more afraid. She might accuse him of trying to rob the bank! He might go to jail for acting like this. For a moment he almost broke into a frightened apology. He wanted desperately to forget the whole business, to creep away and forget everything. But the fear and torment showed on his face as anger and wildness.

"How much do you want?" Annie asked, taking care to keep back where he couldn't grab her.

Ricky blushed, ashamed of the way he had talked to old Annie. "All of it," he said in a subdued voice. "I have to buy something important."

"Well, don't just stand there," Annie said. Her fright over, she was her old snippy self again. "You know enough to make out a withdrawal slip. Hurry now. I want to have *some* time to finish my lunch."

29

Ricky filled out the slip and pushed it toward Annie. "I thought for a minute we were going to throw some punches," he said, grinning.

"Here's your money," Annie said disapprovingly. "What are you going to buy . . . a revolver?" With that she turned her back, marched to the table, sat down and resumed eating her lunch.

Ricky looked down at the five ten-dollar bills in his hand. He'd done it. He'd done something big without a session with his parents first. He'd done it without asking.

His mouth was dry, his legs shaky. He'd proven to himself that he had guts. Now should he give it back to Annie and ask her to forget the whole thing? He *could* wait.

A car went past the bank. It might have been any stock car driven by a farmer or a townsman, and the money might have gone back. But it wasn't a stocker. It went by with that special sound that seemed to draw all the blood in his veins after it. The sound of high compression breathed out through duals. The deep, throbbing race-car sound of straight pipes, full of the promise of lightning acceleration, of power, of speed.

Ricky's head lifted, his eyes shone. A rod! Link had one. Jerry had one. Sherm had one. Chub had one. And in just about five minutes Ricky Madison would have one!

2

It was a block away from the square on a side street, and it didn't look like the kind of garage you'd want to take a new car to. A big, unpainted frame building with a red gas pump in front, and rusted scraps of junk piled along the outside walls. In the weedy lot next to the garage, with a hand-lettered FOR SALE sign on the windshield, was the car.

He walked around it slowly, lovingly, taking in every beautiful detail he already knew by heart but had to see again. From the front bumper, which had to be straightened, to the back, which was missing, it was a dream car. It was a '39 Ford coupe, originally black, but now the rusty shade of an old top hat. It didn't matter that the fenders were battered and rusted through—they'd come off. And if the door on the driver's side had to be wired shut, that was all to the good. It wouldn't be so likely to fly open so he'd be

31

thrown out if he happened to roll the car on a turn. Anyway, it was safer to get in and out of a car on the curb side.

He opened the good door, letting out a rush of hot air that smelled of dust, old upholstery and metal. The seat and the insides of the doors were torn and covered with black grease smears. The grease of age and use. He felt the usual momentary disappointment that the gearshift lever was on the floor, not up under the wheel. But he comforted himself with the thought that the fancy sports cars like the Jags and the Nash Healeys had their gear boxes on the floor. And that was good enough for him!

No doubt about it. This was the car that had been made for him. He slid under the wheel, sitting on loose and broken springs, staring forward through a windshield that was pitted and discolored from the ravages of the weather.

He sat there a long time, his hands resting on the wheel, his eyes looking out over the front of the hood. Once he had it, he could make changes. Strip off the fenders. Sand off the old finish and repaint. As he saved money, get spinner hub caps, chrome head nuts and carb stack. Add another carb as soon as he could, and some day finned high-compression heads complete with a dual exhaust system.

Some things might be done sooner. Milling down the old heads would boost compression. Might re-bore, too, and have the ports polished and relieved at the same time. It wouldn't be too expensive, and it would give him something to go with until he could buy the speed equipment he wanted. It was easy to lower the rear end. He could do it himself with shackles until he could afford to chop and channel.

It wouldn't take too much to make a real street rod out of this coupe. It wouldn't be a track racer, and it wouldn't look as good as some other cars, but it wouldn't be easy to beat around town and out on the country roads. There was a lot a guy could do if he was willing to work.

He sat behind the wheel dreaming and planning until Merle Connor returned to the garage from lunch driving an ancient two-truck. Merle saw Ricky in the coupe, and it being too hot to start work right away, he strolled over to the car to kid Ricky with a sales talk.

Merle was in his thirties, a dispirited man in baggy brown coveralls and a greasy red leather cap he wore winter and summer. He was always renting some old building or shack and starting up some kind of fix-it service. He had been through lawnmowers and sewing machines and electrical work, and now he had a garage. Wherever he went, he seemed to be a magnet that at-tracted all the stray junk and metal rubbish in the town. Even at home, in his yard, his kids' playthings were mainly old car seats or broken vacuum cleaners or parts of metal beds that Merle had carted around aimlessly in his truck until the children unloaded the things at home.

Merle leaned against the wired door of the coupe and picked his teeth with a bobby pin that had some-how ended up in his pocket. This done, he reached into a pocket for a cigarette. He dug again for a kitchen match, flicked it into flame with his thumbnail, and blew smoke in Ricky's face. "Well, kid, you ready to buy yet?"

Ricky thought of the money in his pocket, and a feeling of panic came over him. The moment his father returned to the bank Annie would tell him everything. He felt sick. *What have I done? What have I done?*

"Mighty good car here," Merle said, thumping the tinny door with his fist. "Just got her in, and she'll probably be sold this afternoon. Showroom condition. Still has that new smell."

The car had been sitting there for months.

"She's a nice one all right," Ricky agreed, patting the steering wheel.

Merle yawned. He hated to go back to work, but he was bored with the talk. They'd gone over the same ground a hundred times. He pulled the greasy red cap down over his eyes and let his cigarette hang from his lips. "Kid," he said, tired of everything, "if you want this car so much why don't you buy it?"

Ricky was stung by the annoyance in Merle's voice. By the implication that since he'd never bought anything at the garage, he never would.

The revolution that had begun with a successful skirmish against Annie Myers flared up again.

"Maybe I will buy it," Ricky said.

Merle had heard that before. "Yeah?" He flipped his cigarette away. "When? The year two thousand?"

34

"Maybe right now," Ricky said, afraid to listen to himself.

Merle straightened up. He caught the sound of money in Ricky's tone. That was the way the kids sounded when they were ready to buy. Bold and scared. But as he swung around to look at the slender brown boy in the car, Merle's interest faded. Anybody else, maybe, but not Ricky Madison.

"Your pa would skin you alive if you bought a car," Merle said. "You know that."

Ricky's lips tightened. The fear and uncertainty in his mind retreated before the outraged feeling that surged through him. *Everybody* telling him what his father would or would not let him do. *Everybody*. The whole town knowing more about it than he himself did. Even Merle.

Ricky reached in his pocket and pulled out his money. He held the bills up in front of Merle's face. "Who you listening to?" Ricky demanded, his voice aggressive and shaky. "This, or what you think my father would say?"

Merle shot a quick look at the money. The game was over. "That don't look like sixty-five dollars to me," he said disinterestedly.

"Sixty-five?" Ricky looked hurt. "I thought the price was fifty."

Merle chuckled in a way to indicate that Ricky was talking like a child. "Kid," he said, "you just don't know about car prices. They've gone up since the last time I talked to you. There's a big demand for good

35

used cars now. A big demand. Matter of fact, sixty-five's pretty cheap for this car." He glanced at Ricky to see how he was taking it. An adult could have bought the car for twenty-five, and he'd be glad to get rid of it, but these kids were different. When they got the fever for a particular car, they *wanted* it. Ricky had been mooning over the coupe for months. It was just a question of how far he could be pushed.

"Yeah," Merle said, turning his back on Ricky. "I turned down sixty for it this morning. The market's real good now. Real good." He turned again, suddenly, hoping to catch Ricky off-guard, but Ricky made no attempt to conceal the hopelessness he felt. If he hadn't been sure he wanted the car, he was sure now. Now that somebody else would probably buy it.

"Fifty's all I got," Ricky said dully, looking at the money in his hand as though it had betrayed him. "Well, if it ain't enough, I guess it just ain't enough." He slid across the seat and got out of the car, his lower lip protruding.

Merle shook his head. These kids! No effort to bargain. No brains. Whatever they had, they'd spend. If they didn't have it, they gave up. He walked around the car to join Ricky. "Well, it's enough to buy her *with*, even if it ain't enough to buy her *all*," Merle said. "Of course, I hate to do business that way. All that extra trouble and book work, and forms to fill out for the government. . . . I don't know. . . ."

Ricky looked at the coupe, thinking hard. The old doubts began to come back on him, but he shut them out. Made believe the world began and ended right where he stood. "I'll do 'er," he said defiantly. "I'll give you fifty dollars down and pay the other fifteen a dollar a week. How's that?"

Merle scratched his unshaven chin. He had Ricky in his pocket now. The thing was to keep the price down to what he was sure the kid would be able to pay. It could go up a *little* more. "Well, it ain't that easy," Merle said reluctantly, leaning against the coupe. "Sixty-five was the cash price. On terms, it would have to be seventy-five. Book work and all that stuff. And I think that other feller might be back with a cash offer of sixty-five. The one I told you about. He had the money on him. I imagine he'll go up another five. Sure would like to see you have it, of course, but I can't just *give* you ten dollars, can I?"

"I guess not," Ricky said, not knowing how to fight back. All he knew was that he had to have the car before it was bought out from under him. "I guess I can do it for seventy-five."

"You won't regret it," Merle said, taking Ricky's fifty and tucking the bills in his coveralls. "Clean that car up a little and you can probably turn right around and sell it for a hundred."

Ricky followed Merle into the garage where he signed to pay the remaining twenty-five dollars in twenty-five weeks, and the deal was over. It was Ricky's car. Merle took an ignition key from the nail it had been hanging on, and handed it to Ricky. "She's all yours," he said in a tone of relief. "Don't drive too fast, now." Chuckling at his own joke, Merle went into the large part of the garage where he had a flat tire to fix. He didn't mind the idea of working at all.

Ricky looked down at the small tarnished key in his hand. It was funny, the difference it made knowing the key belonged to him. It wasn't just a key to a car, it was a key that had unlocked the cell he'd been living in.

He shook his head, biting his lips in a kind of puzzled grin. He felt so *different*. Like he'd come to Merle's garage a kid, and suddenly turned into a grown man. Like he'd shed what he used to be the way a snake crawled out of an old dried skin. That was just exactly the way he felt. That was it, all right. That was the difference. He wasn't a kid any more. He had a car. He'd caught up with the other guys. He was as big and as independent as anybody . . . even his father.

He'd sure found out something. The difference between being a kid and a man was something you had to discover for yourself. You couldn't sit around and wait for somebody else to tell you when your kid days were over. When you felt they *were* over, and you *did* something about it, then they *were* over. It was just that simple. He'd never feel like a kid again because he wasn't a kid any more.

Ricky tossed the key in the air and grabbed it with a quick, striking motion on its way down. He had a key, and it fit his car. Now there was a job to be done. To take that old car out on the road and find out right now how fast it could go.

3

When Ricky walked out of the garage toward *his* car, he noticed things that had escaped his attention before. Now that he had fifty dollars in the car and owed another twenty-five, he saw for the first time that the tires were so bald the cord showed in patches on two of them. There was a sag to the left that suggested a broken spring, and an appearance of being out of line that indicated the car had been wrecked, and maybe had a sprung frame.

Now that it was his he stood looking at it out of perplexed brown eyes, his thumbs hooked in his belt, and wondered if he had been cheated. For a moment he experienced that awful sensation of knowing what it was to regret achieving a long-sought goal. But only for a moment.

He climbed in the car carefully, wiping his feet on the grass outside before placing them on the filthy

39

floorboard. He held the key tightly between the thumb and forefinger of his right hand, and his hand trembled as he inserted the key in the ignition lock. He turned the key, shoved in his clutch and kicked the starter.

It wouldn't start.

The motor turned over laboriously about two and a half times as the tired battery gave of its weak juice, but it didn't catch. Ricky had been anticipating a motor that caught at once, and a quick sound of power. Biting his lower lip, he tried again, fearfully, afraid he might flood the carburetor, or run the battery down. The sound of cranking was deeper, more groan-like, dangerously tired. He gave up and sat back, perplexed and sweating, disappointment gnawing at his stomach.

Merle looked out of the garage. "What's the matter?" he yelled. "Can't you start?"

"She won't catch." Ricky looked hopefully at the mechanic.

Merle strolled toward the car with maddening slowness. He poked his head inside and looked at the dash. "For one thing," he said laconically, "you're out of gas. I had about a gallon in the tank, but I guess one of your friends must have took it."

"Gas," Ricky said, feeling like a fool. "Yeah."

He climbed out of the car, and with Merle to help, pushed it over to the red gas pump.

"How much?" Merle asked, unscrewing the gas cap.

Ricky felt in his pockets. Not even enough for a gallon. He'd hoped Merle would offer to fill the tank for free, as a gesture in honor of the purchase, but he was afraid to suggest that generosity to Merle.

"How about adding a dollar's worth to my account?" Ricky asked, trying to sound casual.

Merle hesitated. He didn't want to give Ricky any more credit, but he couldn't think of any other way to get rid of him and the car. "Well, all right," he said, reaching for the hose. "But just this once."

Ricky got back in his car with a feeling of relief. Once was all he'd need of Merle's cheap gas. After this, he would be getting the best ethyl gas from one of the good stations, and after *that*, he'd be burning his own fuel mixture.

"Okay," Merle said. "Turn her over."

This time the car started. Ricky let it idle a moment to warm up. Also to give himself time to get up nerve to put the car in gear and drive away. It wasn't that he didn't know how to drive. He'd driven his friends' cars enough to have confidence in his ability. He didn't know where to go. Now that he had his car, he didn't know where to drive it. He couldn't drive around town without being seen, and he wasn't ready to risk that yet.

A happy inspiration struck him. The lake! He almost whooped as he thought of how the others would look when they saw him drive up in his own car. They wouldn't believe it until he proved it to them. But that was what he ought to do first. Let the guys know that Ricky Madison was his own boss, and he wasn't going to be left out of things any more!

"You're gonna use up all your gas," Merle said. "Ain't there some place you want to go?"

Ricky nodded, grinning. He shoved in the clutch, wrestled the gearshift lever into low, and eased up on the clutch. The car shivered violently as the clutch strove to engage. Ricky eased up on the gas. The car bucked and died.

"Don't be afraid to give her plenty of gas," Merle advised. "As long as you let that clutch out slow she won't jump out from under you." He stood back, grinning at his joke.

Ricky tried again, his lips tight. his face wrinkled with tense concern. This time he moved. As soon as the clutch engaged—and it seemed forever until it did —the car stopped shaking sideways and up and down, and shuddered forward with a whine of grinding gears.

The car slowed almost to a halt before Ricky could fight it into second, but he made it, and it was with a surer touch that he finally shifted into high. He tried to see if the rear was safe, but when he looked in the rear-vision mirror all he could see was a thick cloud of blue smoke rolling out behind him. But he was on the road, and moving. He exhaled a tremendous sigh of relief, settling himself more comfortably behind the wheel. He was soaked with sweat, and tired, but he looked about alertly as he drove, afraid some careless driver might run into him before he was well started. In a few minutes he had driven across the outlying streets of town and was on the graveled back road that led to the lake.

Bouncing along the back road at a noisy twenty-five

miles an hour, Ricky relaxed enough to enjoy the driving. He fought ruts and dips happily, felt the hot wind hit against his face through an open window, and grinned with pleasure as he pressed on the accelerator and the car responded to his touch.

A rod of his own at last! He ignored the rattles and the trailing blue smoke. A little fixing here and there, and he'd be matching wheels with anybody. Maybe even reinforce the body with pipe, fix a rollover bar, and enter the stock-car races. With the money he won he could buy another car for street use. Something newer and flashier.

He liked the idea of being a stock-car racer. He imagined the gravel road under him a track, with himself at the head of a string of speeding cars. He tromped on the gas pedal. The car responded slowly and noisily, motor whining, loose fenders celebrating each bump in the road with tinny, banging sounds.

A turn came up. He gripped the wheel, hunching over it the way his friends drove. He wanted to drive with one hand on the wheel and the other resting on the gearshift knob, but he was still too unfamiliar with the car and fast driving to try it.

Just as he reached the turn he got scared. He pulled his foot off the gas pedal, instinct guiding it to the brake. His plan was an easy touch of the brakes and then power, but there was no easy touching with these brakes. His foot went almost to the floorboards before the brakes grabbed all at once. The tail end of the coupe started to change positions with the nose as the left brake grabbed harder than the right. Ricky wrestled with the wheel, his foot glued to the brake pedal, his skidding wheels churning up a shower of dirt and stones as the car bounced to a stop half turned around in the road, the motor dead.

"Chicken!" Ricky snarled at himself. He'd only been doing forty, and he'd ridden around that turn at sixty with other drivers. Stock-car racer! Maybe Sharon was right when she suggested he ride out on his bicycle. That was his speed.

He started the car again, driving toward the lake. In low gear he tromped on the gas pedal, tearing the insides of his car as his wheels spun in the loose gravel. In second he held it wide open again, trying to find out how fast it would go in that gear. Thirty-nine! A miserable, crawling, creeping, shuddering, wavering thirty-nine! He slammed into high gear and headed down a straight stretch, furiously wanting to redeem himself for turning yellow at the curve.

He got the car up to fifty, leaping and bucking from one side of the road to the other, kicking up a thick trail of dust that mingled with blue exhaust smoke. The car kept trying to leap off the left side of the road, but he gritted his teeth and fought it back. Another turn came up. Turns were frequent on this back road. He glared at it as though it were a personal enemy. This time like a race driver!

He approached fast. Like a race driver. Like he was pushing a Jag, or an MG in a road race. He had it planned. A quick downshift when he reached the clump of sumac at the beginning of the turn and he

could go around wide open. Clutch in. . . . Hit that
gearshift hard. . . . Jam it into second! . . .

It wouldn't go!

The outraged ancient transmission screamed and
spat out the teeth of second. The whirling gears, refus-
ing to mesh as they were forced together, fought with
a deafening metallic, grinding yowl. Ricky tried to
control the lashing shift lever with one hand and steer
with the other. He came on the turn in neutral, floating free, without power to pull him around. He made
a desperate try to get back into high again, but he
failed.

He hit into the turn with inertia thumbing its nose
at his attempts to pull his front wheels around. He felt
himself drifting, and the drift became a slide on the
loose footing. Because he could slide he didn't roll,
but he was sliding toward the ditch, his hands glued to
the useless wheel. A low moan of fear forced itself
through his rigid lips as he felt the battered coupe go
into a spin, trying its best to turn over. For some reason, even as he hung on to the wheel he kept his foot
pressing down on the gas pedal, racing his motor vainly,
as though wishes were torque and hope was the trac-
tion he needed and didn't have.

He felt his wheels leave gravel for grass. The rear
wheels touched first, were slowed, and the front end
of the car slammed around to head toward the fields.
Momentum carried the car forward, throwing Ricky
from side to side as the coupe left the road and headed
into a shallow, broad ditch. There were three or four

45

hard jolts and then the car got hung up on a small hummock, and came to a sudden stop that threw Ricky against the wheel and knocked the breath from his body. A protecting arm that he brought up in front of his face hit the windshield with a numbing shock. He half-rolled off the wheel and fell onto the seat and then slid to the floor, where he lay shaking from head to foot, his breath coming back in jerky sobs.

He didn't try to get up for several minutes. Even after his breathing was normal, and his trembling had stopped, he lay where he had been thrown on the car floor, his eyes wide and unblinking.

He felt something he didn't understand. It was like despair, and regret, and hopelessness, but also something more. It was like a terrible weariness and feeling of futility. The years of longing, of wishing, of struggling to be something he didn't quite know . . . suddenly it all weighed down on him, made him tired . . . tired. . . . He wanted to close his eyes and sleep. Sleep and escape the torments, the explanations, the effort of keeping up, of being. Just sleep and escape the bother . . . forever. . . .

He felt himself growing numb, and losing consciousness. He let his mouth fall open, and kept his eyes wide and staring. He had the feeling that if he lay real still he would cause himself to die. There was something familiar about the way he was lying and looking. As though he'd lived through this moment before, a long, long time ago.

A shiver of fear went through him. Now he remembered. It had been a newspaper picture, taken a few minutes after an accident. He'd seen it when he was ten years old, and he'd looked at it for hours. A picture of a teen-age boy killed in a wreck. He'd been sprawled on the floor of his car, mouth and eyes open, expressionless . . . dead. . . .

Ricky made a sound as though he were going to be violently ill. He sat up suddenly, hitting his head on the underside of the dashboard. He didn't even pause to rub it as he crawled out of the car and felt the ground under his feet again. It was better, once he was outside. The sun was shining, the fields looked pleasant and peaceful. His car didn't seem to be damaged at all. The black mood left him, and he pulled a piece of grass to chew on as he walked around the coupe to see how it had fared.

He seemed in luck. Not one of the old tires had blown. As far as he could tell, the wheels were still as much in line as they had ever been—which wasn't saying much. He got down on his knees and looked under the car. No oil or water had leaked out.

He got back in the car and tried to start it, but it wouldn't catch. He got out again and made another circle. It wouldn't help him if he did get started. He was hung up on the hummock, and the only way he could get back on the road was to wait until somebody came along to give him a tow.

His predicament did not cause him any feeling of shame. Rather, as he stood by the side of the road and looked at his skid marks, hoping his friends would be the first to find him, he felt a growing sense of pride and daring.

Wouldn't the guys stare when they found out that he not only had a car, but he'd put it in the ditch trying to take a turn too fast. It would be real evidence that he had a lead foot and wasn't afraid of anything. Proof they wouldn't have to worry about *him* keeping up on the road.

Looking at his car, he felt a little regretful that it was still on its wheels. If he could have done it without hurting the car too much, it sure would have been something for the guys to come along and have him point out casually that he'd actually rolled his rod the first time out. That would give them something to talk about, all right!

Ricky strolled around his car again, thumbs hooked in his wide belt, a reckless swagger in his walk. That had been *some* ride, all right. Too bad Sharon hadn't been with him. Boy, he sure would have made her squeal.

He had a momentary vision of the way he would have liked the mishap to take place. Of Sharon gasping at his boldness as he hit into the turn at ninety, with the others on his heels. Then the tire blowing on the corner, and his masterful efforts to control the car. Then her squeal of fright as they slid into the ditch, while he jockeyed the car with split-second decisions. Then the slow rollover, with Sharon clinging to him for support, holding him close as he was unavoidably thrown against her. Holding each other close as they turned over and over and over and over, slow-motion-like, never in danger, floating gently through the air with their arms locked about each other as they turned over and over and over. . . .

It was funny about him and Sharon. They'd known each other ever since they were runny-nosed kids fighting over a shovel in the sand pile. Then she'd got a crush on him just at the age when he hated girls. She'd tagged after him and sent him presents, and he had to treat her real mean so the other guys wouldn't kid him.

When he finally got rid of her, it was when all the other guys were getting interested in girls, and they gave her the rush and he was left out. When he tried to move back in, confident she would be happy to have him at last, she didn't want him.

There had been an awful, miserable period when he was so in love with her he did everything but crawl to her on his hands and knees to get her attention. Then it was her turn to take cruel advantage of his devotion. She ordered him around, sent him on fool errands and mocked him for serving her. She let others insult her without caring, and went out of her way to find insult in the compliments he tried to pay, openly scorning him because he did not dare argue with her, disdaining him because he alone treated her with respect. Because he lived for her smile, she gave her smiles to others; because he longed to touch her, she avoided the slightest contact with him. She was nice only when he seemed about to give her up—then she would have a kind word for him, or a smile. And when she had him at her heels again, she would return to her scornful acceptance of his homage.

49

Then, that too had stopped. He quit following her around like a little dog, and she ceased tormenting him. Suddenly they who had known each other from childhood were strangers. She seemed all at once to leap years ahead of him, and become an attractive young woman while he still remained a boy.

They saw each other every day, and they went many places in the same crowd, but it was as though they shared no past. He always looked at her, though they seldom spoke, and everything he did or said was for her benefit, though he went out of his way to ignore her.

But no matter what he did, or what he said, she never seemed to notice, as though there was no communication of any sort possible between them. She seemed to have shut him out, to look through him and never at him, as though he didn't exist. And now, when he thought of her, it wasn't as the little girl who had tagged after him, or as the girl he had been a slave to. He saw her in his mind as he would see a picture, motionless, remote, aloof, unreal. . . .

He jumped as a car stopped behind him with a dragging sound. He turned to face an old farmer driving a pick-up truck. "Anything wrong, Bub?" the farmer asked.

"Uh . . . no," Ricky answered. "I've got some friends coming for me. I think I had . . . it was a busted spindle or something."

The farmer nodded, looking at the coupe. "That the one Merle Connor has?"

"Yeah," Ricky said. Noting the look in the farmer's eye, he added, "I was trying it out."

"Anything's apt to be busted on that car," the farmer said. "And probably is." He slid behind the wheel of his truck, waved a finger at Ricky and drove off.

Ricky looked at the retreating truck. "You wait until I've had this car awhile," he shouted. "You won't be making fun of it *then*."

He spat on the ground, hitched up his Levis, and sat down in the shade of his coupe to wait for his friends and dream. As long as he made himself think about the problems of fixing up his coupe, he could get so interested he could forget to think about what would happen when he returned home, and had to face his parents.

He was there for more than an hour before he heard the sound of familiar motors coming his way. He scrambled to his feet and stood by the side of the road, shading his eyes as he watched for them. First he saw their dust, and then the cars came into sight, one after the other, sliding around a turn half a mile from him. He watched them come with an excited smile on his face. For the first time in his life he didn't have to envy them, to feel inferior, to resent their freedoms. When they were close enough to see him, he waved them to a stop.

They came up fast, hitting their brakes and sliding, turning their wondering, incredulous faces toward him as they saw and understood at once who it was and what had happened. They backed up noisily, gunning and braking violently, until they were close to him.

Link Aller leaned on the door of the Chevvy convertible he was driving. He looked at Ricky with a glint of superior amusement in his black eyes. "What'd you do, boy?" he drawled. "Steal a car?"

"Steal nothing," Ricky answered, leaning nonchalantly against his coupe and hooking his thumbs in his belt. "I bought it."

"You *what?*" Chub yelled from his Ford Tudor.

"I bought it," Ricky said truculently, not prepared for the way they were acting. As though it was a joke. "I suppose you thought my folks could stop me."

"Naw," Link whooped. "We figured Merle paid you to take it off his hands."

The girls giggled. Ricky ignored them all but Sharon, who was riding with Link. She didn't seem to be paying any attention to what was going on, but was filing her fingernails. He wanted to shake her, and make her acknowledge that she knew he had bought a car.

"What happened?" Sherm asked, getting out of his car and joining Ricky. The other boys took their cue from Sherm and gathered around too, sitting on their heels or standing slumped to one side.

"Aw, you know," Ricky said loudly, so that Sharon would hear. "I hit the turn too fast, and when I kicked her in the . . . kicked her . . . she didn't have enough dig to bring me around. So . . ." Ricky made a careless gesture with his hand. "I flipped her."

The moment he said it, he was sorry. He hadn't

meant to tell such an obvious lie, but it had just slipped out.

Chub looked at the skid marks in the gravel. "I don't see where you rolled over," he said. "And your car . . ."

"I didn't mean I *rolled* it," Ricky said, angry that he was on the defensive as usual. "When I said flipped, I meant I flipped off the road in the ditch."

"Then you oughta say you ditched it," Chub said. "Not go bragging that you flipped when you didn't flip."

"I know how I *meant* the word," Ricky said. "It's not my fault if you took it some other way. You don't even know if I said flipped or slipped."

Link Aller winked at the others. "I didn't know this heap could go fast enough to slide on gravel," he said, touching the coupe with his booted toe. "I've had it on the road. It's a real turtle."

It was all going wrong. For a moment Ricky felt like walking away and leaving them and his coupe, but he knew that would be too childish. Instead he shrugged his shoulders and spat. "I won't argue with you," he said, trying to sound uninterested. "But I'm in the ditch and I need some help to get out. You guys want to help me out, or prove I couldn't be there in the first place?"

It was the right thing to say. This time they laughed with him, and moved to help.

Sherm, who was closest, backed his car around until it was near enough to be hooked to Ricky's coupe by chains. Ricky got in his car and started his motor. With his car in reverse, Sherm towing, and the other boys pushing by hand, he was soon back on the road. The chains were unhooked and the boys gathered to hear the sound of Rick's motor and discuss his car. They were pleased that he had wheels, but it wasn't their way to come right out and say so. Their way of welcoming him as an equal was to rib him.

"I know she's not perfect," Ricky said seriously as he gunned the motor and a cloud of blue smoke rolled out of the exhaust pipe. "But at least I've got my own rod."

"Rod!" Chub howled, wrinkling his round face in dismay as the fumes enveloped him. "You don't call this a hot rod, do you? Man, it's more like a warm stick."

Link grabbed one of the fenders and shook it. "Look at that wing flap," he said wonderingly. "This heap must really fly when it moves. Just like a bird."

"Listen to that mill," Sherm said, cupping his hand behind one of his big red ears. "Must have at least eight pounds of compression right down the line. Man, I'll bet those valves have holes in 'em big enough to stick your head through."

Ricky tried to head off more of the same. "I got a name for it," he said, feeling like a traitor. "I call it the shot rod."

He felt angry and guilty when the others laughed. It was as though he'd told something shameful about a friend who trusted him.

"Well, let's get on back to town," Link said. "Want a tow, Ricky?"

54

"I'll get there," Ricky snapped. "Maybe before you do."

"You might—if I pushed you," Link teased, with a proud look at his convertible. It was bright yellow, with chrome exhaust extensions and Buick portholes along the hood.

Ricky looked sullen, but didn't answer. He just felt like giving up. After all the waiting, and torment, and all the trouble he was in, the big moment of his life had come, and it had been flat. The guys hadn't welcomed him at all. The way they acted toward him and the coupe, it made him feel more like a kid than ever. A big fool kid.

Only Jerry Long stayed by him as the others moved toward their cars. Quiet, thoughtful Jerry, who was his best friend.

"How did you get your dad to okay it?" he asked.

Ricky didn't look up. "I didn't," he said.

"That's not so good."

Ricky lifted his head. "Why not? You guys all did the same thing, didn't you? If it was good for you, why isn't it good for me? I'm not a kid any more. Can't you see?"

Jerry scuffed the gravel with the toe of his shoe. "I had to fight for mine," he said, "but my dad agreed before I went and bought it."

"I tried it that way," Ricky said. "You know my folks. They didn't say yes and they didn't say no. I . . . I don't know *what* they said. You know how they do it. You've been around."

"Maybe you should have waited," Jerry said. "Any-

55

way, you could have done better than this . . . car. What did Merle try to stick you for it? Last I heard, it could be had for twenty-five bucks."

"I made a good deal," Ricky said, mentally kicking himself.

Jerry looked at him. "How much, Ricky?"

"I told you. A good deal."

"We've been buddies a long time," Jerry said. "I know when you're faking. What was it, thirty-five?"

"Worse," Ricky admitted, looking ashamed. "Forty."

"I told you you should have waited. We'd have gone with you and run it down until Merle let it go for twenty. You've got to learn not to go off half-cocked. See you in town." Jerry walked to his car, shaking his head.

Ricky was last in line when they started. But once they were under way the thrill and glory of being under his own wheel at last made him impatient. They were ahead of him, making him eat their dust, but he was through being the guy who always trailed behind. They still didn't believe that he'd caught up with them in every way. Maybe they'd believe him if he proved it.

He began to crowd Jerry, riding close, almost blinded by dust and riding into a shower of stones that flew back through the dust to rattle against his hood and windshield.

Shot rod? A warm stick? He faded to the left and pulled closer, starting to nose past. He was almost even with Jerry when they came to a turn, but Ricky didn't fall back. With the others watching he'd rather roll than give. They swept into the turn, and putting on the power, he went sliding past Jerry, speeding blindly into the dust, trusting that no other car would be coming from the opposite direction. For a moment on the turn, control of his car was vague. A chuck-hole bounced him toward Jerry's car, but as the cars almost touched Ricky kept his foot on the gas, pulling ahead in a burst of noise and flying stones.

"You crazy or something?" Jerry yelled furiously. Ricky couldn't hear, and didn't look over to see how Jerry was taking being passed. He was already on Chub's trail with the gas pedal pushed to the floor. One by one, he was going to take them all before they reached town.

He took Chub next, and then Sherm. They let him clatter by, puzzled by the fierceness of his driving, wary of his recklessness. He was new to them as a driver. They didn't yet know how close he could be trusted, so they gave over, and let him roar past in a lopsided rush of speed and noise.

And Ricky, exulting as he pushed past them, trying to catch up with the past in a single burst of speed, was hardly aware that his feelings of triumph were shot through with hostility. That, as he passed one friend after another, his thrill was not so much one of victory as of revenge.

A warm stick, eh? He was showing them. He closed in on Link Aller's car, which was leading the pack. Link had always led, from the days when they were little kids. No matter what it was, he'd always been the first to try something new and succeed at it, from riding a two-wheel bike to smoking to going with girls to having a car. Always the first, always seeming to be looking back at the others with a derisive smile on his face as he challenged them to be his equal. Always staying a step ahead of them all, a mile ahead of Ricky. It wouldn't be complete until Link had eaten some of his dust.

He drew up alongside Link, looked over, and received a crooked, sardonic grin in return. He pressed the accelerator against the floor with all his strength, intending to spurt past Link, but for some reason he didn't pull ahead.

Wide open now, hanging on to the wheel of his lurching, straining car, he pushed at the gas pedal with every ounce of pressure he could bring to bear, as though hard pushing would make his car go faster. But Link stayed at his side, driving the convertible easily with one hand, and grinning.

The ride was getting too wild for Ricky. Bumps threw him in the air, he landed heavily, his car fought to run off the side of the road. He was scared, afraid a bad hole would toss him off the road or into Link's car. Suddenly afraid of what would happen if one of his thin tires blew. Afraid of the tortured grind and scream of his over-worked, over-heated motor, of the twisting strain on the chassis, of the beating his springs and shocks were taking. Yet he hung on, ready to risk death rather than give way to Link.

He risked another look to see how Link was taking his breakneck race and was shocked to see the easy, mocking grin still on Link's mouth, and the relaxed, one-handed driving. As though Link were all alone on the road, and drifting along at thirty. Even Sharon, sitting beside Link, held her hair down with one hand and looked as calm as though she were sitting in a parked car. And *he* thought he was making a wild race of it!

A car approached. Ricky focused his eyes on it, sighting over the wheel as though aiming a gun. The road wasn't wide enough for three. Somebody would have to give. Somebody else.

Ricky glanced at Link again. Link's grin was tighter. He could yield or he could pull ahead, to let Ricky in behind him. But he saw Ricky's determination not to yield, and Link responded by matching Rick's speed to the mile, so they stayed abreast.

Ricky knew it. He knew Link was forcing him to the limit and keeping him there, testing him, sure that Ricky would give at the last moment, break, and pull in behind the convertible.

The car ahead loomed larger. The driver slowed as he saw the two cars bear down on him at top speed.

Ricky saw the car slow down and waver as the driver tried to make up his mind. But he wouldn't give. He *wouldn't!* Not to Link. Not any more. He straightened his arms and braced himself. There was going to be a crash. They'd both hit the oncoming car. There was always the ditch. . . .

The driver of the approaching car made the needed move to avert disaster. He pulled off the road and went into the ditch, a fraction of a second before the two racing cars roared past, showering him with dust and gravel. As he flashed by, Ricky caught a glimpse of a man's staring face, and saw the lips moving. He didn't hear the man hoarsely begging Providence for a gun with which to kill the drivers of the cars that had driven him from the road.

"Oh, God. . . ." Ricky gasped as he saw the car ahead go into the ditch, and then was by it. "Oh, God. . . ."

And then Link lifted his hand in a farewell gesture, and without seeming effort or strain his car shot ahead, leaving Ricky to fight the blinding dust and spray of pebbles and stones that flew up from under the tires. It was with a mixed feeling of frustration and relief that Ricky gave up, eased off the gas pedal and was kind to his tortured machine.

In town again, he pulled up alongside Link's yellow convertible where it was parked in front of the drug store. Link and Sharon were already in the store. Ricky pushed through the door as the other boys drove into the square and nosed into place beside his car.

Link and Sharon were sitting side by side in a booth. Link looked amused as Ricky came in, Sharon angry.

"What happened to you?" Link asked. "When I shifted into high, you were gone."

"You just wait," Ricky said. "Anybody can beat that old heap now, but you just wait."

"You . . . *fools!*" Sharon burst out. She wanted to say more, but she was too angry to speak.

"By the time I've got high-compression heads . . ."

Ricky began seriously, looking at Link, "and dual springing ignition, and . . ."

"You *fool*, you," Link said in a high voice. "You kuh-razy duh-river."

Sharon moved away from Link. Ricky looked at her with a reckless smile on his lips, but when she did look at him for a moment, there was nothing but disgust on her pretty face.

"Nuts," Ricky thought. "First she's snotty because I don't have a car, and now she's mad because I have one. *Nothing* pleases women!"

"Man, man, man," Sherm Lucas kept repeating as he clumped into the drug store. "Ricky, you're a wild hair if I ever saw one."

"Nuts," Chub said, sitting down beside Ricky. "Just plain, ordinary nuts! That's what you are. Boy, if you're gonna be driving, *I'm* gonna take flying lessons. I don't want no part of no road *you're* on."

Ricky smiled sarcastically, pleased with himself. "I scare you out?"

"Running somebody off the road isn't a game," Jerry said as he joined the group. "I thought we were going to have some bodies to carry home."

"I don't understand you guys," Ricky said. "You all turning chicken or something? I didn't do anything you guys haven't done." He looked around with what he hoped showed as careless courage. "You just wait until I get that mill hopped-up. Then you'll see."

"You'd better fix that busted spring and get some decent rubber on your wheels first," Jerry said.

"You're a menace right now. You looked like you were traveling sideways."

"Tell you what I'd do," big Sherm said thoughtfully. "Before I added any speed equipment I'd get a good valve and ring job. No high-compression heads are going to do any good if you've got rings like rubber bands."

"From the sound of that transmission," Chub added, "I'd suggest you get a new set of . . ."

"Yeah, sure," Ricky hooted. "I'd buy a new car too, if I had the dough. Don't you think I know what I want? But it's what you get, not what you want that makes you fat."

"What you've got will make you dead if you don't fix it," Jerry said. "If you could only see yourself on the road, you'd be afraid to sit in that thing when it was parked."

"What do you want me to do?" Ricky demanded. "Give up my car and quit driving just because you guys don't like it?"

"It ain't that, Rick," Chub said. "But it ain't safe."

"Look who's talking about safety!" Ricky cried. "I suppose you never ran anybody off the road. Remember the time when you sneaked up on Jerry? He was doing a good eighty, and you came up behind him and bumped him with your car. I was with you! Was that safe?"

"Aw, that was different," Chub said. "I wasn't on bald tires with a mill that might shell out on me any second."

"It's different because it's me," Ricky said defiantly. "That's what's different."

He was sure of that, too, and it made him feel helpless. How was he ever going to convince them that he was one of them? What would it take to make them stop acting like he was the only one who didn't have the right to drive? It was bewildering. He'd thought once he owned a car he'd automatically take his place in the group. Instead they were jumping all over him.

"I guess maybe you guys are just sore because I took you with my old heap," Ricky said.

"Aw . . . haw!" Chub snorted, his round, shining face creased into deep wrinkles of contempt. "I could take you without getting out of second. Any time you say."

"Why didn't you?" Ricky challenged.

"I didn't want to."

"Yeah," Ricky said sarcastically. "You *like* to be passed, don't you? Don't all of you? You just love it when somebody passes you. That's why you always pass right back again—if you can."

Jerry poked Ricky with his elbow, hoping to tone him down. He was just making a fool of himself. "Talk sense, Rick," he muttered.

"I am talking sense," Ricky said stubbornly. "I'm ready to match wheels with anybody here any time."

"I wouldn't waste the gas," Sherm said, yawning.

"Chicken," Ricky said to him.

Link, who had been sitting quietly, smiling at his fingertips, looked at Ricky with his usual insolent smile. "At least Ricky proved he wasn't chicken," Link said, his black eyes holding Ricky's gaze. "Didn't you, Ricky?"

Ricky felt his skin tingle under that knowing, penetrating, mocking look. *He knew I was scared. He knew it all the time. He knew I wanted to chicken out. He knew. . . .*

"I suppose so," Ricky said tightly, forcing himself to return Link's stare. "For all anybody cares. If you guys want an exclusive club, I guess that's your privilege."

He looked quickly at Sharon, but she was sitting with her chin in her hands, her eyes closed, a bored look on her face. Ricky shrugged and got to his feet, his heart filled with bitterness against them all. He had to face his parents now. And he had counted on having the guys behind him, to give him courage. But now . . . what had it all been for? What was the use? He felt like getting in his car and smashing into a wall or running off a bridge. That would satisfy everybody!

He walked out without saying good-bye, his head thrust forward, a brooding, petulant look on his face.

He got in his car, slammed the door shut and slid under the cracked wheel. Tinny, lopsided, beat-up piece of junk! He started it, listening angrily to the weak motor. He was just about to slam it in reverse and back away from the curb when a fat hand came to rest on the door of the car where the window was rolled down. Ricky looked up and into the heavy, sweat-streaked face of Arnie VanZuuk. There was nothing threatening in Arnie's manner, but he represented the law. the Big Don't, all the don'ts in the world wrapped up and delivered in one restraining package. Ricky's mouth tightened. It wasn't enough that everybody else was hopping on him, Arnie had to add his weight.

"You bought the car, Ricky?"

"Yeah." He stared right back at Arnie. It was his car. He had a right to buy a car without being third-degreed by the cops. Nobody else would have been questioned.

"You drive careful, yes?" Arnie said it pleasantly, but it was still an order. It was Arnie's way, making his orders seem like asking a favor.

"Sure," Ricky said curtly. "I'll be careful. You don't think I'd want to wreck my own car, do you?"

"Heaven forbid!" Arnie exclaimed, but the irony of his tone was lost on Ricky.

Ricky was anxious to get going, but Arnie's hand was still on the car. Ricky wondered what else the fat joker wanted.

"You been already for a drive?" Arnie leaned down a little, his blue eyes bright and questioning in his red face.

"A little," Ricky said. "Shakedown run." He stared back at Arnie defiantly. If there'd been a complaint from the guy they'd run off the road, he'd complain right back. Say the other guy was driving like he was drunk.

"That's all right," Arnie said mildly. "You got a driver's license, I suppose?"

Ricky's mouth hung open. It was the one thing he'd

forgotten all about. Caught! The first time out, and in trouble already.

"I . . . I don't have it with me," Ricky stuttered, avoiding Arnie's eyes.

"You should carry it," Arnie said. "Maybe you get stopped by a highway patrolman instead of me. They like you should carry it all the time. It's the law."

"It's home," Ricky said. "In my room. I'll get it right away."

"All right," Arnie said, nodding his big head. "The next time I see you, you show it to me, all right? If I find you another time without it, I have to give you a ticket."

"I'll have it," Ricky said. "I promise."

"That's a good boy," Arnie said, withdrawing his hand. "Is easier to keep out of trouble than get out. I been looking over your car. You need tires."

"I'll get some as soon as I can," Ricky said. "And I'll fix the spring, too." A note of self-righteousness crept into his voice.

"That's nice," Arnie said. "And the straight pipes? When are you getting them?"

"As soon as . . ." Ricky broke off, seeing how he had been trapped, knowing now that he hadn't been fooling Arnie about anything with his sincere line of chatter. "I better go home and get my license," Ricky said.

"Don't forget it," Arnie said, stepping back.

Ricky put his head out of the window. "I really do have one," he said seriously. "Jerry drove me to the county seat one day, and I passed the test in his car. 1

do have one. I'll show you right now if you don't believe me."

Arnie smiled slowly at the thin, over-anxious face, the earnest brown eyes. "I believe you, Ricky," he said soothingly. "What makes you think I wouldn't believe you?"

It was in Ricky's mind to say that cops never believed anything good about young guys with cars, but he didn't say it. It was something he'd heard enough about, but he'd only heard it. When it happened to him, that would be time enough to sound off.

"I just wanted to be sure," Ricky said. "See you later."

He'd intended to back up in a rush, and peel down the street with a burst of speed, but Arnie's being around made a difference. He backed slowly and carefully, and made a slow, easy start forward. He looked back toward the sidewalk, and saw Arnie watching after him. He didn't like that. He had never minded Arnie's looking at him before, but now it was different. Now that he had a car Arnie wasn't only the fat old cop he chewed the rag with in the drug store. He was somebody to watch out for.

Ricky waited until he was out of the square before he picked up speed. He meant to take a run to the edge of town, then go home and clean up his car a little.

And have it out with his folks.

4

When he swung into the drive behind the house he had all his arguments ready. He had something to fight for now, and it wasn't going to be easy to get him to give up his car.

It all depended on how they acted. The more they bawled him out the more he'd hang on to it. But if they made some kind of a reasonable proposal, he might let his dad take the car back to Merle's and get the money. The way Merle had stuck him! He hoped Merle wouldn't tell anybody.

Ricky sat in his car with the motor running for a few moments before he shut it off. Then he stayed behind the wheel, waiting. His mother would hear the motor, and she'd come out to see who it was. She always did, when someone drove up.

He looked around the inside of his car with less than pleasure. It was pretty cruddy. Now that the novelty

68

of the purchase had worn off, and he needed more gas, and he *had* raced with the guys, and he *had* been cheated, he was more than willing to meet his parents halfway, get his money back, and look around for a real buy.

The back door of the house opened and Ricky's mother came out to see who had driven up. Seeing Ricky at the wheel of the battered old car, she walked toward him slowly, her face furrowed with concern. He watched her come, feeling his face reddening with guilt.

"Whose car are you driving, Ricky?" she asked, stopping a few feet away from him. "You know your father doesn't want you to drive other people's cars. He . . ."

Ricky looked at her silently, hopefully, shame and defiance mixed in his wide-open brown eyes, the stubborn set of his mouth. She knew the look, and guessed what it meant.

"Yours." She said it as though something she had dreaded for a long time had finally come to pass.

He looked at her feet, noticing every detail of how her sandals were made. "I guess it is, Ma."

He expected the questioning to begin now, the "why did you do it?" the "you can't keep it," and the lecture designed to shame him and make him agree to give up his car. He was prepared for it. He had his answers ready.

But when he looked up again, wondering why she didn't scold, he was bewildered. She was distastefully but calmly looking over his car.

69

"Is this the best you could do?" she asked critically. "It looks awful."

"It's all I could afford," Ricky said, watching her warily, expecting her manner to change.

"What did Dad say about it?" she asked. "Did he think it was all right?"

Ricky shook his head, as though trying to clear it. What his mother was saying didn't make sense. "Dad hasn't seen it," he said, looking guardedly at his mother.

"You mean he let you go *alone?* The least he could do was go with you."

Ricky twisted uncomfortably behind the wheel. Something was going on that he didn't understand at all. What was his mother driving at?

"Dad said when he left home he was going to let you buy a car," his mother said. "The least he could have done was go with you, and see you weren't cheated."

Ricky's head sank forward until his chin touched his chest. Now he saw their game. Now. Oh, no, *they* wouldn't scold him, or try to fight the car away. He should have known *that.* They had some smooth easy scheme cooked up, the way they always had. They were going to make believe they had been *just about* to buy a car for him, and make him feel guilty and childish because he hadn't waited.

They'd pretend they were all for his having a car, then they'd start chopping away at him. *What about the gas, Ricky? What about repairs, Ricky? You were cheated, Ricky. We'd have bought you a better car if you'd waited, Ricky. You acted like a child, Ricky. You were cheated because you didn't ask us, Ricky.*

70

He knew the routine. They'd drag his welfare into it somehow, and by the time they got through agreeing that he deserved to have a car, they'd have him ready to give it up. That's what *they* thought. That old trick wasn't going to work any more. The harder they tried to show how foolish he'd been, the more he'd hang on to his car and prove he *had* made a good buy.

Ricky climbed out of the car and got the garden hose out of the garage. He filled a pail with water, added detergent, and sloshed it around until it was sudsy.

"I wasn't cheated," he said. "You wait until I've got the car washed and polished. Once I get the dirt off, you won't recognize it. I'll be glad to take you for a ride when it's all cleaned up, Ma." He looked at her hopefully.

She was still looking at the car as though it were some stinking carcass a dog had dragged in their yard and left there.

Ricky shrugged. It was no use trying to explain to his mother. She was like all women. All they looked at in a car was the upholstery and the color of the paint. If it looked clean and new, they thought it was good. They didn't know anything about what mattered under the hood.

"Watch out, Ma," he said, getting ready to wash the top of the car. "I don't want to splash you."

She stepped back, watching him work, jealous of the devotion with which he touched the shabby surface of the filthy coupe. She was disappointed that her son should be so simple-minded as to feel that ownership of a broken-down old car was his highest goal in life. But there was more than disgust and disappointment in her mind as she watched her lean tanned son carefully scrubbing the rusty hide of his car. There was fear, and the fear bred hatred for every inch and ounce of the old coupe.

In the driveway, parked in front of the garage, it was an ugly, misshapen toy. An eyesore, but harmless. But once the motor was started, it ceased to be a toy or an eyesore. It became a threat, a deadly enemy. The moment it began to move it endangered the life of her son.

How many other boys there had been who had followed the siren sound of a gasoline motor. How many others who had washed and polished their cars, spent loving, greasy hours fussing with the motors, shining the chrome, caressing the iron monsters as though they were loved ones of flesh and blood.

How many others there had been whose devotion, whose care, whose tender concern over every scratch and dent had been repaid with death. And now, there was one in her drive. There was a boy washing the old wounds of his car. And there was his car, a discolored, battered, abandoned thing that her son had rescued from the junk yard. His machine, that he would care for and pamper and rejuvenate until it had power and speed. Until its voice would urge him to go faster and faster. Until it repaid his care and devotion with . . . death. No. Not her son. Not *Ricky*. Not that way. . . .

"Look, Ma!" His pleased voice broke into her morbid thoughts. She looked at him standing by his car with his denims and yellow shirt soaked with water, directing a spray from the hose against the car. His face was eager, bright, and full of life. "I've just started, Ma, and look at the way that finish is coming up."

"I see, dear," she answered mechanically, as she had often responded to his demands when a child to look at the cave he had dug or the tower he had built. And not knowing what else to do or say, she went back into the house to prepare the evening meal.

Looking out of the windows over her sink she could watch him. It was silly of her to let a superstitious dread weigh her down. Other boys had cars and were careful, and weren't hurt. Ricky would be careful. Ricky had good sense. Yet, as she looked at the car he had bought, rusted, torn, sagging, it seemed the embodiment of dissolution, a machine cadaver. Old, dead, already decaying, it had been on its way to the graveyard. Why had Ricky interfered? Why had he held out his young hand to it, called it back to breathe life into it once more? She did not believe in luck, yet she felt that it was bad luck, tragic luck that Ricky sought to revive a machine that belonged with the dead of its kind. That it would not be held back, that it would go on to die, and that it would carry him with it.

Ricky was polishing the car and knew it was time for his father to be coming home. Despite the many heroic scenes in his mind in which he convinced his father that he had a right to the car, Ricky was scared. It hadn't been too bad with his mother, but with a thing like this, he knew that it was his father who would launch the major attack. Purposely he kept his back to the street, so that he wouldn't see his father until the last moment. He bent to his work, rubbing furiously, actually disappointed that one application of polish didn't restore the new, gleaming finish to the worn-out, checked paint.

Ricky turned to pick up a clean rag and saw his father just reaching the house. He was walking quickly, his arms pumping. For once he didn't look neat and composed. The feeling of dread that came over Ricky was so great he moved numbly, picking up the clean rag and rubbing the side of his car without really seeing what he was doing.

He heard his father walk up the drive and stop. Ricky's hand slowed, but he kept rubbing. He felt he should turn around, but couldn't.

"Ricky."

His father's voice was quiet, but unsteady.

"What, Dad?" He tried to focus on his polishing.

"Turn around, Ricky."

Ricky turned, his eyes on the polishing rag he held in his hands.

"Look at me, Ricky."

Ricky looked up quickly, then bent his head again. But he breathed easier. His father's face wasn't angry. It had looked disturbed, but not angry. Ricky felt self-confidence coming back. Getting the car had knocked his parents off their pins. He really had the upper hand, now. He'd showed them.

74

"Look at me, Ricky."

Ricky looked up again, and this time his head stayed up.

"Why did you go into the bank and threaten Miss Myers in order to get your money? You didn't have to go behind my back to get your money."

"I didn't go behind your back," Ricky answered, turning red. "I wanted my money, and when I left home I just went and got it."

"And bought this car."

"Yes."

"I'm sorry you did it that way."

Ricky didn't answer. Now his dad was going to try and make him feel ashamed. But it wouldn't work.

"Your mother and I talked things over after you rushed out of the house," Ricky's father continued. "We decided we were going to let you have a car. We thought you were old enough, and mature enough to be trusted. If you'd waited half a day. . . ."

The only reason he's telling me this, Ricky thought, is because I've *got* a car. Sure, they were *just about* to let me have one! In another two years! Trying to make me feel like a louse.

Ricky's fear had left him now. Instead he was almost amused by the way first his mother and now his father were wriggling on the hook. He'd bought his car against their wishes, and since they couldn't make him take it back, they were trying to make it seem getting a car was *their* idea, and he shouldn't have beaten them to it.

"Now," his father was saying, "I don't know. The way you acted doesn't seem very mature to me. I don't think you can be trusted with a car."

"I seem to have one," Ricky said. "I bought it with my own money, so I guess it's mine."

"I wouldn't be too sure of that!" his father snapped, stung by the insolence in Ricky's tone.

"I *bought* it!" Ricky put his hand on the car, as though touching it would give him courage. "It's mine!"

"Let me tell *you* something," Mr. Madison said deliberately, as though talking to a difficult client at the bank. "You are sixteen years old. You can't make a contract to buy anything, if I don't want you to. And the man who sold you the car can't enforce the contract if I want it revoked. I can force you to return the car and get back every cent you spent for it."

Until that moment, Ricky had been half-hoping it would be possible to return the car after establishing his independence with its purchase. But the way his father was making a point of his being a child without authority to buy the car, made him determined to fight for it.

"I don't want to take it back," Ricky said stubbornly. "If you make me, I'll leave home like I said. I'll do it, too."

He saw his father hesitate. The threat was working. They knew he meant business now.

His father smiled somewhat bitterly. "All right, Son," he said softly. "I was going to do you the favor of letting you return the car, but maybe it will be best if we do it your way. Maybe it will teach you a little lesson if I insist you keep the car."

He's pitching a curve, Ricky thought. I'm set for it.

"I called Merle Connor," Mr. Madison went on. "I found out that you contracted to pay seventy-five dollars for a car that isn't worth thirty-five. My first impulse was to keep you from being cheated. But since you are so determined to prove your independence, I won't interfere. As far as I am concerned, my boy, it is your car, and you're stuck with it. Whatever the terms are, you'll have to meet them. The expenses of this car are all yours."

"That's all right with me," Ricky said. "I can earn enough to pay for it."

"Uh huh." His father straightened his coat. "Now . . . how about your insurance?"

"Insurance?" Ricky looked blank. It had never entered his mind.

"You know our state law, don't you? Either you carry insurance or you prove that you have a financial ability of ten thousand dollars."

"Well . . . I'll just get insurance," Ricky said.

"How?"

"What do you mean, how?" Ricky felt himself being driven in a corner. "Like everyone else."

"No insurance company will write you up," his father said. "Not until you're twenty-one. Unless, of course, I got the insurance for you, with the company that I insure with. You'll need me or some other adult to get that insurance for you. And even then there's a question of whether or not you'll get it."

77

"Suppose I don't get any insurance?" Ricky demanded. "What then?"

"All right," his father said. "Let's assume you drive without being insured. Suppose you are in an accident, someone is injured, and you are sued for damages. And we'll suppose the court upholds the judgment—let's say for twenty thousand dollars.

"The first thing that will happen, you'll lose your license and your car. There isn't much more that can be done until you're twenty-one, but when you reach that age, you reach manhood with a mortgage on your life. The people who have the judgment against you have first claim on everything you own and everything you earn. Until you paid off the amount assessed against you, you would be a prisoner of that debt. It might take the rest of your life to pay it off."

Ricky had no answer to that. They had him again.

"However," his father continued, "I wouldn't allow you to drive without insurance. Not so much for your protection, as for the protection of anyone you might injure. I know your thinking. If I use the insurance factor to make you give up the car, you'll feel I tricked you. I told you I wanted you to keep the car—if you can. But I also want to be sure that you're not a menace to others. Of course you'll have to pay for the insurance."

"I'll pay it," Ricky muttered. "How much will it be?"

"Somewhere around forty or fifty dollars a year."

78

Ricky looked trapped. "I don't have that much. I'm broke."

"You should have thought about that before."

"If you get it for me, could I pay you back a dollar a week?"

"Will you be able to? You have to pay on the car, you'll have operating expenses, repairs, a license to buy later on. How much are you earning now?"

"Well," Ricky said, "if I get that job at the grocery store I . . ."

"Get the job before you make any promises," his father said. "You bought the car, and you can keep it if you can pay for it. But before you can drive, these other matters will have to be taken care of."

"You don't have to worry, Dad," Ricky said earnestly. "I'll show you I can take care of the car."

"I don't suppose I have to tell you that if I find out you're misusing the car, I'll insist you give it up."

"Gosh," Ricky said, "I couldn't be reckless in this old car if I *wanted* to. I bet it wouldn't go over forty miles an hour if you had it wide open. But I'll be careful. With everything it's going to cost me, I'd be a fool to risk getting in a wreck!"

Mr. Madison smiled slightly at the self-righteous tone that had crept into Ricky's voice. "I trust your judgment, Ricky," he said. "But from the looks of your car, I wouldn't do very much driving until I had better tires on it, and fixed it up a little."

"That costs mon . . ." Ricky began, but let the sentence go without finishing it. Instead he looked critically at his car. "I see your point, Dad," he said in as mature a tone as he could muster. "And taking care of those weaknesses is the first thing I'm going to do. I don't believe in taking chances."

Mr. Madison nodded. He looked tired. "I wish you had waited, Ricky."

Ricky looked down at his moccasins. "I couldn't wait any longer. I *couldn't*."

Now that it was over, and he could keep the car, Ricky felt a sense of triumph, and exultation. He would get the job and earn the money to pay for his car. And he'd drive where and when and how he felt like it. He didn't take his father's threats too seriously. After all, they'd denied him the car until he'd bought it. They wouldn't be so quick to take it away. Not now that they knew he meant business. Next time he talked about leaving home, they'd believe him.

"I'm going in," Mr. Madison said, buttoning his coat. "Your mother will have to be convinced you can keep the car."

"She already is," Ricky said. "She thinks you told me to go and buy it. She's kind of mad because you didn't see that I got a better one."

A pained look showed on Mr. Madison's face. "I should have known that somehow I'd come out on the short end," he complained. "Whatever happens now, she'll think it's my fault."

"I guess she will, Dad," Ricky said. "I've got an idea. Why don't we take this car back to Merle and get me a better one that Mom likes?"

Ricky's father shook his head. "Too late, Ricky.

You couldn't wait for my choice. You just make the best of yours."

When his father left, Ricky went to the far side of his car and sat down by the front wheel, where they couldn't see him from the house.

Stuck. His father knew it, his mother knew it, the guys knew it and *he* knew it. Trying to act like a big shot, he'd really shown himself up for a dope. No wonder they were laughing at him, the way he had let Merle cheat him. No wonder Sharon had looked at him with disgust. He'd just proved that he was a worse kid than she thought.

Payments . . . insurance . . . license . . . parts. . . . He was stuck for a couple of hundred bucks, and he'd have to take that grocery job now. And what did he have to show for it? A junker nobody wanted.

But he'd show them all! He'd prove he hadn't been cheated. He'd rebuild his car until he had a rod that could match wheels with anybody. It could be done—maybe. Then they wouldn't sneer at him. Not after he showed them what he could do. That was the ticket all right. Work quietly, and make a real bomb out of the coupe. And then, some day when they were all giving him a rough time, invite Link to drag against him. Boy, wouldn't they stare when what they thought was a worn-out junker suddenly racked them all up. Ricky grinned, thinking about it, seeing his coupe leaving Link and the others behind as it exploded with a burst of speed that beat anything the guys had ever seen before. Yeah . . . it would come. . . .

"Ricky. . . ."

They had come up so quietly he hadn't heard them, but there they were, at the head of the drive. Link, Chub, Sherm and Jerry, sitting in their cars, looking warily in his direction.

Ricky scrambled to his feet. "It's all right, guys," he yelled. "I keep it."

"Good enough," Jerry yelled back. "We brought you some stuff."

While Ricky watched with glowing eyes, the boys took the "stuff" out of the trunks of their cars. Ricky shook his head in wonder as each of them came toward him rolling a tire and carrying other equipment.

"We thought you might need these gummies," Jerry said, leaning his tire against Ricky's car. "They're all better than the ones you've got on."

"Gee," Ricky said shakily. "I sure appreciate it."

"It wasn't nothing," Link grunted. "Just old stuff we couldn't use. I brought an old spring, too. It's good enough to keep that junker of yours from riding on the door handle."

Chub added to his tire gift a dented chrome extension for Ricky's exhaust pipe, a death's-head gearshift knob, and a radio antenna. Ricky was grateful for the antenna, even though he didn't have a radio. It gave him a place to mount and fly the thinning squirrel tail that Sherm had brought along with some extra chrome acorn nuts for the heads.

Ricky looked at their friendly, half-ashamed faces. They wanted him to be one of them!

"Gee, guys," he said shakily, looking at the treas-

82

ures they had brought. "I'll never forget you guys. Any time I have anything you need, you just ask."

They laughed good-naturedly, hands in pockets, looking down at their feet, self-conscious over this rite of welcoming Ricky into their ranks.

"We're just trying to make sure you won't explode when you're out with us," Jerry said.

Link came back with his spring and set it down. "You checked it very much?" he asked Ricky.

Ricky shook his head. "I meant to, but I was in a hurry."

"How about now?"

Ricky was reluctant to have his friends examine the car. He didn't want them to see how bad it really was. But that was what they wanted to do, and he couldn't say no. "Okay. But I can tell you in advance what's wrong with it."

"Start her up," Link said. "If she'll start."

Ricky started his motor and got out again while it idled. Link lifted the hood and unscrewed the radiator cap. The others watched him while he listened to the water being pumped through, then put his scowling, dark face down where he could see in. "Bubbles," he said tersely, shooting Ricky an almost derisive grin as he straightened up.

Ricky's heart sank. Bubbles could mean a cracked block or cracked head. If that were true, he was really in for trouble. He'd need a new head, or a whole new motor.

"Turn her off," Link said.

When the motor stopped, Link pulled out the oil dip-stick and examined it closely, then ran his fingers along it. Ricky stood back a little, not wanting to seem too anxious.

"No water or bubbles," Link said. "I guess the heads and block are okay. Probably a blown head gasket. You'll want new ones anyway, when you tear this mill down and clean it up."

"I thought maybe it was a head gasket," Ricky said. "The way it was overheating."

"Smoke from your oil breather too," Link said. "But you didn't expect good rings, did you?"

"Not any," Ricky said, grinning feebly.

Link got in the car and pressed the starter without turning on the key. "She clicks," he said. "Starter drive teeth are worn." He turned the key and started the car. He gunned it a few times, and clouds of dark smoke rolled out of the exhaust.

"I imagine my carburetor needs work," Ricky said, looking at the dark smoke.

"Get new jugs," Sherm said. "Don't fool with that old one."

They walked around to the back of the car. Ricky was prepared for the next symptom, afterburning. The put-putting at the tailpipe indicated leaky exhaust valves. He put his hand down to touch the muffler. It was hot to his touch. Well, a valve and ring job was to be expected. It was expensive, though. Everything was expensive.

Link shut off the motor and got out of the car again.

"I'll road test her for you after we get new rubber on," he said.

"I already did that," Ricky said. "I know what it needs. All I have to do is get the money to fix it up."

"I still think you ought to take it back," Jerry said.

"You guys don't understand," Ricky said, making up his story as he went along, needing to convince them and himself that he ought to keep the car. "I wanted an old junker. I'm going to take this car and work on it until it *is* something. Then I'll sell it and buy something decent. I'd be afraid to fool around with anything good until I knew more about it."

"Say . . ." Chub's round face creased into a wide, admiring smile. "You got something there, boy. Why didn't I think about that? Can I help? There's a lot I'd like to learn—on your car."

"I can always use help," Ricky said.

Link, who had been leaning against the coupe, listening, finally spoke. "You can't work without tools. What are you going to use for equipment?"

"I'll figure out a way," Ricky said. He stepped back and looked at his car. "I'm going to take a picture of this old wreck, and write down everything that's wrong with it, and everything it takes to fix it up. If it works out, someday maybe I can own a speed shop or something. There's a big future in building custom cars."

"Around here?" Link laughed.

"Why not? People around here have as much money as they do in California. And I'll bet if there was a place to have cars customized, there'd be plenty of guys who'd want the work done."

"If it works out, you let me know," Link said. "Maybe I'll let you do some work on my car. Put air in the tires, or something like that."

"You'll know if it works out," Ricky said. "You'll know from my dust."

"I'll see that day," Link said sarcastically.

"I know you will," Ricky said defiantly.

"See you in my rear-vision mirror," Link said, moving off. He got in his convertible, started it, and raced the motor for Ricky's benefit. It sounded mellow, tight, powerful. Link put the car in low gear and cracked it. He burned rubber as he took off.

"You'll have to go some to drag with him," Jerry said to Ricky.

"There'll come a day," Ricky said.

"You serious about that speed shop idea?"

"Sure I'm serious."

"You don't have much to start with."

"I've got more than Henry Ford had," Ricky said. "I've got a Ford that already runs, and I've got ideas. A lot of them."

"I'll help," Jerry said. "You know that."

"If I need you, I'll yell." He said it, but in his heart he was vowing that he wouldn't call on any of them. He'd do it alone, somehow. Prove to them all that he knew what he was doing.

When Jerry, Sherm and Chub left, spinning their wheels as they showed him how their rods could dig in,

Ricky loaded the tires they had brought into the trunk of his car. He was about to drive away when he got out of the car again and went into the house. His father and mother were in the kitchen.

"Did you see what the guys brought me?" Ricky began. "Four tires and a lot of other stuff."

"That was nice of them," his mother said. It had been decided not to make an issue out of Ricky's action.

Ricky turned to his father. "I've got a question, Dad."

"What?"

"I want to drive over to Merle's to change tires, but I don't know if I should, without insurance. You never know what might happen."

Ricky's father looked pleased. "I like the way you're starting off, Ricky. I'm glad you came to me with that question. As a matter of fact, I've already filled out your application. You can sign it now, and you'll be covered."

"That's swell," Ricky said. "Real swell."

"It's on the living room desk."

Ricky went into the living room to sign. His father and mother exchanged glances. "Seems to be working out fine," his father said.

Ricky's mother nodded without much enthusiasm. "It's his first day. We'll see what happens after three months."

When Ricky came back, he was carrying his camera. He explained to his parents why he was taking a picture of his car. "A year from now, you won't recognize that coupe," he vowed. "It will be the classiest car in this town."

"Then what?" his mother asked.

"Then I'll sell it at a profit, get another old car, and do the same thing. It shouldn't take too long before I can open my own . . . garage."

"Your own . . . garage!" Ricky's mother looked at him in dismay.

"Sure," Ricky said brightly. "I can hardly wait."

"But what about college? Ricky, a *garage*. . . . Is that all you want to be, a mechanic?"

"What's wrong with being a mechanic?" Ricky's voice rose. "You don't know what kind of a future there is in building custom cars, that's all. What do you want me to be? A *school teacher?*"

"We'll talk about that some other time," Mr. Madison interrupted. "Right now, why don't you get those good tires on your car."

"I guess I'd better," Ricky said, still bristling. He went out feeling that a new fight was developing. First against his having a car, now about what he wanted to do in life. His parents were just going to have to understand that it was *his* life, and he was going to live it the way he wanted to.

Inside the house, his parents were keeping the issue alive.

"I don't care what he thinks he wants to do," his mother was saying. "Ricky will go to college."

"Of course he'll go," his father said. "But he still has two more years of high school. There's plenty of time to talk to him about it. He'll forget these wild schemes long before he's ready to go on to college. And the less we argue about them, the sooner he'll forget them. You wait and see."

Merle Connor saw Ricky drive up to the garage and waited for him to come inside. Merle had all his arguments ready about why he couldn't take back the car.

Ricky came in hesitantly. "Hi, Merle," he said when he saw Connor.

Merle nodded.

"I've got kind of a favor to ask," Ricky said.

"You bought the car fair and square," Merle said. "I don't see how I can take it back."

"I don't want to bring it back," Ricky said. "I want to fix it up." Ricky sat down on the running board of a truck. "Everybody thinks I got a junker," he said. "I want to prove I didn't, and I've got a plan. If I came down here in my spare time and helped you around the garage, would you let me use your tools so I could work on my car? And maybe give me some advice?"

"I don't know," Merle said, searching for a cigarette. "What can you do?"

"I learn pretty fast," Ricky said. "And of course I'd buy all my parts from you. You could probably help me get some bargains."

"Well," Merle sat down and pushed his greasy red cap back on his head. "Would you want to keep the place clean and change tires and stuff like that?"

"Anything you say," Ricky promised. "I've got some tires to put on the coupe now. You can have the old ones if you want them."

Merle scratched his chin. The idea of a free helper appealed to him. If he had somebody to keep the place clean, he might get more business. Might become the biggest garage in Dellville, with all kinds of equipment. Then he could get a car dealership, and go somewhere.

While Merle thought, Ricky outlined his plan for rebuilding the coupe, selling it, and starting over again, with the idea of having a regular custom shop.

"Fixing up old cars would only be the beginning," Ricky said. "Shoot, a guy who pays five thousand bucks for a big car gets one that's exactly like all the others. If we were set up to customize that car, and make it the only one of its kind, I'll bet we'd get a lot of customers who wanted their cars to look special. They do it in California, so I don't see why we couldn't do it here, do you?"

"Kid," Merle said slowly, squinting at his cigarette, "I think you got something. You come in and help me, and I'll let you use my tools. And if you sell that car and make some money, I'll come in with you as a partner."

Ricky let out a big sigh. "Boy, oh, boy," he said wonderingly. "What a day *this* has been! I'm on my *way!*"

5

Ricky wasn't aware that his parents had stopped eating and were watching him. His left arm was on the table, curved protectively around the dish of pudding before him, his face was directly over the dish, almost low enough to touch. His spoon scraped noisily as he dug after the last few lines of chocolate.

"Wouldn't it be easier to eat the dish, Ricky? I'm sure it would be quieter."

Ricky straightened up and pushed the dish from him. "That was good," he said, looking at his father.

"It would be just as good if you didn't play you were eating from a trough."

"I'm sorry. When something's good, I get so interested in eating, I forget everything else." Ricky patted his chest. "Notice how I'm putting on weight? I feel *heavy*."

"It's about time you got some flesh on those bones,"

his mother said. "But you'd gain just as much if you paid some attention to your manners."

"All right," Ricky said wearily. "I'll be refined." He sat up straight and tried to look prim. "May I be excused, please?"

"Don't get offended," his father said. "The reason we want you to keep your face out of your dish is so we can see what you look like. The only time we see you any more is at meals."

"I'm busy," Ricky said. "Working at the grocery store all day, and then on my car at night. I don't have much free time. If I can be excused, I'd like to go now. I promised Merle I'd be down right after supper."

"Must you hang around that garage every night?" Ricky's mother asked. "Can't you stay home one evening?"

Ricky stood up. "I've got work to do," he said. "We've hardly started getting my coupe in shape."

Ricky's parents exchanged glances. It was time they talked to the boy.

"We were just wondering, Ricky," Mr. Madison said, "if it's such a good idea for you to spend so much time with Merle Connor."

"What's wrong with Merle?" Ricky demanded, getting on the defensive. "I'm learning a lot from Merle."

"We appreciate the help he's giving you," Ricky's father said, "but you spend all your free time with him, and I don't know whether Merle is the kind of person a boy should be around so much."

"Why not?"

"For one thing, dear, he's an older man, and married, and . . ."

"You and Dad are married and older than I am," Ricky said. "And you want me to stay around with you."

"Don't be ridiculous," Ricky's father said in an annoyed tone. "And don't make fun of your mother. Is that what Merle is teaching you?"

"I'm not being ridiculous and I'm not making fun of Mom," Ricky said loudly. "I don't see why you and Mom have to pick on Merle just because he's good enough to let me use his place to work on my car. And help me too. That's more than a lot of people have done."

"That part is all right, Ricky. We don't mind your spending some time on your car. But when you spend all your time playing with it, it's time we stepped in."

Ricky leaned against the wall. "I wouldn't call it play," he said. "I've got a lot to learn before Merle and I go into business together."

His parents looked stunned, and Ricky was pleased. They thought he was just kidding around with his car. They'd see he was serious now. He wasn't playing with a big toy, he was planning his life's work.

"I . . . I don't understand," Ricky's father said.

"It's simple," Ricky answered. "We're fixing up the coupe together. If we can sell it and make a profit, Merle's going to be my partner, and we're going into business together, making custom cars. In four or five years we'll have something. You wait and see."

"Four or five years," Ricky's mother repeated. "But . . . what about your plans for college?"

"I'm not going to college," Ricky said. "Merle doesn't think I have to."

"*Merle* doesn't . . . Ricky, are you out of your mind? What does Merle know about . . . about . . ." His mother was so upset she couldn't find the right words.

"Merle knows a lot about cars," Ricky said. "More than I could learn in college, I bet."

"Is that all you want to know in life?" Ricky's father asked, trying to remain calm. "About cars?"

Ricky nodded. "I told you. I want to build custom cars."

Ricky's mother answered him angrily. "Cars . . . cars! For the sake of cars you intend to give up everything and become a partner of the most shiftless, worthless, unsavory— Is that your ambition in life? To be like *Merle?*"

"Merle's just as good as anybody else in this town," Ricky said defiantly. "And he knows a lot that other people don't know."

"I'm sure he does," Ricky's mother said bitterly. "What an ideal you picked."

"Now wait a minute," Ricky's father said. "Son, if you want to build custom cars, there's not a thing wrong with the idea. But that's even more reason why you should go to college. Building cars is a job that takes an engineer as well as a mechanic. You could study engineering and design and metals, and when you graduated you would be equipped to take other people's cars and work on them. That's a big responsibility, you know."

"You can't beat practical knowledge," Ricky said. "That's what Merle says."

"Son, I'm not saying anything against practical knowledge. It's essential. But you get that at college too. The point is, with what you are learning now, plus your college education, you'll be able to get ahead in life, and make something of yourself. Not be another Merle."

"All I want is my own speed and custom shop," Ricky said, looking at his parents with a plea for understanding in his eyes. "If I'm good, people will come to me and I'll go places—places I want to go. I don't want to go to college. I want to stay here and start my business."

"Is that your ambition in life?" his mother asked dully. "To be a mechanic?"

"If that's your name for it, I guess it is," Ricky said. "You don't know what kind of future there is in custom cars, that's all. You'll see."

"I see," his mother said. "I see the Merle Connor of the future." She got up and began to clear away the dishes. When she bent over to get a plate, Ricky saw a tear fall to the tablecloth. He looked at his father, but his father also looked as though he were in mourning.

"I . . . I guess I'd better be going," Ricky said uncertainly.

His mother answered, her voice choked with tears. "Go on. . . . Go to Merle Connor. . . . *Be* like him. . . ."

95

Ricky moved his shoulders uncomfortably and went out. He was disturbed and shocked by the way his parents had reacted to his plans. He'd thought they'd show some interest, but all they had shown was disappointment. Acted as though he were a moron or something.

College! What was so special about college? A lot of people went to college and came out just as dumb as they'd gone in. But his folks thought that when you went to college something big happened. You were a wheel, and better than anybody else just because you'd gone to school. College! Fat lot any of those profs would know about souping up a V-8, or chopping a top! Four years wasted, that's what it would be. And somebody else would have the custom shop. The way his folks acted! As though you were somebody inferior if you did any work with your hands, or got grease on you. All they thought about was manners, and keeping a white shirt clean from breakfast to supper. And they called that living!

His coupe was waiting for him in the driveway. In the month he'd had it, it hadn't changed much on the outside. He had fixed the spring, and it rode level now, but the real progress had been made inside.

He got in and started the motor, smiling as it sounded tight and even. He could thank Merle for that. He'd gone to Merle with a lot of fancy speed ideas, and Merle had just sat there looking greasy and cynical, smoking a cigarette, listening. When Ricky had finished talking, Merle had thrown away his cigarette and yawned.

"You through dreaming out loud, kid?"

"I'm not dreaming."

"You might as well try to hop-up the kitchen stove as what you've got here."

"But . . ."

"Butt's a short cigarette. The first thing you have to do is get this thing so it will run good, then you can worry about getting it to run fast. You ain't planning to buy a new motor, are you?"

"I can't."

"All right. We'll start with what you've got. Get all the tired parts fixed, and then maybe you'll have something to work on. Try to put soup in it now is like trying to put soup in a sieve."

That's the way they had started. When he was through with his chores around the garage he would get busy on his car. For all the information he had picked up reading the auto magazines, he didn't know where to start. It had taken Merle, standing by lazily, spitting, directing him with a kind of impersonal sarcasm, to teach him the basic approach to rebuilding a car.

At first Merle had been content to stand around and direct and haw-haw at Ricky's stupidity. But the way Ricky had hung on, grimly trying to learn, had quickened Merle's interest. It wasn't long before Merle was neglecting the tires people had brought to be fixed, and the other minor jobs he attracted, to give full cooperation to Ricky.

Ricky hadn't done much driving in that month, but Merle, always an accomplished borrower of tools he didn't have, had taken him on a tour of how to put strength and vigor back into tired iron.

They'd pulled the motor and gone over the frame from stem to stern, tightening, straightening, replacing worn bolts and shims, checking cables, brakes, assemblies.

Turning to the motor, Merle had shown Ricky how to do a valve and ring job, and while the block was out, Merle had loaded it on his truck, along with the heads and the flywheel.

"I know a guy runs a machine shop owes me a favor," Merle had said. "Watch the garage while I'm gone." In a few days he made another trip, and when he returned there was a proud grin on his unshaven face. The block had been ported and relieved, to allow better breathing and escape for the exhaust gases. The iron heads had been milled to boost compression, and the flywheel lightened.

"You get some speed equipment now," Merle had grunted, "we got something to hang it on. Now you're ready for that straight pipe."

That was their weak spot. Anything they had to buy.

They had worked on the body too, in that month. Nothing fancy. Just what it took to iron out the dents, smooth it, and get it ready for leading, scraping and repainting. Ricky wasn't anxious to do much body work until he had worked out a good design, and it would take a body shop to do the job. Lowering blocks had sufficed to pull the rear end down in the hot-rod tradition, and from here on in, it was just a question of what he could afford to buy and put on. Fixing the interior was last on his list.

He drove to Merle's easily. Already his car was something to be proud of. Cracking the gas pedal brought instant response. No flat spot, no bucks and leaps, no clouds of smoke. It wasn't a rod yet, but it would be. Meanwhile, it was a lively stock job—well, maybe just a little better than stock. It was good, and solid, and going places, and he had Merle to thank for it. And his parents were trying to turn him against Merle. For all the good it would do them.

Merle was waiting when Ricky reached the garage. Outwardly he kept up appearances of being bored, cynical, and slightly contemptuous of Ricky and his coupe. But inside Merle was pleased to see Ricky. At first the kid had been a nuisance with all his questions, but after a while it was good to have him around.

To Merle's surprise he found himself drawn into Ricky's project with almost as much enthusiasm as Ricky himself had. He didn't try to explain it to himself. All he knew was that he stopped being bored when it was time to work on the old coupe. Stopped sitting around wondering what to do after he lost his garage. He was beginning to feel some pride in his place. Once Ricky had cleaned it up and made a place for the tools it looked pretty good. One day he even looked at the outside and thought about *painting*.

The way Ricky jabbered about opening a speed shop, and doing custom work. Why, the kid hardly knew the wheels from the brake drums. But the idea fired Merle. Without the spirit to plan for himself, he easily hooked on to the plans Ricky made. Under Ricky's questioning, things came back to Merle that he thought he had forgotten years before. Items of knowledge about cars and motors. Tricks for improving performance, old formulas for power that he had learned drifting from shop to shop and then forgotten. To his own astonishment he began to read again. First one magazine on cars that Ricky had been carrying. Then he'd asked to read Ricky's entire collection, working his way laboriously through the shop notes and technical articles, often meeting words that were strange to him, but knowing what they meant when he read further.

And in his way Merle too began to dream of the future, with the concrete block building in it that housed the machinery and the parts a custom shop needed. And he, hoping to reach the heights that other mechanics had reached, began to look at Ricky's coupe as the vehicle that would carry him to the goal of success and respectability in Dellville. The kid was right. Fix one up and sell it, and another, and another, and one day they would be bringing in the new Cadillacs and Lincolns and Chryslers to be re-designed and re-built according to the owner's whim. Man, that *would* be the day!

Ricky drove his coupe into the garage and got out. "She runs like a top," he called to Merle.

Merle walked over slowly, a cigarette dangling from his lips. "You been able to take Link Aller yet?"

Ricky scowled. "No. But I will. You wait and see."

"I'm waiting," Merle said. "Got my magazine?"

Ricky took a new issue on car restyling and handed it to Merle. "Lot of good ideas in here."

"For us?"

Ricky grinned ruefully, hooking his fingers in his belt. "Boy, the equipment some of that stuff takes!"

"We'll figure something," Merle said. "If we're gonna have that big future you always talk about."

"We will, Merle," Ricky said, staring at his coupe and seeing the car he wanted to see. "Some day we'll be the biggest thing in the Middle West."

"Until that time comes," Merle said, "how about sweeping down?"

"You bet," Ricky said. He went for his broom and began to sweep. He was proud of the way he was keeping the old garage. It was beginning to look like something. Everything in its place. It was sharp.

"Merle . . ."

"What?"

Ricky walked over to Merle and looked over his shoulder. Merle was looking at the picture of a custom car that had been turned out by a West Coast custom house. Long, low, sleek, with white leather upholstery and a modified Caddy motor.

"We'll do better than that," Ricky said. "Won't we?"

"Sure," Merle said. "Haw!"

"The next money I get ahead," Ricky said, "what should I put on the coupe?"

"What it needs," Merle said, closing the magazine.

"New cam?"

"Not right away."

"Aw." Ricky looked disappointed.

"Don't be all in a rush all the time," Merle said. As he spoke, a certain dreamy quality came into his voice. "The way you get money in little dabs, I'll tell you what I think you ought to do. Get a race-type air cleaner for the carb."

"Stack's better."

"It's dusty country, son."

"Oh . . . yeah . . . of course. What next, Merle?"

"Then you ought to save for dual headers and pipes. You'll pick up some horsepower and performance there."

"And they got that mellow, mellow tone," Ricky sighed.

Merle snorted, but he also was thinking of the sweet deep sound they'd make. "After that we'll beef up the ignition, and then see if we can't put another carb on. Two pots will carry you fine for street use. Then we'll put on a 3/4 grind cam. That might not be according to the book, but since we've got to put on a piece at a time, that's as good a way to add on as any."

"How about stroking and boring?" Ricky asked. "And a high-speed rear end? Once we start, we might as well go all the way."

"We will, we will," Merle said petulantly. "But we ain't millionaires, and I don't have everything we need to work with. I'm trying to keep you on wheels while we get these things done, you sprout. And it won't hurt you one bit if we have to tear that mill down and build it back up three or four times. Kid, there's a lot

102

you have to learn if you're gonna be my partner. A lot."

"Well, the power end will be your department anyway," Ricky said. "I'm going to be the design boy. And I've got some designs in mind that are out of this world!"

"And need a Detroit setup to build, I bet," Merle scoffed.

"Maybe not," Ricky said. "We don't have to use steel. Maybe we can come up with something in plastic or fiberglas that will change the whole body industry."

"Now we just might at that," Merle said, grinning. "So you take that broom and think about it, and I'll read the magazine, and when we're both finished, we'll maybe do a little work on that heap of yours."

"I hear you talking," Ricky said. He took the broom and returned to his sweeping. Someday there would be a showroom with a marble floor, and gleaming, handmade models to show, and he'd have his studio where he'd design those bodies, then work with Merle on the problems of fitting power to the bodies that were drawn on paper.

He could see them now, in a modernistic office, with fancy furniture and lights. Sitting at a huge desk, looking at plans while the newspapermen took their picture. *Top Auto Designers at Work. Nation's Leading Design Team Wins International Competition for Best Car in the World.* Sharon would be in the picture too, of course. She was his secretary.

Suddenly Ricky laughed.

"What's funny?" Merle asked.

Ricky looked at Merle sitting in his dirty, baggy overalls, his face dirty and stark under the harsh lights. "I was just thinking how you'd look shaved wearing a white shirt and tie, getting your picture taken. I don't see it."

"Neither do I," Merle said. "Because when we make our pile I won't have any white shirts. Just a closet full of western sports shirts, with lots of stripes and pearl buttons. I mean to look dressed up!"

Ricky leaned on the broom, still dreaming of the future, and the picture for the paper. "That will be a day," he sighed. "What a day. College . . ."

"What about college?"

"My folks want me to give this up and go," Ricky said. "After I graduate from high school."

Merle felt panicky. If Ricky left, there wouldn't be much point in trying to carry on alone. He knew he'd never have the spirit or the courage to do it himself. Common sense would take over and discourage him. It took Ricky's talking the dream to make it seem real.

"College," Merle said cynically. "What for? So you can be a rah-rah boy?"

"I told them I didn't want to go."

"You don't need *college*," Merle snorted. "You can learn all you need to learn right here, from me. You seen how I fixed up your coupe, didn't you? I didn't need college for that. Gone to college, I'd been as dumb as you were about it. College!"

"Oh, I'm not going," Ricky said. "Don't you worry.

104

I guess I know the best way to learn motors and cars. Right in here, from the ground up."

"Now you're shouting," Merle said. "College. . . . Your dad say that?"

"Tried to."

"He talks like a man with a paper eardrum. I know *you*, sprout. You're gonna get somewhere if you stick with your old Uncle Merle. I'll learn you all you need to know."

"You bet I'm sticking," Ricky said. "And some-day . . ."

"That will be *the* day," Merle said, really believing it. "Connor-Madison . . . that name was made for a custom car."

"It sure has class," Ricky said, and he began to sweep again.

"Merle . . ."

"Sprout?"

Ricky twined one leg around the broom. "You're sure I don't need college?"

"I told you, didn't I?"

"You'd tell me to go if you thought I needed it, wouldn't you?"

"Sure I would. You don't think I want a dumb part-ner, do you?"

"Connor-Madison Motors," Ricky said. "I like the way that sounds. You know, I've been thinking of a sports-car design we might try on my coupe. Suppose we do a real radical. Take her right down to the frame and build something that's got the look of life about it. You know what I mean, Merle? Like it was supposed to move. Lines that don't just sit there. There has to be a sweeping feeling. Something racy, and classy, and . . . alert. . . . Like a good horse with his head up, sniffing the wind, and ready to run."

"That's the old Connor-Madison you're talking about," Merle said. He closed his eyes while Ricky talked, and he could see it. See it plain as day. It was there as long as the sprout kept talking. It was there and he was Merle Connor, custom king of the Middle West. The way the sprout talked, it all became real. The Connor-Madison was real, the new building was real, the people clamoring for work on their new cars were real. As long as the sprout kept talking in that voice that ached with wishing. All that was real. The ramshackle garage disappeared, his history of failure at every job disappeared, his old truck vanished, his ever-growing, complaining, worrisome family faded into a complacent haze. He forgot he was behind in his rent, and on the verge of being dispossessed, forgot he owed for tools, equipment, parts, didn't have enough work to pay his grocery bill, that even his tobacco was bought on credit.

As long as the sprout dreamed out loud Merle Connor dreamed with him. He was good to have around. He believed, and faith was known to have worked miracles. But if he left, and the garage was empty, and there was nobody left to wish aloud, then he was licked, Merle Connor was. And he'd soon be looking for another shanty where he could start another abortive enterprise.

"You don't need no college," Merle said, shaking

his head knowingly. "You stick with me, and we'll go places."

"I'm with you all the way," Ricky said.

Two weeks later Ricky drove down to Merle's after supper as usual. The big door to the garage was closed. Ricky blew his horn, but Merle didn't open up. Frowning, Ricky got out of the coupe and walked around to open the door himself. That's when he saw the FOR RENT sign propped in the window.

Ricky looked around helplessly, his mouth working, but there was no one to talk to, no one to explain. Slowly Ricky got back in his car and drove to Merle's house. The old truck was in the yard, and several ragged little children were playing on it. Ricky walked up to the house, climbed sagging steps, and knocked on the front door. Inside he could hear the sounds of a guitar, and Merle's flat, nasal voice singing a hillbilly song. Ricky felt cheered. If Merle was singing, things must be all right.

The door was opened by Merle's wife. She was a tired-looking woman with straw-colored hair and a pasty complexion. She was in her bare feet, and wearing a shapeless old print dress with a tear in the side. When the door opened a heavy smell of dirty clothes and dirty bodies rushed out.

"I'd like to see Merle," Ricky said.

Connor's wife looked at him for a moment. "He's inside."

Ricky followed her, wrinkling his nose against the smell. There were dirty clothes thrown all over the place, pieces of gnawed bread and jam on the floor. The broken couch in the living room was covered by an old sheet, and there was a baby lying on it, fighting with a swarm of flies for possession of its bottle.

"Merle's in there." Connor's wife nodded toward the back room from which the guitar and singing sounds came.

"Thanks."

Ricky went to the doorway and looked in. Merle was sitting on a chair with his feet stretched out to rest on the bed. He was dressed in baggy coveralls, and the greasy, red leather cap was on his head. He sang with a cigarette in his mouth. There was a bottle of whiskey by his side.

Ricky waited until Merle had finished his song. Then, while Merle was strumming, trying to figure out what to sing next, Ricky stepped into the room. "Hi, Merle. I stopped by the garage . . ."

Merle turned his head. He stared at Ricky with bloodshot eyes that were angry and mean.

"Who are you?" he asked belligerently.

"You know," Ricky said uneasily.

Merle picked up the bottle and took a drink. "Tell me your name!"

"Ricky Madison, Merle. You know."

"Ricky . . . Madison. . . . My name is Merle Connor." Merle's head sagged, and he mumbled to himself. Suddenly he looked up again, his face a dark red. "You ever hear of the Connor-Madison?" he asked, squinting at Ricky.

Ricky laughed hesitantly. "Good old Connor-Madison," he said. "Boy, that's a car that will be a car. It'll be the talk of the state when we get through with it. Right, Merle?"

Merle picked at his guitar, listening. Then he looked at Ricky as though he hadn't seen him before. "Sprout," he said thickly, "you better get out of here. Because if you don't, sprout, I'm gonna mash your face in."

"But *Merle* . . ."

"Git out!" Merle slammed his hand against the guitar. "Git out or I'll kill you!"

Ricky backed up hastily. Merle roared and bawled, hitting his guitar. Mrs. Connor padded to the front door and opened it. "I don't know what you done to Merle," she said. "But he sure has it in for you."

Ricky went out and got in his car. Just before he started the motor, he heard Merle start to sing again. Another mournful hillbilly tune. There were real tears in it.

A small dirty face tried to peek in Ricky's window. One of Merle's kids.

"This your car?" a shrill voice piped.

"Yeah."

"Is it a hot rod?"

Ricky looked at the smudged, wondering face and nodded. "Yeah."

"It's a Ford, ain't it?"

"Yea— No," Ricky said. "It's no Ford. It's a new make. Connor-Madison."

"Con-nor?" the child shrieked, unbelieving. "It's a Ford! Connor's *my* name."

"The only one ever built," Ricky said, starting the motor. "Watch out, sprout, I'm in gear."

He drove away with two sounds in his ears. The shrill child-voice screaming, "It's a *Ford!*" and the tearful chant of Merle Connor singing a song about death in the hills.

6

It was only after he had driven away from Merle's house that Ricky realized what had happened, and what it meant to him.

Merle was out of business again. There would be no more chores around the garage, no more work on the coupe, no more plans about the Connor-Madison. It was all over. Another reason for his parents to say, "I told you so." Something else for his friends to kid him about.

Habit directed him to the town square, and the Dellville Drug. But instead of turning in at the drug store, he kept on driving. They'd know about Merle's failure. They'd be waiting to rib him about it.

Ricky's mouth tightened. Why run away? He didn't have anything to be ashamed of. It wasn't *his* fault Merle had failed. And they had done a lot to the coupe. If anybody wanted any proof of that, he'd go out on the road with them. Just let them try to rib him too much!

Already on the defensive, prepared for an attack, feeling betrayed and belligerent, Ricky parked in front of the drug store. He raced his motor before turning the key. Let them know he was there and not ashamed of anything.

He thought he walked into the drug store with a careless air, but the chip on his shoulder could be seen a mile away. A quick look around as he entered showed they were waiting for him. Sherm, as usual, had his big face stuck in a comic, but Jerry, Chub and Link were standing by the magazine rack, talking. A couple of kids were at the counter drinking sodas. Sharon was in a booth talking to a red-haired girl.

Link was the first to speak. While the others hunted for something neutral to say, Link lifted his head and whistled. "Well, look who's here," Link exclaimed, simulating great wonder. "We thought you'd moved away."

"You know I've been busy," Ricky said, joining the group.

"Ain't your new friend in?" Link asked maliciously. "Is that why you've decided to honor us with your company?"

"I said I had work to do!"

"How you coming?" Jerry asked.

Ricky shrugged. "I *was* coming fine, until today."

Jerry nodded. "I heard Merle lost his place. Too bad."

"Yeah. We were just beginning to roll."

"How much you got left to do?" Chub asked.

"Yeah," Link added. "How is that shot rod of yours? Will it run without a tow yet?"

"It will run the wheels off that gook wagon you're pushing," Ricky said, feeling anger getting control of him.

Link looked amused, but didn't accept the challenge. "You've eaten enough of my dust to know better than that, Ricky," he said in a patronizing tone. "When your car has the guts mine has, I'll be ready. But I don't feel like wasting gas now."

"That's a new way to chicken out," Ricky said. But he knew Link could run away from him, and he was glad to let the matter drop. He moved away from the group and climbed on a stool at the soda counter, turning his back to it and leaning against it. That way he could see Sharon.

Sherm lifted his head. He saw Ricky for the first time. "Hi, Rick," he said cheerfully. "How's the Connor-Madison Special?"

Link howled, and even Chub and Jerry had to laugh. Sherm was so sincere. Sherm scratched his head when they laughed at him, but he didn't mind. When Ricky didn't answer, Sherm went back to his reading.

"Hey, Rick," Link called. "When are you going to start taking orders for custom work? Or do you have so much business you can't mess with Chevvys?"

Chub looked out toward the street. "I see a Ford coupe that could use some work. Maybe that fellow would be interested. Oh . . . sorry, Rick, that's your car."

Link winked at Chub, and talked to him, but loud enough so Ricky would be sure to hear. "I heard a rumor Connor-Madison was going to customize stock trucks and tractors."

Chub guffawed. "I heard they built a hay baler that can reach three miles an hour in a quarter-mile drag."

"No!" Link exclaimed. "If they can do that with a hay-baler, just think what they could do with a manure spreader!"

"With frenched headlights," Chub added.

"And fadeaway fenders."

"And a modified Merc power plant."

"What a bomb!"

Ricky swung around and leaned on the counter. Maybe because he'd known it was coming, it didn't bother him too much. They could rib him all they wanted to, the fact remained that Link was the only one he couldn't outrun on the road. The knowledge comforted him. From now on, he wouldn't shoot off his mouth about what he was doing, or intended to do. They'd find out when he chose Link someday and ran him into the ground. That was the only thing that would shut them up for good.

Link and Chub continued their loud jokes. They were trying to keep the same line going, and it was getting tiresome, even to them. But they didn't want to let Ricky off the hook yet. Trying to be funny, Link got dirty.

Ricky scowled at Link's first dirty comment. At the second he turned toward Link. "All right, Link, take it

114

easy," Ricky warned, He motioned toward Sharon and her friend.

"She's heard worse," Link said.

"She's not going to hear any more out of you," Ricky said, sliding off the stool. He took two or three steps toward Link. He was shaking a little from his sudden anger.

Link looked cynical, amused. "Says who?"

"Says me." Ricky walked forward until he was within a couple of feet of Link.

"Look who's getting a pure mind all of a sudden," Link taunted. "What'd you do? Join the YMCA? Or didn't Merle allow rough talk in his garage?"

"I'm just telling you," Ricky said stubbornly. "Lay off the dirt." He stepped closer to Link. He was a little taller than Link, but Link was heavier.

The humor went out of Link's voice. He didn't like to be crowded. Not by Ricky. "Quit trying to throw your weight around," Link said, trying to stare Ricky down. "You give me orders, you'd better be ready to back them up."

"I am ready," Ricky said, meeting Link's stare.

"Aw, break it up," Chub cried. "What's the matter with you guys?"

They ignored him, standing toe to toe, eye to eye. Jerry touched Ricky's arm. "Come on, Rick. Don't start any trouble." Ricky shook him off.

"Well," Link said.

"Well yourself," Ricky answered.

"You're crowding me."

115

"What are you going to do about it?"

Link grinned. He brought his left hand up for a quick push against Ricky's chest. Ricky knew that habit of Link's, and was waiting for it. The moment Link's hand moved, Ricky lashed out with his left. But Link's hand didn't touch him. There was a blur of motion in which Link's face moved out of range, and as Ricky's left pawed the air, Link came in over Ricky's lead with a hard right. There was a sharp click as Link's knuckles met Ricky's chin, and Ricky went down on the seat of his pants.

He was down only for a moment, but when he scrambled to his feet, humiliated and raging, Jerry and Chub grabbed him and held him while Link stood mockingly in front of him.

"That's all, you crazy fools!" Jerry commanded sharply. "What's wrong with you guys anyway?"

"Ricky just needed a little lesson, that's all," Link said. "He's a little free with his orders."

Rick tried to pull away and attack again. "Simmer down," Jerry said disgustedly. "Haven't you had enough?"

"Let go!" Ricky said hoarsely. "Let go!"

"Not until you get some sense. Come on, Chub. Let's drag him away from here."

"What's the matter with you, Rick?" Chub asked. "Can't you take a little ribbing?"

"Not from that guy," Ricky muttered.

Link watched them pull Ricky away, and then, the victor in possession of the field, he waved a short, impudent salute and walked out.

116

Just at that moment Sherm finished reading the comic book he had borrowed from the rack and closed it with a sigh. He looked around, blinking his blue eyes, seeming to be disappointed at returning to reality. He looked at Ricky and yawned. Then he frowned. "You got a cut on your chin, Rick," Sherm said, pointing with a big finger. "You didn't wreck your car, did you? What happened?"

"Nothing, Sherm," Ricky answered. "Nothing happened."

"That's good," Sherm said. He went to the magazine rack and got another comic book, and in a moment he was again lost to the world.

Chub and Jerry tried to take Ricky's mind off the fight by talking about his car, but he didn't respond. After he had answered several questions with an unintelligible grunt, they decided to leave him alone. They went out, and drove away.

That left Ricky alone with Sherm—which was like being all alone. Ricky sat with his chin in his hands, brooding. Brooding over losing a place to work on his car, over the loss of a dream about building custom cars, over the loss of the fight. Whatever he touched his hand to, he lost. As though he were jinxed.

He was surprised when Sharon took the seat next to him. He'd forgotten all about her. Remembering that she must have seen Link whip him, he felt a surge of shame.

"Thanks, Ricky," she said.

He didn't look at her. "I didn't do anything." He looked down sullenly. He didn't want her to get any idea that he had been fighting over her. Women liked that. He hadn't lost any fight over *her*.

"You did a great deal," Sharon said. "You stopped his smutty talk."

"Yeah. With my chin," Ricky said bitterly.

"I like what you did, Ricky," Sharon continued. "You know . . . most girls don't like to hear dirty talk, and for some reason or other a lot of boys go out of their way to talk that way in front of us. So thanks for what you did."

Ricky took a drinking straw from its container and began to unravel it. "You never did like it," he said. "I remember when we used to play together, when we were little. You used to run and tell if I said naughty words."

"Once I put sand in your mouth," Sharon said.

Ricky turned toward her, laughing. "Do you still remember *that?*"

Sharon nodded and laughed, blushing.

Ricky looked at her with a feeling of delight in his heart. What ever gave him the idea that Sharon was like a cold statue? Why, she was just the way he always remembered. Soft brown hair, gray-green eyes that were warm and friendly and bright, the sprinkle of freckles across her nose, and the smile, and that soft lower lip. . . . Why . . . he knew her . . . they were old friends!

"We haven't seen much of each other lately," Ricky said. "You kind of froze me out."

"I remember when you froze *me* out."

Ricky laughed again. "That was when I hated girls. But later . . ."

"That's when I didn't like show-offs."

Ricky reached for a new straw and began to peel it. "Was I a show-off?"

Sharon watched his fingers at work. "That's what I liked about you tonight. You weren't trying to show off. You were yourself."

"I wasn't much in the mood for showing off. I never meant to be one. I thought you were stuck-up, and didn't like me at all."

"I didn't think I was acting like that," Sharon said.

"Funny. How we think we're acting one way, and if we could see ourselves, we'd see we were not like that at all."

"That's right."

They looked at each other and smiled. As though they had been waiting for years until they could break through the invisible barrier between them and be to each other what they wanted to be. Just in the looks they exchanged there was so much they told, so much they understood.

"You . . . uh . . . got any plans for the evening?" Ricky asked.

"Nothing special."

"Want to go roller-skating?"

Sharon nodded. "My skates are home."

"So are mine. We'll pick them up. How about the rink at Selmar? It's kind of late to go to Des Moines."

"I like Selmar's rink. I wish we had one in Dellville."

"So do I," Ricky said, taking his car keys from his pocket. "But you know good old Dellville. Nothing. The nothing town."

They walked to the door together and he opened it for her. When they got in his car they looked at each other again, smiling, their hearts beating faster. Ricky started the car, letting it warm up for a moment before driving. Just like that, his amazed brain was trying to convince itself. Just like that, without working at it, Sharon was his girl. Looked like that jinx had been broken.

Ricky went through the house like a whirlwind, taking the steps three at a time on the way up, coming down in three big jumps.

"Ricky!" his father yelled from the living room. "What's going on?"

Ricky went into the living room carrying his skates, his face beet red. "Dad . . . Mom. . . . I'm going skating at the Selmar rink. I . . . uh . . . I'm taking Sharon . . . gotta rush. . . . 'Bye. . . . I won't be late."

He was out of the house in a rush. A moment later they heard his car drive away.

For a long moment Ricky's parents looked at each other. Then they began to laugh.

"Whew!" Mr. Madison said, taking out a handkerchief and patting his forehead. "Just like that!"

Mrs. Madison looked quietly pleased. "I rather think a certain young man will be spending less and

120

less time with Merle Connor. I wonder. . . . If Sharon suggested that Ricky go to college . . ."

"Don't break up the romance," Ricky's father warned. "Right now, her big job is to take some of his attention away from that car. And she's the little girl who can do it."

"Sharon's a nice girl."

"I know," Madison said. "Nice and sweet and pretty. That's the kind that drives you crazy."

"What a way to talk!"

"You mean what an age to be. . . . Anyway, I think Ricky is suddenly going to be less of a problem. Wait and see. He'll be yelling for a chance at college."

"I'm glad he chose Sharon," Mrs. Madison said.

"Me too. She lives so close Ricky won't need the car to see her. Maybe he'll let me borrow it some night. I could take you roller-skating."

"We have a car."

"A *stock* job," Ricky's father said, grinning. "You know, I've been reading some of Ricky's magazines. They're kind of interesting. It's amazing what some boys have been able to do. Some fathers even helped. It sounds like a nice father-and-son hobby."

"You're a little old to go speeding around the country in a hot rod."

"I'm not that old," Madison protested. "You know, I really would like to drive Ricky's car and see what it's like. But I don't want to ask. Not after the way I've nagged him about it."

"The next thing," Mrs. Madison said, "you'll be

wanting to date teen-age girls. You can't be a high-school boy again, so don't try."

"I don't want to be a high-school boy. But I still think it would be fun to learn something about motors. Take that family sedan of ours. . . ."

"A perfectly good, satisfactory car."

"It's transportation," Mr. Madison admitted. "Dependable transportation. But I've been reading in Ricky's magazine, and I think we could get better performance out of it. Better mileage, smoother operation, more power, better . . . acceleration . . . better . . ."

"Better put that magazine away and go back to your fishing magazine," Mrs. Madison said. "One hot-rod driver in the family is one too many. Did you see tonight's paper?"

"Not yet."

"Look at it."

Mr. Madison picked up the Des Moines evening paper and looked at the front page. It showed the picture of a smashed car, and the headline,

TEEN-AGER KILLED,
THREE CRITICALLY INJURED IN WRECK
RACE ON COUNTRY ROAD ENDS FATALLY FOR FARM YOUTH.

"This takes the fun out of it," Ricky's father said.

"There's a story like that almost every day. Won't they ever learn?"

"I suppose there is some way to slow them down," Madison said. "But I don't know what it is. What will it take to slow down other drivers, with new cars coming out boasting of motors over two hundred horsepower? Teen-agers don't drive them. And what about drunken drivers? Killing someone with a car because you're drunk is even worse than doing it because you're young. Why pick on teen-agers? I know they have more accidents than other age groups, and something should be done to correct that, but we can't single them out. Not the way so-called adults drive."

"You're beginning to sound like Ricky," Mrs. Madison said.

Madison smiled. "Darling, that's the nicest thing you've said to me in a week. When Ricky starts talking like me, you and I are going to be old and gray, Maggie."

There was a big juke box at one end of the roller rink, and it played a lot of waltzes. The rink was crowded with boys and girls from small towns and farms in the area. It was a good-natured crowd, full of laughter. They liked to skate, and there were few pauses in the music or the rolling thunder of skates.

Ricky and Sharon skated well together. Perhaps because they had once played together and remembered kinesthetically, if not consciously, how to cooperate. Skating side by side, holding hands, they matched stride for stride in an effortless, gliding circle around the rink. Other times they entwined arms as dancers, turning, swaying with the music, smiling happily and somewhat sleepily under the spell of the music and the drum-roll of skate wheels. When they took time out for Cokes and hamburgers they smiled at each other over the paper cups, and then they went back to let the music carry them along. They didn't talk much. They didn't have to.

When they knew the last dance was coming up Sharon sensed the change in Ricky. He was no longer relaxed, or dreamily content. She could feel by his arm that he was tense, and there was a certain detachment about him, a sense of his being apart from her.

She looked at him curiously as they sped over the smooth floor. He was looking around at other couples, and when some of them left the floor, he suddenly guided her to the sidelines.

"Let's finish out the dance, Ricky."

"We don't have time," he answered. "Change as fast as you can." He was pulling at his laces hurriedly, racing to get back into street shoes.

"What's your hurry?" Sharon asked. "It's not late."

Ricky stood up. "Come on."

"But I only have one skate off."

"Change the other one in the car," Ricky said, pulling her to her feet. "Let's go."

He went out as fast as he could pull her along. They heard several motors starting, and Ricky groaned. "We'll be the last ones out of here!"

"What difference does that make?"

"Get in."

Ricky had the car started in a flash. Lights were going on all around them, and cars were moving. Ricky shifted into low and shot ahead, slewing around on the graveled parking strip as he headed for the exit.

There was a mad dash going on for that exit. Cars of

every description, from every corner of the lot, were leaping and bucking across the parking lot. Clouds of dust rolled up from under spinning wheels. There was a din of horns. Horns that blew, honked, tooted and blatted.

"Oh, Ricky!" Sharon shouted indignantly.

"Hang on!" he shouted back. With his thumb pressing the horn he drove his coupe into the center of the pack. The dumpy shapes of other rods loomed up suddenly, then faded; the roar of straight pipes was deafening. The traffic streams converged on the exit, drivers jockeying to edge one another out of line, to fake their way through.

Ricky bore down steadily, shooting through holes between cars that seemed barely wide enough to walk through. In the din of motors and horns and shouts there was an occasional blunt sound as unlucky drivers tangled fenders.

Sharon cringed as they closed with other cars and then stopped inches short of collision. She looked at Ricky. He was hunched over the wheel, his head forward, his eyes wide, his lips pulled back in a grin of wild excitement.

A Tudor loaded with boys and girls tried to cut across Ricky's line of travel. He didn't give. His horn blasted and he drove forward, happily aggressive, ready to ram before he would veer away.

"Give, you crazy . . . give!" Ricky yelled to himself. The other car gave, and he shot past in a burst of triumphant speed, working his way into the clear. A coupe like his own appeared at his side, holding with

125

him hub to hub. He was being chosen. He cracked the gas and shot ahead. The coupe at his side stayed with him. Rocking crazily, the two cars roared at top speed in second toward the intersection with the main highway.

"Rickyyyyy!"

He didn't even hear her. The race was on and he had his coupe wide open. They would have to stop when they reached the highway, and the winner would be the one who backed off last. Ricky held, riding fender to fender with the other coupe while both motors screamed in shrill protest.

Ricky's face was rigid now. Frozen in a grin of defiance. He was like one hypnotized as he hurtled through the dust toward the highway. Then, luckily, the other driver backed off. As soon as he nosed ahead, Ricky pulled his foot from the gas pedal. Second gear and quick stabs at the brake brought him sliding to a stop just as he reached the highway where a private policeman was directing traffic. The policeman started toward Ricky, flashing a red light.

"Not tonight," Ricky said lightly. He saw a small break in highway traffic and nosed into it. The car he cut off honked at him. Ricky laughed derisively, and a moment later was pulling around the cars in front, with the gas pedal to the floor. A few minutes later they were alone on the highway, with the speedometer indicating eighty.

Ricky laughed. "How'd you like that?" he asked proudly. "Guess we showed 'em."

126

"Showed them what a fool you are!" Sharon said angrily. "Slow down."

Ricky looked pained. "But, Sharon . . ."

She looked at him with widened eyes that were serious and afraid. "I told you, Ricky. I didn't like you when you tried to show off. I still don't."

"I wasn't showing off," Ricky protested, grinning. "I didn't want to get caught in the traffic."

"Ricky, listen. Slow down or let me out."

"Aw . . ." Ricky glanced toward her. In the glow of the instrument panel he could see that she was deadly serious—and very pretty. His foot eased up on the gas pedal. "I was only trying to get you out ahead of all the dust."

"I can do without those favors, thank you."

"All right, we'll do it your way." He slowed the car to ten miles an hour. "We may get hit from behind, but if you think it's safer, you're the boss."

"Please don't act like L . . . like a smart aleck, Ricky."

He knew whose name she was going to say. It hurt.

"Nice fifty okay?"

"Just fine."

"Fifty it is."

They rode along quietly, the old feeling of closeness coming back—until headlights showed behind them. Again Sharon could feel Ricky grow tense, his eyes haunting the rear-vision mirror as he watched the car behind come up.

"Ricky . . ."

"Yeah?"

"No racing."

"I'm not racing."

"You're starting to."

"What do you want me to do?" he demanded.

"Back to fifty."

"I . . . all right. . . ." He cut his speed, but pouted like a child. A moment later a new sedan swept by them, its red taillights pulling away rapidly.

"Now that guy will go around bragging that his car took a rod," Ricky complained.

"What difference does that make?"

"It makes a difference. Guys shouldn't brag about things they can't do. Boy, if I'd been alone he never would have passed me!"

"Grow up, Ricky," Sharon said. "What disgrace is there in being passed?"

"I don't know," he said, frowning. "I just don't like it. There's something about having another car go past that's like an . . . insult. It's like saying your car isn't as good as that one."

"That doesn't make sense."

"It might not on paper, but it does when you're driving. And I'm not the only one," Ricky added. "You'd be surprised how many people in stock cars are the same way. I've followed more than one man or woman who didn't go over forty until I tried to pass. And the minute I tried to go around, they speeded up. And *that's* against the state law."

"You don't have to be like that," Sharon said. "Let's have a nice ride home."

Ricky looked at her again, and felt a funny gnawing sensation in the pit of his stomach. The wide eyes did that, and the little spray of freckles that he knew were on the nose, and that soft red lower lip.

"It is a nice ride home," Ricky answered. "And I'm in no hurry to get there. Are you?"

Somehow he knew that she had answered by moving closer to him. Not more than a fraction of an inch, perhaps, but he knew. She had moved, and it was an answer. She began to hum one of the songs that had been played at the roller rink. Ricky smiled and sang the words.

"You have a nice voice," Sharon said. Her head was turned toward him, the wide, serious eyes taking in the details of his face.

"Best tenor in the Dellville High Glee Club," Ricky said. "I'll be the best baritone after my voice settles down. I'm not bragging. That's what Mr. Stuart said last year."

Sharon wrinkled her nose and giggled.

"What's funny?" His voice was guarded.

"You."

"Funny ha-ha or funny queer?"

"Funny nice."

"That's a funny way to say it."

"Do you know a better way?"

"Way of what?"

"Saying somebody's nice?"

Ricky's right hand dropped away from the steering wheel. He moved it in the darkness until it touched Sharon's hand. Then he paused, waiting, his heart pounding. There was a slight answering pressure. He clung to her hand, feeling new sensations that threatened to overwhelm him. Then he raised his arm and put it around her. She moved toward him, nestling against him, her head on his shoulder, the clean smell of her hair so good it almost made him cry. With her right hand she clasped the fingers of the hand around her shoulder.

"Sing again," she said softly.

"What?"

"Something nice."

"Will you join in?"

"That's why I want you to sing. You start."

He started to sing a dreamy romantic song. Something he'd always thought icky, but which had suddenly acquired a new meaning. Sharon picked up after the first bar. Her voice was low and sweet.

The speedometer indicated forty-five, then forty.

A car swept past, honking. Ricky hardly cared.

7

They entered Dellville as quietly as the twin pipes on the coupe would allow, trailing the subdued throatiness of the mufflers through wide, dark, tree-lined streets. It was almost midnight, and no other traffic moved. The town seemed in full sleep, and nothing disturbed its rest.

"Peaceful-looking town," Sharon said sleepily, looking at the neat white houses that shone softly in the moonlight. Big white houses, with big shady yards, where there was plenty of room for children to play.

"Dead burg," Ricky answered. "Not even a place to get a sandwich after eight o'clock."

"I'll make one for you."

His right arm was still around her. He squeezed with it. "I'm not hungry."

"You said you wanted a sandwich."

"Uh-uh. I said you couldn't get one. In case you did want one."

"Well, in case you do want one, I'll make one."

"Your folks would like that," Ricky said. "My raiding the refrigerator after they're in bed. They are in bed, aren't they? Or do they wait up?"

"They might be up," Sharon said, "but they don't wait up for me. They trust me."

"Do they trust me?"

Sharon laughed, hiding her face with her hand.

"What's so funny about that?" Ricky demanded, feeling a bit resentful.

"The idea of their not trusting you," Sharon said, and giggled.

"I know they think I'm just the harmless little neighbor boy," Ricky said. "But I'm not as much of a kid as they might think."

"Oh, don't get ruffled," Sharon said. "They know I've put sand in your mouth before, and I can do it again."

"I don't know if I like this being trusted so much," Ricky said. "Makes me sound pretty dull."

"There's nothing dull about a good friend."

"How good?"

"Fishing?" she teased.

"Yeah. You biting?"

Sharon leaned toward him and bit him lightly on the lobe of his ear. Then she giggled softly.

"You're crazy," Ricky said, grinning from ear to ear. He turned at the corner and drove toward Sharon's house. Suddenly he straightened. "Your folks are up tonight. There's a light in every room. And there's Arnie's prowl car!"

Sharon sat up and stared through the narrow windshield. "I wonder if anything . . . happened," she said worriedly. "Somebody might be sick or hurt. . . . And I was gone all the time. . . . Ricky . . . I'm scared."

Ricky nosed the little coupe to the curb. "There's our car too," he said, his brown eyes showing his confusion. "What would my folks be doing here at this hour? Maybe it's a card party or something."

"With *Arnie* here?"

"It's not against the law to play cards."

Sharon was fumbling for the door release. "I hope nobody's . . ." She couldn't say the word "dead."

"It won't be anything bad," Ricky said. "You wait and see."

He joined Sharon on the sidewalk and reached for her hand, but she pulled hers away to bite her nails as she hurried toward the house.

When they walked across the porch, Ricky could see Sharon's folks, his own, and Arnie, all in the living room. At the sound of footsteps they all turned to look at the front door.

"Oh, golly," Ricky whispered. "They're waiting for us. Do I have any lipstick on me?"

"Probably," Sharon said. She could see all her family now, and they were all right, and she felt giddy with relief.

"What a time . . ." Ricky mumbled as Sharon opened the door. He licked his hand and rubbed it across his mouth, hoping for the best.

They weren't prepared for the reception that was waiting for them. The moment they entered the living room, blinking self-consciously in the light, the two mothers sprang forward, clasping their children in their arms.

"You're safe!" Sharon's mother said in an emotion-choked voice. Then she began to cry.

"It wasn't you . . . it wasn't you. . . ." Ricky's mother murmured, kissing him impulsively.

"Watch out, Mom." Ricky pulled away. "Now you probably got your lipstick all over me. Didn't you?"

Everyone in the room stared at him, seeing for the first time the lipstick that was smeared over his face in half a dozen places. And then they laughed. The fathers and mothers, their laughter still echoing of tears, Arnie's bull-like bellow that threatened to shake off his huge belly, and even Sharon's sudden, helpless, ashamed laughter, all at the sight of Ricky's indignant, blushing, red-smeared face.

"Oh, my dear God," Sharon's mother said, putting her hand on Ricky's arm. "At first I thought it was blood."

"Why should it be blood?" Ricky asked. "We weren't in any accident or anything. What's everybody here for? What *happened?* I . . . I'm sorry if I kept Sharon out too late. . . ."

"Didn't you hear the news?" Ricky's father asked.

"No." Ricky looked around at their serious faces.

134

"What happened? We . . . uh . . . didn't have the car radio on. I . . . uh . . . don't have one."

"We know you went skating in Selmar," Ricky's father said. "About an hour ago there was a news flash that a car was in a wreck in that area. The report said the car was too badly wrecked to tell at once what model it was, but it was a black Ford hot rod. There was a boy and a girl inside. They were too badly . . . too . . . they couldn't identify them. And there were roller skates in the road. The police said they thought the car was in a race, but they're not sure. When you didn't come home, we began to worry. It sounded like your car."

"It wasn't us," Ricky said, half-aloud, but with the look that was on his face no one laughed or smiled. He was thinking. Was it the coupe he had raced to the intersection? The Tudor he had cut off? The tall blond kid he'd stood next to when buying hamburgers? The cute red-haired girl in the green skating suit? Which ones? Which ones? They were kids he'd seen, who had been alive when the music was playing, who'd skated and danced and laughed and run for their car . . . and never made it home. Which ones? It seemed terribly important that he know, so he could say "I'm sorry" for more than a name.

"Well, your chicks are home," Arnie said, putting his too-small blue cap on top of his head. "I go now."

"Wait," Sharon's mother said. "I'll make coffee."

Arnie's blue eyes twinkled. "Ah, ah," he chided. "You know the way to keep a Dutchman in the house. For good coffee, I stay all night." Arnie chuck-

135

led. "This town. . . . You can't get a cup of coffee after eight o'clock, and what I make for myself . . . pfui! Even the drunks I arrest won't drink it to cure their hang-overs. For good coffee I stay!"

Sharon moved quietly to Ricky's side and nudged him. He followed her out of the living room, and up the stairs. "Where are you taking me?" he asked her.

She looked back. "To wash your face."

"Just like old times," Ricky said. "You were always dragging me up here and trying to scrub me."

"Your face was always dirty."

Sharon took a towel and washcloth from the linen closet. "Do a good job." She handed them to Ricky.

"Since I'm going to wash it all off," Ricky said in a low voice, "how about getting some more on first?"

"Don't be greedy," Sharon said. She turned him around and pushed him toward the bathroom.

Ricky washed his face, careful not to splash. When he was through, he drew a comb from his back pocket and gave his brown hair a couple of licks. He looked at himself carefully in the mirror, making sure all the lipstick was gone. When he went out in the hall, Sharon was waiting for him. She had put on fresh make-up. Not much, just enough to look good.

When they went downstairs, the dining room table had been set. Sharon's mother had mentioned coffee, but there was cake, and cheese, and sandwiches were being made in the kitchen. Arnie was already seated at the table, his cap off, his round sunburned head nodding happily.

136

"Arnie," Sharon's father said when they were on their second cup of coffee, "you've seen more than your share of highway accidents. What are we going to do to cut the accident rate?"

"Drive more careful," Arnie said.

"How are you going to make people do that?" Ricky's father asked. "We have laws, but no one takes them very seriously."

"How you gonna stop somebody from jumping off a building?" Arnie asked. "Only one way. Keep him from getting on the roof."

"You can't do away with automobiles."

"Then you have accidents." Arnie nodded as Sharon's mother motioned to fill his empty cup. "Most from carelessness, but sometimes the machines go bad. People make mistakes, and machines break down."

"There must be some way to make people drive more carefully," Sharon's father insisted. "We need tougher laws."

"When the law gets too tough, the courts don't convict," Arnie said, taking a piece of cheese. "Besides, you have to enforce a law. That takes policemen. We've got a handful of highway patrolmen to cover the state. People who want to break the law, or be reckless, they're willing to take the chance the patrolman ain't around. The only fellow that can enforce the law all the time is the fellow that breaks it."

Arnie turned his big head to look at Ricky. "How we gonna make sure Ricky obeys the laws, for instance? We might do it if we had him staked on a rope,

137

like a cow, and watched him all the time. But when he's out of sight, he's the one who makes or breaks the law. It's got to come from inside. Right, Ricky?"

"I guess so," Ricky said guardedly.

"I know," Arnie said. "I been the police force here a long time. We got a good town because just about everybody has made up his mind to obey the laws. I'm around for the few people that don't want to obey. If we had a lot like that, I couldn't do anything to keep order."

Sharon's father filled his pipe, got it going, and leaned on the table with his elbows. He looked directly at Ricky. "The state gives teen-agers the right to drive if they pass the required written and road test, right?"

Ricky nodded.

"In other words, in order to get a license, you have to prove that you are as competent to handle a car as I am, or your father, or mother, or any adult. Right?"

"That's right."

Mr. Bruce puffed on his pipe, watching Ricky through the smoke. The others were quiet. "Why is it, then, that teen-age drivers have the highest percentage of accidents of any age group?"

"I don't know," Ricky said. "I didn't know they did."

"They do. I want your honest opinion now. Are teen-agers dumber than the rest of us when it comes to understanding the law?"

"I don't think so."

"I don't either. Perhaps teen-agers don't know how

138

to handle automobiles as well as old ladies and grown men. Is that it?"

Ricky smiled. "I think the average teen-ager can out-drive the average adult. When it comes to handling a car . . ."

"They're terrific," Mr. Bruce said. "I know. Good reflexes, good eyes, good muscle control. All the things that make them good athletes and all that. Do you agree?"

"It sounds logical," Ricky said.

"Then what's wrong?" Mr. Bruce asked. "You pass the same tests, you understand the laws, you are superb drivers. . . . Why do you have so many accidents?"

"Well," Ricky said reluctantly, "I suppose we drive pretty fast—"

"That's not the reason," Mr. Bruce interrupted. "I'm on the road a great deal and I drive fast. Most of the people in this state drive fast. There are many accidents because of high speed, but the fact remains that the teen-agers have more accidents than anyone else. Why?"

Ricky shook his head. "I don't know why. Just bad luck."

"No. Not entirely. I'm not pointing the finger at you, Ricky. I don't know how you drive. But I'll tell you where the fault is—between the ears. And maybe in the heart."

Mr. Bruce put his pipe in the corner of his mouth and looked at Ricky. "You know, but you don't care. You want the privilege of driving, but you refuse to recognize the responsibility that goes with it. I've met a lot of teen-age drivers on the road. Some of them were a pleasure to meet, but most of them weren't."

"Those children who were killed tonight while racing," Ricky's mother said. "What a terribly stupid way to die."

Ricky's father had been taking in Bruce's opinions with a thoughtful, yet impatient look. The moment he had the chance, he cleared his throat, touched his glasses, and spoke.

"I've been thinking, Bruce," Ricky's father said carefully, "and I agree with a great deal you've said. But let's bring it home. Ricky's a teen-ager, and we know he's more likely to have an accident than an adult. Yet, we can't condemn him in advance. We can't refuse to let him drive because he might have an accident."

"Wouldn't that be better than waiting until he has one?"

"It might be safer, but would it be better? The way I look at it, as long as the state of Iowa allows a sixteen-year-old to drive a car if he passes the tests, he has a right to drive. Unless his behavior is unlawful to the extent that the law can deprive him of his right. If the law is wrong, let's change the law, but we can't treat our kids like second-class citizens without giving them a chance. Why penalize the responsible teen-ager for crimes the others commit? You can't do it any more than you can prevent me from driving because my neighbor, who's the same age, is a careless driver. You can't indict a generation."

140

"They're indicting themselves," Bruce said. "Look at the record. Arnie, what do you think?"

"I think it's time I go look around the town," Arnie said. He looked from parent to parent, and then at Ricky and Sharon. "I think the answer ain't what we can make the young ones do. It's what they feel inside. You two dads . . . you were my problems twenty years ago. I remember. And you didn't have cars."

"We were a little wild, but we didn't kill anybody," Mr. Bruce said.

"You would have, if you'd had cars," Arnie said. He got to his feet, puffing with the effort, the coffee already making his face shine with sweat. "But twenty years ago there was a depression, and you didn't have enough to eat, let alone buying cars. Not many reckless drivers then, but there was worse. There was young people without hope, and without spirit. I used to see you sitting on those benches in the square where the old men sit now. You were like old men then. You didn't have nickels for sodas and money for cars and gas and movies and roller skating. You sat and talked like old men. That was worse."

Arnie put his blue cap on his head. "That was good coffee, Mrs. Bruce. Good coffee." He paused by the door, looking at the two families seated at the table. "We get another depression, the car killings slow down too. Or a big war. When all the young fellers are killing with guns, the highways get a little safer. Is a depression better? Or a big war? Maybe we got to look for some new answers. I wish I knew some."

Arnie tugged at his gun belt, touched his fingers to

141

his cap and went out, walking heavily across the front porch and down the steps.

No one spoke after Arnie left. Ricky picked at cake crumbs on the table. The fathers smoked. The mothers looked sad. Sharon looked sleepy.

The radio, which was still on, was tuned to a late disk-jockey show. It was playing a tune that made Ricky lift his head. It was the one he and Sharon had sung together. He looked at her, and she smiled and turned her eyes away.

The music stopped. The disk jockey came on. "Folks, we interrupt our music to bring you a bulletin from the news room. The two teen-agers killed in the accident near Selmar earlier this evening have been identified as Ronnie Bridges, seventeen, a farm youth of near Dellville, and Sue Traynor, sixteen, of near Selmar. The two young people were killed when the car in which they were returning home from a roller-skating party went out of control on a gravel road. It is believed the Bridges boy was racing with another car, but police have not yet been able to locate the other driver. We return you now to music on records, brought to you every night at midnight by the Gratz Brewing Corporation, makers of that smoother, finer, mellower-tasting Gratz Beer . . ."

Mr. Bruce turned off the radio. He looked at Ricky. The boy's thin brown face had a long, sad look on it. He looked tired, and very young. Bruce turned to Ricky's father. "Madison, I want to say something that I mean in a friendly way."

"Yes?" Ricky's father looked surprised. But they were old friends, and could speak frankly.

"You were right in saying you shouldn't refuse Ricky the right to drive. I can see that."

"There are arguments to the contrary," Ricky's father said.

"Well, I just want you to see my position in this. I want our children to go places together, but not in Ricky's car. I don't want to sound like an old maid, but I'm afraid. Ricky might be a good and careful driver, but I'm not willing to take the chance. As long as this teen-age situation is so bad, I don't want Sharon riding anywhere with Ricky or any other teen-ager."

"But, Dad!" Sharon protested. "How can we go anywhere or do anything without a car? Roller-skating, or the outdoor movies, or the ball games. . . . We don't have anything like that in Dellville. What will we do?"

"I don't know. There must be some activities you can find in this town. But until these teen-age accidents are cut down, you're not to go driving anywhere outside of Dellville."

"But, Mr. Bruce," Ricky said, "I haven't had any accidents. I haven't even been near any."

"I know, Ricky. We've been lucky in Dellville so far. Ronnie Bridges is the only boy in this area who's been killed—so far. But I know how you boys drive, Ricky. It's only a matter of time before another one of you is killed. And I won't risk Sharon's life, even if you two would. As a matter of fact, I'm going to call

143

the parents of other girls in Dellville. If we get to-gether, and refuse to let the girls ride with you until your driving habits are safer, I think we'll get results."

"But, Dad . . ." Sharon gestured helplessly with her hands.

"I know it will be dull," Mr. Bruce said. "But I think the boys will find it worth while to examine their attitudes and driving habits if they have to go dateless for a while. And I'd rather you live a dull life for a while than meet the most exciting death. Madison, what do you think about it?"

"Well, John," Ricky's father said, "it's a poor parent who won't do what he thinks is right to protect his child's life. All I can say is, I hope it works."

"It would have worked with us, twenty years ago."

"Then it ought to work now."

Mr. Bruce turned toward Ricky. "No personal in-sult meant, Ricky. Believe me, you're more than wel-come to come over any time and to take Sharon in your car within the Dellville city limits. But that's as far as she can go in your car."

Ricky and Sharon exchanged despairing glances, and Ricky was already trying to figure some way to get around the ban. To be stuck in Dellville again, even with Sharon, was a horrible prospect.

Ricky turned in at the drive behind his father's car, shut off lights and ignition, and got out, slamming the door of the coupe. He went in the house and up to his room, tight-lipped with anger.

He switched on his light and sat down at the desk

his father had built for him years ago. It was covered with old magazines about cars, scraps of paper with drawings on them—some his own ideas about body styles and trim, some traced from magazines.

He looked around his room. It was an almost square room, with painted grayed-green walls. The walls were covered with pin-ups of cars he had seen and admired. Beautiful, sleek custom jobs, like the one he was going to design and build. He snorted angrily. The Connor-Madison. Aw, what was the use?

All the time Sharon had been going with other guys, it had been all right for her to ride in their rods. But now that she was going with him, the ban was on. Whatever the excuse was, he knew the real reason. Just because he'd played in their sand pile when he was little, they still thought he was a kid. He'd show them, somehow. He'd show them.

There was a knock on his door. "Come in," Ricky said sullenly. His father came in, in shirtsleeves, wearing slippers.

"Can I talk to you for a minute, Ricky?"

"Sure." The sullen look stayed on Ricky's face. Another lecture? He was ready for it.

"Too bad about Sharon," his father said, sitting on the bed.

"There's other girls," Ricky answered.

"I can see her father's point," Madison said. "If you were my daughter instead of my son, maybe I'd do the same thing. It isn't that I think less of you because you're a boy, naturally, but it's a different situation."

"Yeah, I guess it is," Ricky said.

145

"Rick . . ."

"What?"

"Tell me something. Straight. Man-to-man."

Ricky looked at his father curiously. There was a new note in his father's voice, a new comradeliness in the way he sat in the room.

"Do you ever race with the others?"

"Well . . ."

"No bull, now. The straight stuff."

"Well, yeah, I do, once in a while. You know how it is. . . ." Ricky laughed apologetically. "One guy kind of chooses you, and you . . . uh . . . kind of go along."

"Long races?"

"Sometimes. We kind of like to see who can get home first. You know."

"What do you do most?"

Ricky looked thoughtful. "Look for guys to drag with. You know. . . . You've got your rod, and he's got his, and you get to wondering which one has the most guts, and so you find out."

"Where do you drag?"

Ricky looked vague. "Here and there."

"I want to ask you," Ricky's father said, leaning against the wall, "do you ever have any reason for racing or dragging or speeding other than for kicks?"

"Sure," Ricky said. "You put speed equipment on a car and you have to test it somehow. To see if it's working right."

"So you use the streets and highways."

"Where else?"

Mr. Madison looked thoughtful. "Tell me, Rick, do you think you fellows would slow down on the streets and roads if you had a drag strip?"

"Would we!" Rick exclaimed. "You're not just a birding, Dad. Hey . . ." A delighted smile appeared on Ricky's face. "What do you know about drag strips?"

Madison chuckled. "More than you think. I've been reading your magazines, Ricky. Now I've read about these hot-rod clubs around the country that have drag strips, and I've read about communities and police forces that have provided a place for them, and supervised them. I've also noticed that wherever there is such a club with a strip, they pledge themselves to safe driving at all times, and cooperation with the law. Would that work in Dellville?"

"You just give us the chance!" Ricky exclaimed. "If we had a place we could hold drag races, we could have fun and it would be safe too. With even starts and the right timing equipment, we'd soon find out how good our cars were. Boy, if the town would meet us half way and give us a place, it wouldn't have to worry about *us* any more!"

"Well, I was thinking, Rick. A drag race is just an acceleration race, and it can be run in a quarter of a mile. Now the road to Cosgrove is straight as a string for almost half a mile out of Dellville. And there is a dirt road that runs near it. Why couldn't you and your friends form a timing association, and ask the city for permission to use that stretch of road one afternoon a week for drag races? In return, you would pledge to

147

drive safely, obey all laws, and cooperate with the police wherever you drive. That ought to be a fair exchange."

Ricky was out of his chair, pacing. "We've talked about it, Dad, but we never had the nerve to ask. We thought it would be turned down. Golly, we'd do everything the other clubs do. Have rigid safety requirements for the cars that enter, and all the rest. If other towns did the same thing, we could have town teams, and regular drag competitions. Reliability runs, too. That's where you have to drive cross-country maintaining a certain average time, without going over certain speeds. It's a real test of good driving. We could have all that!"

"And it would slow you down on the roads?"

"Dad, I know the guys. If we had a place of our own, and a time, we'd clobber the first guy that fouled us up by racing or being reckless on the roads. Really!"

"Then," Mr. Madison said, getting to his feet, "why don't you get your friends and work out a petition to the city council. That road is within the city limits for over half a mile. I'll do what I can to talk up your plan, and you come to the next council meeting with the petition and information about your club. Okay?"

"Oh, gee, Dad," Ricky said, his voice quivering. "I didn't know you . . . anybody . . . oh, gee, what a break it would be for us."

"I've thought about the problem a great deal, Ricky. As far as I know, it's the best answer. If we can make dragging a respectable, supervised sport, it will be safer than football. It's my way to save your life, buddy."

148

"Thanks, Dad. You're a swell guy."

"Well . . ." Mr. Madison took off his glasses and polished them on his sleeve. "We get that strip, and maybe I'll take the sedan out and choose you." He grinned.

"I'll hop it up for you, Dad," Ricky said eagerly, wanting to please. "We could make a real bomb out of the sedan. A real bomb!"

"Good night, Ricky," his father said, laughing. "Don't stay up all night planning your club."

"Dad," Ricky said, standing straight, "I'll see to it that you become an honorary charter member of the Dellville Timing Association."

Mr. Madison was still chuckling when he returned to his bedroom. Ricky's mother was seated at the vanity, brushing her hair. "What was all the shouting about?" she asked. "It sounded awfully happy for a boy who has just been told he can't take his girl riding."

"The patient is making a fine recovery," Madison said, unbuttoning his shirt. "I think he'll live."

8

The petition had been signed by eighteen boys, twelve of whom owned their cars. Sharon had typed it, and Ricky, as founder and first president of the Dellville Timing Association, had been chosen to present it to the city council.

Shortly before the council was scheduled to meet, all the members of the DTA gathered in the Dellville Drug, some with their girl friends. The place was jammed with non-purchasing patrons.

The petition was in a brown manila folder, and lay on the counter of the soda fountain. Ricky stood near it, and Sharon stood next to him. There was a loud hum of excited conversation, laughs, yells and loud shop talk. Big things were happening in old Dellville. Big things.

Sharon looked at her wrist watch. "You'd better get started in a minute or two. It's almost time."

150

Ricky made a pained face. "I'm scared. I wish somebody else would read this."

"You won't be scared once you start reading."

"I hope not." Ricky looked around for something he could use to bang for attention. Right next to him, oblivious to the noise, Sherm was deep in another comic.

"Hey Sherm," Ricky said. "I need something to use for a gavel. Let me have your head, will you?"

Sherm reached in his pants pocket and pulled out some change. He held his hand out to Ricky without looking up from his book. "How much do you need?"

Ricky whooped and slapped him on the shoulder. "Good old Sherm. I don't need any."

There being nothing to pound with, Ricky got up on one of the stools and cupped his hands over his mouth. "Hey! Quiet! Shut up!"

The noise subsided a little as those nearest Ricky turned to see what he wanted.

"It's almost time to go!" Ricky shouted. "Time! Time!"

The noise lessened to a normal hum. Ricky leaned down and picked up the petition. "Has everybody read the petition?"

"Yes!"

"Is there anybody here who hasn't signed it?"

"Has signed it?" The question came from the back of the crowd.

"Has *not* signed. Has not. Who ain't signed?"

"I haven't!" A boy pushed his way forward.

"Read it and sign it," Ricky said. "And don't get it

dirty. Remember, you guys," he shouted to the crowd, "you gotta stick to what you signed. No chopping corners on our part. Understand?"

"*Yo!*"

"Now do all members have their membership cards? The ones we mimeographed."

"Yo . . . yo. . . ."

"Now all you guys with cards . . . have you all paid your dues?"

There was a loud mass groan.

"Come on, you guys," Ricky said. "If you haven't paid, come up with the two bits. Sharon will take your dough."

"She'll take yours too!" someone yelled from the back of the room. Everybody laughed, and Ricky grinned. It had been a good-natured shout.

He looked out over the crowd. Golly, to think *he* had organized this club, and worked out most of the program. And the way the others were following his lead. It was a wonderful feeling, this being a leader. Terrific. Beat anything he'd ever known. They'd have a swell club. Maybe what he was doing tonight would be the beginning of a new era in Iowa driving. There might be hundreds of clubs, and he'd be the first state president, maybe. He'd be known, anyway. Boy, leading all these guys was something. He'd be lying awake nights worrying in case one of the members got careless and violated the safe-driving pledge. That's what it meant to be a leader. Worries. He'd crack down on the first one that was reckless.

"We'll all go over together," Ricky said. "Let's try

152

to keep quiet and not be rowdy. No horseplay or stuff like that. We've got to convince the council we're serious, or they might turn us down. Okay?"

"*Yo!*"

"Let's go! Let's go gettim!" Ricky jumped to the floor and picked up the petition. The others fell back to allow him through, to lead them across the square. To lead them to the new era in Dellville. An era of real sport and fun.

Making his way through the crowd, Ricky saw Link standing in the background, a cynical smirk on his face. But Link had signed. Link had joined. Link didn't want to be left out. Boy, the day would come when he'd whip Link in a drag race with everybody watching. Everybody. A lot better than winning a private race on some back road. The day would come when he'd leave Link in his dust.

Ricky marched out of the drug store with Sharon at his side and headed across the square with the members of the DTA close behind him. At the entrance to the building which was the city hall, he turned. "Remember, guys. Easy up the stairs, and quiet inside."

Nervous now, and perspiring, Ricky climbed the wooden stairs to the big room where the council held its meetings. He took a front seat, and the others filled the chairs around him. There were few chairs, and most of the boys and girls ranged themselves along the wall.

The council was already seated at its table. Mayor Travis, a red-faced retired coal dealer, sat at their head. Buell Jones, the city clerk, sat to his left, busily writ-

153

ing. Two council members, Gus Vorkle and Charles Trumm, sat to Ricky's left as he faced the table. The other two, George Reynow and Ricky's father, sat to his right.

Ricky looked at his father and grinned. His father smiled back and winked, giving him a small sign that meant "Courage."

Having keyed himself for this moment, Ricky was in a sweat to stand up, argue his case, win it, and depart triumphant on the shoulders of his friends. He sat on the edge of his chair, ready to spring into action. Tonight, to make a good impression, he was wearing his good brown trousers and shoes, a white shirt and a tie. The tie was choking him, but he kept his hands away from it. This was too serious a business to jeopardize it by looking sloppy. It was all right for the others to wear jeans and undershirts and boots, but he had to look responsible. That's what his father had said. He looked at Sharon, sitting next to him. She wore a crisp white blouse and a plain, pale green skirt. It made her look older . . . lovelier. . . .

The mayor sat back in his chair and beamed at the young people. "My, my," he said aloud. "We seem to have quite a nice turnout of young folks tonight. It's a good thing to see our young people take this kind of an interest in their city government. Yes indeed."

The Mayor smiled at his joke. Everyone else roared. It was a good omen, the Mayor joking with them. A good omen.

Ricky got to his feet. "Mr. Mayor," he said, his voice breaking under the tension. "I have here a petition of which I am desirous to place before this body. It . . ."

Mayor Travis held up a restraining hand. "Not just yet, son. Don't rush the city government. We've got some other business on hand before we get to you folks. So you young folks just relax and be patient, and let us do the city business, and be quiet, and we'll get around to you in due time. You can sit down, son."

Ricky had been holding the petition at arm's length. Suddenly it got very heavy. He pulled his head down in his shoulders and sat down, his face aflame with embarrassment. He felt like sinking through the floor. Mayor Travis had made him seem like a fool. Even some of his club members had giggled at him. He risked looking at Sharon from the corner of his eye. She wasn't amused. That helped restore him to a calmer state.

"Guess I spoke too soon," Ricky whispered to her.

A piece of paper, folded over, bounced on his leg and fell to the floor. He picked it up, then looked to see who had thrown it. He saw his father pointing to himself with a pencil. Ricky opened the paper. It read: *Don't get rattled. And for Heaven's sake watch your grammar. Don't try to be a lawyer. Make it simple. Dad.*

Ricky looked at his father, nodded, and put the piece of paper in his pocket. Some of the glory had departed from the evening.

Ricky sat back and waited while the council went to work on other problems. Most of the business was done in a low tone that couldn't be heard ten feet away. The council members droned on and on about this problem and that. Garbage . . . water . . . assessments . . . millage . . . city engineer . . . estimates . . . surveys . . .

Every new item immediately became an intricate problem. Speaking in their bored, monotonous voices, the council members voiced their opinions, smoked, conferred back and forth, and droned and droned and droned.

It became very hot and close in the council room. The air, stale and motionless to begin with, turned murky and strong from the smoke of cigarettes and cigars. The boys and girls standing around the room got bored and restive. They fidgeted, yawned, slumped and tried to find a comfortable way to wait out the boring details of the council meeting. After almost an hour they looked for some diversion. They found it by bumping one another, pinching, tickling and snatching hats.

Someone grabbed a girl's compact and passed it on. She tried to get it and, leaning over too far, started to fall. She grabbed at a boy for support. He put out his hand to hold her, but she didn't like the place he had chosen. She slapped his face. The slap echoed sharply in the room and was followed by a wave of laughter and shuffling.

Mayor Travis looked up, his eyes watery and tired. "Let's be quiet back there!" He thumped his gavel on the table. "I'll have to ask you to leave if you're not quiet."

Someone mimicked the Mayor's expression, and

those around him giggled. The giggle spread like a ripple across a still pond. The council members looked up, annoyed. Mayor Travis banged his gavel. "Please be quiet back there. This is city business, and it is important, even if you think it's funny."

The members of the DTA put on their meekest expressions and tried to be quiet. Ricky turned around several times, scowling at them. But even though he had a chair, his back ached, and the foul air was giving him a headache. He felt sweaty and dirty, and very, very tired.

The monotony was more than some of the crowd could stand. After more than an hour they began to slip away. They went out quietly, but they went down the stairs as heavily as they could, and once they were outside, they yipped and yelled with relief. Some of them got in their cars, and Ricky closed his eyes in silent suffering as he heard them rip past the city hall, with straight pipes blasting.

Something like two hours and thirty-five minutes after the council began its meeting, it was ready to hear the petition. Ricky was half asleep, his throat parched, his head splitting when the big moment came.

The Mayor tapped with his gavel. "I believe you had a petition, young man. . . ."

Ricky stood up, his legs numb. "Yes . . . sir. I have a petition that I would like to read at this time."

Ricky's voice sounded dead and flat, just as had the others. By now there were no more than half a dozen members of the DTA in the room. Arnie VanZuuk had come in, and was sitting to one side, soaked with

157

sweat and dozing, his hands folded over his stomach.

"If you will just file the petition with the city clerk," the Mayor said, "it will be read and considered by this council in due time, I am sure. Now if there is no further business . . ."

"Mr. Mayor." It was Ricky's father, his voice crisp. "I believe the petitioner has a right to read his petition before this body if he so desires."

The Mayor licked his lips. "It's late, and hot, and we've had a hard evening. I don't know what purpose it would serve to hear any further business at this time."

"Mr. Mayor," Ricky's father answered, "I believe it was understood that the council would hear the petition tonight. This petition is no surprise to us, and these young people have waited patiently for their turn to bring their business before this council. I believe we owe them the right to listen to what they have to say."

"What's the council think about it?" the Mayor grunted.

"Let him read it," Trumm said, yawning. "Get it over with."

"All right, boy," the Mayor said. "Get on with it."

Ricky cleared his throat. "This petition is being made in the name of the Dellville Timing Association. It is signed by eighteen members."

Ricky looked at the council. The Mayor was sitting back in his chair, breathing through his mouth. Vorkle was doodling on a pad in front of him, Trumm's head was back and a cigarette dangled from his lips. Reynow sat slumped in his chair, a look of tired suffering on

158

his face. Only Ricky's father looked interested. He smiled at Ricky, and nodded for him to continue.

"To the City Council of Dellville, Iowa.

WHEREAS: there are a number of young men in and around Dellville who own automobiles that have been modified with speed equipment, and

WHEREAS: it is well known that there is a good deal of fast and sometimes reckless driving in and around Dellville, and

WHEREAS: this same fast and often reckless driving is a common problem in all communities of this and other states, and

WHEREAS: many accidents and too many deaths and injuries result from unsupervised speeding and racing, and

WHEREAS: the young people of Dellville are interested in keeping Dellville a safe and sane town, and

WHEREAS: it has come to our attention that other communities have solved their problems with the hot-rod drivers by mutual cooperation on the part of the authorities and the drivers, and

WHEREAS: we believe the same program that has saved lives in other communities would also save lives in our community, and

WHEREAS: it takes an organization of young drivers to carry out part of the program, it has been

RESOLVED: that we the undersigned, constitute the charter membership of an organization to be known as the Dellville Timing Association, and

RESOLVED: that the purpose of this organization shall be to promote safe driving on the part of all members and their friends, and to cooperate in every way with the legal authorities of the community, and

RESOLVED: that the further purpose of this organization

159

will be for the furtherance of driving sports automobiles in supervised competitions, operating under strict safety rules. It is our belief that such activity can become a popular and constructive sport. And

RESOLVED: that every member of the Dellville Timing Association, in exchange for the privilege of entering his automobile in the competitions, and in return for the privilege of membership in the organization, does faithfully vow and aver that he will abide by all rules and regulations of the organization, that he will drive his automobile with due caution, consideration and courtesy at all times, that he will not break any laws of the state or community, and will not engage in any drags, choose-offs, rat-racing, or other dangerous or reckless activities while upon the public highways and streets of said state and community. And

BE IT FURTHER RESOLVED: that in order to carry out this program of safety and the development of driving and engineering skills, it is necessary to have some place where supervised competitive driving can take place, and

BE IT STILL FURTHER RESOLVED: that we, the members of the Dellville Timing Association do hereby beg and petition the City Council of Dellville, Iowa, to set aside the first half mile of the concrete road that leads to the town of Cosgrove, such setting aside to be once every week or two weeks, as the Council deems fit for the purpose of holding Association-sponsored acceleration trials under the supervision of the police or other competent authorities. And

BE IT STILL FURTHER RESOLVED: [Ricky's voice was giving out. He spoke in squeaks and rasps] that we of the Dellville Timing Association go on record as being strong in the belief that if such a program of mutual assistance were carried out, the problem of dangerous driving by teen-agers would disappear from the scene.

160

"Respectfully submitted to the City Council of Dellville, Iowa, by the Dellville Timing Association. Signed by eighteen members."

Ricky wheezed to a halt and carried the petition to Buell Jones and dropped it on his desk. Then he returned to his seat. Sharon gave him a quick smile of praise, but he was too tired to smile back. He was so tired that what he had read didn't even make sense to him.

Mayor Travis roused himself and blinked at the council. "You have heard the petition. What is your pleasure?"

Gus Vorkle put down his pencil. "I heard it. What I want to know now, is what the deuce it's all about? I couldn't made head or tail out of all that mumbojumbo."

"What's this about the Cosgrove road being used as a race track?" Charles Trumm demanded. "Eh?"

Ricky stood up. "We've got this timing association we just formed, and we need a place to run our drag races. The idea is, if the city lets us have a place for the races, we'd pledge not to race or break any laws on the highway. And our members have to have their cars inspected for safety, and abide by . . ."

"Just a minute, young fellow," George Reynow interrupted. "What you were saying, you want the city to turn one of its roads over to you for a race track. If we don't, you'll race on all the highways. Sort of a blackmail proposition, I'd say."

"And it's about time you young fellows got it

161

through your heads that you obey the laws because they're on the books," the Mayor added. "You don't come up here and tell us which laws you'll obey and which you won't. I guess not."

"You're not being fair!" Ricky's father shouted, his sharp face taut and angry. "I explained this proposition to all of you, and you all seemed to agree with it."

"You're prejudiced because you've got a boy here speaking his piece," Gus Vorkle said. "The more I think this over, the more I'm against it. The idea of the city providing a race track! What we want to do is get rid of this hot-rod driving, not encourage it. If we give 'em a track, it will look like we're telling them to build hot cars. We'll have every crazy souped-up jalopy in the state coming down here to race. I don't see it."

"But you don't understand!" Ricky cried. "If it's supervised . . . if we have a place, we won't want to use the highways. . . . It's for *safety*. . . ."

"Boy, *you're* the one who doesn't understand," the Mayor said. "It's about time you and all the others like you understood that we're sick and tired of these hot rods. If something isn't done we'll see that the legislature raises the driving age. Then where'll you be?"

George Reynow pursed his mouth into a prim, tight circle. "Seems to me the young people of this town don't appreciate anything wholesome. Dellville opened a recreation center where these young folks could get off the streets, but they never went near it. *Never* went near it. My wife used to supervise there. Said the only thing these boys wanted to do was annoy the girls. Now they're asking us to provide them with a race track. I think a curfew would do them more good. There isn't one has any business being out after nine o'clock."

Ricky's father was about to renew his argument for the boys when he noticed Ricky moving toward the council table, a stubborn, fighting look on his flushed face. Madison waited to hear what his son had to say, proud of the way Ricky was fighting for his idea.

"Mr. Mayor," Ricky said, "I don't think I made myself very clear. Maybe it's my fault. We're not asking for a race track, and we're not trying to blackmail the city either. We're trying to help solve a problem. Right or wrong, sir, the state lets us get driving licenses when we're sixteen, and most of us manage to get hold of cars. That's just a plain fact. Right or wrong."

He supposed they were listening. They didn't interrupt.

"We also know that teen-age drivers have a lot of accidents," Ricky continued. "That's why we formed the Dellville Timing Association. It's to promote safe driving in safe cars. And it's also to give us a chance to experiment with cars and engines and learn something. That's why we want what we call a drag strip. To give us a chance to work on our cars, and have competitions, and make it worth while for everybody to drive safely. They've done it in other places with good results, and we'd like to do it here. Otherwise we *know* there'll be drags in the streets and on the highway. You can't stop them."

Gus Vorkle shook his head. "That's just a new way

163

of saying what you said before. No matter what you call it, you want the city to give you a race track and encourage hot-rod driving."

"You kids are just car-crazy," Reynow added. "You don't have any business owning cars anyway. This city tried to do something for you young people. We had a recreation center. You didn't appreciate it, that's all."

"The recreation center was fine for the little kids," Ricky said. "But we're too big to sit around and play checkers with the little kids."

"If you're that big, you're big enough to get a job and keep out of mischief," Reynow said.

"I have a job," Ricky flared. "And if I'd rather work on my car in my spare time than sit around and play checkers in a dirty old store room, I guess that's my privilege."

Mayor Travis banged his gavel on the table. "It won't do any good to sass the council, son."

"I'm not sassing," Ricky said. "I'm trying to explain. There's a problem we're trying to help solve. . . ." He looked around helplessly and saw Arnie. "Arnie," Ricky said. "What do you think about our idea?"

Arnie removed his cap and brushed the back of his hand across his forehead. He had been all for the idea, but now that the council had turned against it, he had to be careful. They could take his job away. A couple of them thought he was too old and fat and lazy to be a policeman anyway.

"Who knows?" Arnie said. "Could be a good idea. Worth a try, maybe."

Ricky had expected full support from Arnie. He remembered discussions they had had on the subject. "You told me the other day it would make your job easier," Ricky said. "Remember?"

Charles Trumm snorted. "Part of our trouble in this town is a policeman who's looking for ways to make his job easy. We need some new blood on the force if you ask me. Somebody who's willing to get out there and run these law-violators down. Somebody who'll make these lads respect the authority of the police."

Arnie regarded Trumm mildly with his blue eyes. "You try taking that tired prowl car and running down a full-race Merc," Arnie said. "Or any young, skinny cop. See how many fellers you run down."

There was an appreciative chuckle from the few members of the DTA who were still around.

"There you have it," Trumm snapped. "A bunch of reckless boys and a lazy policeman whose idea of law enforcement is to have Dellville sponsor crazy driving. I'm against it. Let's have a vote, Mayor. We're just wasting our time."

The Mayor tapped with his gavel. "You have heard the petition. All in favor of the race track say aye."

"Aye!" Ricky's father spat the word out angrily.

"Opposed signify by the usual sign."

The other councilmen grunted their negative vote.

"Nays have it. Motion is defeated. If there is no further business before the council, we stand adjourned." The gavel tapped. The meeting was over.

Ricky's father put a comforting hand on his son's

shoulder. "Don't be downhearted, son. It's only the beginning. These things take time."

Ricky looked down at the petition in his hands. The useless, scorned petition. There went their plans, there went the Dellville Timing Association. All right. If that's the way they wanted it, he'd show them! Boy, the next time he caught one of those councilmen on the road! . . . He'd ditch him! He'd run him off the road! Smash him! Try to be decent, and what happened? They tromped all over you. You had to fight them. Show them. Defy them. Let them catch you if they could!

9

They drove around the Dellville town square at dusk, not like cars, but like a file of jungle cats on the prowl.

There were five cars, and tonight Ricky Madison's black coupe was in the lead. Behind him were the other rods. Link in his yellow convertible, Jerry in a gray Mercury club sedan, Chub in a black Ford Tudor, and Sherm in his maroon Plymouth sedan. Their combined motors sounded like a group of fighter planes idling at the head of a strip.

Hearing the motors, Arnie VanZuuk pushed himself to his feet and stood just inside the door of his front office at the city jail. He watched the cars go around and around the square, a thoughtful look on his grizzled, heavy face.

He couldn't see the drivers, yet he knew who they were and what they looked like. Each one hunched over his wheel, eyes always on the move, darting from

167

the instrument panel to the road ahead, to passing cars. Watchful eyes, ready for anything that meant a chase or being chased. Eager eyes, anxious for an excuse to open up, to make the big thunder, to spin rear wheels and race . . . race . . . race. . . . Angry eyes, hoping to find some stock car driving too far on the left side of the street, so they could force him over toward the curb. Watching for a car going twenty-eight miles an hour in a thirty-mile zone, so they could crowd it, hurry it up. Watching for men and women who made careless or illegal turns, so they could jam them up, and feel righteous about it.

Arnie stepped back as the five cars came around toward his side of the square. He didn't want Ricky to see him. As long as the boy felt unobserved, he would drive slowly. But if he thought he was being watched by a policeman, his pace would change. He would speed up, chop the corners with tires skidding, *proving* he was going to drive the way he wanted to. Daring a pursuit.

Arnie rubbed the side of his bulbous nose with a thick finger as the five rods idled by. Ever since the council had turned down the drag-strip idea, and the girls in town had been forbidden to ride with the boys, the boys had gone hog-wild. They had declared war. In two weeks his office was piled high with reports from the police in other towns about what the Dellville boys were doing. They were mad, and they were taking it out on everybody. It would take a violent shock to slow them down a little. Like killing some-

168

body, or getting one of their own group killed. But even that wouldn't last.

It was darker now. Arnie followed the circling cars by watching their lights. In a few minutes they would park, and soon they would be off again, like a flight of taloned birds looking for victims. Off to race each other, or go to Missouri and smuggle back fireworks, or to tangle with other drivers in other towns.

Another year or two would make a difference, Arnie thought as he saw them park. Another year or two and some of them would be going in service, or getting married.

Marriage was best. As soon as the first one married, it broke up the gang. Soon another married, and then another. And all of a sudden instead of wild boys he had young fathers who took their little ones to Sunday school and joined the Rotary and the Chamber of Commerce.

Ya. . . . Soon they were fathers and *they* would come to him to complain about how their little ones were in danger from the wild driving of the new teen-agers. In a few years they would become a part of the town.

The trouble was now, while they didn't feel a part of anything. When they thought everybody was against them, fighting them. How to keep them alive now? That was the big problem. Not to enforce the law, but to keep his boys alive until they calmed down and belonged to the town again.

Dellville . . . such a pretty town, such a quiet

town. Big houses, big yards, quiet streets, nice people. A wonderful town for children—until they became big children.

The fat policeman stared wearily at the darkened square. They were his problem. His people. But what could you do? If you left them alone, they got in trouble. If you tried to guide them, they felt it was a duty to disobey and show their independence. Somewhere there was an answer. Whatever it was, it would have to be something that made the boys *want* to cooperate. It had to come from inside them. Then it would work. Only, what *was* that magic something? The drag strip they had asked for? It was worth trying. If it saved one life it was a success.

Arnie turned and walked back to his desk, lowering himself into his chair with a weary groan. "A bunch of silly boys and a lazy policeman," he said aloud in a defiant voice. "Any smart, lively people in this town got any better ideas? Bah!"

Around the square and around the square and *around* the square. Dellville at dusk was always the same. The stores all closed, except for the Dellville Drug. A light at the jail. A light in the cafe, open until eight. A few lights on under the shabby, stubby marquee of the Plaza Theatre, now showing the same cowboy movie for the third night.

Darkened windows. An entire side of the square dead for the night. In the middle, the vacant, deserted store room that had once been the recreation center. The windows scarred with torn posters and advertisements of contests and carnivals long past.

170

A town asleep with its mouth open before it even got good and dark. Everybody at home watching television, angry at cars that went by and disturbed the picture.

A goose horn sounded behind Ricky. Link was getting tired of going around the square. Ricky switched his thinking to what they might do for a little excitement, and swung in to park in front of the Dellville Drug. One after another his friends came by and nosed into the curb until the five cars were together in a tight line.

Ricky got out and went to stand on the sidewalk in front of his car, thumbs hooked in his belt. The others joined him, forming a rough circle. For a while nobody said a word. Ricky stood with hunched shoulders, staring at the trees in the square. Link fired up a cigarette and squatted on his haunches. Jerry, his hands pressed against the small of his back, looked at the sky. Chub put his weight on one leg and toyed with a knife that shot out its blade at the touch of a button. The click of the darting blade sounded regularly, monotonously, and they listened to it, not knowing why. Sherm stared at the tips of his boots and whistled one note over and over.

They seemed to be waiting for something to happen, to be listening, anticipating, as though they expected the town to throw aside its cloak of darkness and silence and burst into light and life. They waited, and listened, knowing that nothing would happen, hoping hopelessly that something might.

Something was wrong with Dellville.

It had always been such a wonderful place to live, with its big houses and big, shaded yards. Ever since they could walk, they had always been able to find things to do together in Dellville. Huts to build, a sand-bottomed creek to swim in, rabbits to hunt, watermelons to steal. It had been a complete little world with everything in it that anyone could want. There hadn't been a dull moment.

Then it had changed. It had deserted them. Something had happened to Dellville.

Suddenly the town had withered, become drab, dull, empty. The backyard huts were rotting shacks, the creek had become too shallow to swim in, the rabbits were spiritless quarry, the watermelons lacked flavor. The houses needed paint, the yards had shrunk.

Dellville had changed. It had become cold. And from the time they had bought their cars, it had become hostile.

They stood around in the darkness and waited. Waited for the miracle that would restore Dellville to them, and make it the warm, friendly, interesting town it used to be. But there was nothing. Nothing but the fleeting memories of the past, when Dellville had filled every need, when it had been a complete, satisfying world to live in. When it had cared. . . .

And because they felt the town had run out on them, turned on them when they needed it most, they felt lost, homeless and resentful. They wanted to lash out in protest against the silence and the darkness, fight off the sleepy placidity that threatened to engulf them before they had a chance to roar and stomp. The town was quicksand beneath their feet, and they felt themselves sinking into the dusty deadliness of its routine. But they would not sink out of sight quietly. They might go down, but they would go down fighting.

This was Dellville, of the happy, sunny past, of the empty present, of the bleak, withered future. Town like a sleeping snake, that awakened at their step only to sink its fangs in their legs. The way it had just done. . . .

One by one they tired of staring at the sky, at the trees, at their shoes. They watched Ricky for a sign. It was his night to decide. Of them all, he was the most rebellious, the most resentful, the most restless. The intensity of his revolt against what he was and where he was convinced them that because he was always moving, he knew where he was going.

Ricky finally moved toward the door of the drug store. The others fell in behind him. They went in and took possession of the first five stools at the soda fountain. Sherm, last in line, pulled a new comic book from the rack as he went by and settled himself to read.

In the light they became individuals, with all the trademarks of boys at an age when they are something of what they used to be, something of what they will be, and not at all sure of what they were.

Black-haired, aggressive Link; round-faced Chub; wavy-haired Jerry; thin, brooding Ricky; placid, husky Sherm. With the exception of Sherm, lost in the world of the comic book, these boys who differed in

173

appearance shared a similar inner resentment. The world was against them, and they wanted to carry the war to society.

"Des Moines?" Ricky asked.

"Why Des Moines?" Link grumbled.

"Why not?"

They leaned on their elbows, staring at the mirror behind the counter, the placards, the merchandise on the shelves. Mouths spoke and words came out, but their attention seemed to be elsewhere.

"We've got some firecrackers left over from our last run down to Missouri," Jerry said, his handsome features showing a look of innocence.

Chub watched his knife blade flick in and out. "Let's not give Arnie a bad time. We shoot 'em off around here, he'll get a lot of complaints."

"So what?" Ricky challenged.

"Arnie's a good guy," Jerry said. "Let's not give him a bad time."

"Come off it, man. Worrying about a *cop's* feelings. . . ."

"Arnie ain't just *any* cop," Jerry said. "He's been pretty decent with us."

"He sure backed us up on the timing-association deal, didn't he? The minute they mentioned his job, he chickened out on us."

"All right. But are we going to be better off if they fire Arnie and get some guy in here who's always giving us a bad time?"

"I didn't say we ought to give Arnie a bad time,"

Ricky said. "I'm just saying a cop's a cop. And they're all the same. If you're young, and you're driving a car, everything you do is wrong."

There was no denying that. They all believed that.

"Some guy with a big car does something wrong, and the cops beg his pardon all over Hell's half-acre for stopping him," Ricky continued. "All we have to do is drive down the street and it's, 'Hey, you young punk, where do you think you're going?'"

"Money talks, man," Chub said.

Link lit a cigarette and blew a cloud of smoke at a fly that was walking on the counter. "The only way to get by with driving a rod is to buy the factory rods that cost five thousand bucks. Look at the way they've hopped up Caddys and Lincolns and Chryslers and them other cars. The same way we do it. Only when we do it, it's some kind of crime, but when the factory builds them like that it's automotive progress."

"Yeah," Ricky agreed indignantly. "Detroit's boasting about building cars that will go a hundred and twenty. *We're* not buying those cars, and they're not track racers. They're stock cars to drive on the highway. Old Gus Vorkle was shooting off his mouth in the barber shop yesterday about how fast his new car could go. And *he* was raising Cain about us speeding."

"It all depends," Jerry said, "whose big fat ox is gored."

"Boy, I feel like goring somebody's ox tonight," Ricky said. "What do you say, guys? How about a run to Des Moines? There'll be a lot of open car windows, hot as it is."

"I'm with it," Link said. "Let's go."

They dismounted from the leather-topped stools and went out to their cars. They stopped for a moment on the sidewalk, breathing in the disturbing fragrance of the country night. The irritating sweetness of the air made the darkened town seem unbearable. They had to go where there were lights and people or burst.

"Keep your girls at home," Ricky said to the darkness. "See if we care."

"There's always girls hanging around downtown Des Moines," Chub said.

"There's plenty in all the towns," Link added. "We don't need Dellville for that. I'd rather find one that lived somewhere else anyway. Girls in this town talk too much."

Ricky went back to the drug-store door. "Hey, Sherm!" he yelled. "Come on!"

Sherm ambled out. "Where to?"

"Des Moines."

"Des Moines? What for?"

"To watch the state legislature kiss the governor's foot, stupid."

The prospect of raiding the city to find new girls added to the excitement of their original plan. It didn't matter what they did in Des Moines, as long as they found some action. Even if they just raced through the city and got the cops to chase them. It was getting away from Dellville. It was living.

Ricky slid behind the wheel of his coupe and pulled

176

the door shut. In a moment his engine blasted into life, and the sound made his blood run fast. He backed away from the curb in a rush, shifted, and gunned his car ahead. His buddies were right on his tail as he circled the square, blasting its silence before they headed away into the night.

This was no leisurely circle they made, but a loud, purposeful swoop. They had a goal in mind, and they were on their way. The lassitude, the slouching, the sloppy movements were gone. Now, firm in the saddles of their motored mounts, faces tense in the glow of their instrument panels, they were off on a raid.

Their tires burned defiantly against streets they knew to boredom. They would be running back to these streets before long, seeking their shelter and protection. But now, leaving them, they gunned their motors, split the night, and thundered their resentment against the dark dead town that wouldn't let them live. And they pointed their noses along the concrete path that offered a temporary escape.

Across the dark fields, beyond the gentle slopes and rolling pastures there was a city. A city where the lights stayed on all night, where stores were open, where people were awake. A city of many streets, where they would be strangers. Where they could blow off steam without worrying that any moment Mom or Dad or Uncle Fred would come upon them and see. . . .

Arnie heard them leave. So they had conferred and they had decided, and they were off like a band of young bucks looking for scalps. He recognized the meaningful note of the gunned motors, the screech of rubber, the bellowing exhausts.

One . . . two . . . three . . . four . . . five. . . . They took the final turn around the square and thundered away, their echo ringing with defiance. He heard them as they reached the edge of town and the open highway. Heard the powerful, receding sound of their engines striving for peak rpm.

By now they were moving like the wind, almost bumper to bumper. Night or day, it made no difference. He had chased them, he knew. They would travel at eighty, ninety and more, on their way to somewhere. Throttles open, up hill and down.

Please God the tires would not blow, the steering assemblies would hold, there would be no unlighted tractors or wagons in their way.

10

Slowly, almost quietly, Ricky led the reconnaissance through downtown Des Moines. The heart of the business district was confined to an area about four blocks square, and although the stores were closed, it was here they would find other rods to choose.

They were not the first into town. Ricky's alert eyes picked out the lowered and hunched outlines of other rods parked along the streets, or moving along them. When he passed he looked at their license plates. Most of the rods were from out of town.

As he moved past each parked car, or those coming toward him, he gave each one a quick going-over, and received one in return. It was almost as though the boys with the hot cars could sense one another approaching. Ricky would get a glimpse of a boy, dressed much like himself, and look into eyes that returned the challenge of his stare. Sometimes there would be a girl with the other driver, or another guy.

At each passing there was a moment when their eyes locked, and they gave each other the cold bold stare, sizing each other up, always as potential antagonists, never as potential friends. In that momentary exchange there was a dare as well as an appraisal, and then they broke contact—for the moment.

Retained was a quick estimate of the other car, and from that, some estimate of the driver. What might be under that other hood? How much guts did the other guy have? The boys whose engines were a mass of chrome speed equipment proudly came out with the hoods off. They were the elite. They could ignore challenges from the slightly modified mills that powered the average rod. Ricky looked for rods that he hoped were in his class, where it was 50 per cent driver that counted, and the power was even.

The first drag came up suddenly, the way they usually started. A black coupe, almost a twin of his own, that he had seen parked on Seventh Street.

Ricky stopped for the red light at Fourth and Grand, and the other coupe slid up beside him, inches away, hub to hub. Ricky looked over trying to appear careless. There were two boys in the other coupe. When he looked, the driver raced the motor for a moment. Ricky touched his gas pedal. Then they both watched the light.

Ricky was in low, with his clutch in. The moment the light changed (give or take a fraction of a second), Ricky's clutch was coming back and his gas foot was moving toward the floor.

The little coupe shot forward with a tremendous roar, rear wheels screeching. The other coupe moved with him, matching his wheels turn for turn. Wide open in low, the two little cars rammed forward until the red light at Fifth made them slam to a quick stop that made the cars nose down toward the pavement.

A green light and they were off again, wheel to wheel, racing madly to be first to the red light at Sixth. Again they made it a dead heat.

Sixth to Seventh was the same story. A combined roar of straight pipes, the squeal of rubber against asphalt, a mounting scream of laboring transmissions and the shrill drag of braked rubber.

When the light changed at Seventh it caught a pedestrian halfway across. He was in front of the other car when the light changed, but Ricky waited. The man walked in front of Ricky, and when he did, the other coupe took off. Ricky spun his wheel as he angrily set his car in violent motion. He swerved, missing the pedestrian by inches, and took off after the other coupe. It was waiting for him at the next light.

Green light again. The other coupe leaped ahead. Ricky didn't jump with him. He moved ahead slowly, shifted into second, and watched the light at Ninth. When he was fifty feet from the corner, he saw the light change begin. Down went his foot on the gas pedal. By the time he reached the corner he was moving fast. He flashed by the other coupe, passing on the right, and opened up. There wasn't another light until Twelfth Street. He laughed to himself as he almost hit peak rpm in second before he had to brake for the

Twelfth-Street light. When the other car pulled up alongside him, he turned toward it with a grin of triumph on his face.

It wasn't the other coupe. It was a prowl car.

The light changed. Ricky drove across the intersection and pulled over to the curb. The prowl car pulled in ahead of him. He turned off his engine, and looking up to watch one of the policemen walk back to him, he saw the other coupe cruise by slowly. The guy next to the driver thumbed his nose. Ricky didn't know if it was meant for him or the policeman.

Ricky had his driver's license out before the policeman paused by his window. He knew the routine. And he knew the best thing to do. He assumed his meekest expression.

The cop held out his hand and Ricky handed over his license. The cop examined it and handed it back. Then he flashed his light at the steering column, so he could read the registration card. He didn't say a word, and Ricky, having learned his lesson in previous encounters with strange police, wisely held his tongue.

The policeman pulled a ticket pad from his pocket and let it rest on Ricky's window. Ricky looked at it, then at the policeman. He was a big guy. Not fat, but big. He looked hard, but not mean.

"You trying to earn one of these, son?"

Ricky looked at the book of tickets. "No, sir."

The policeman's words hadn't been hostile, but his voice wasn't friendly.

"Your license says you're from Dellville. Right?"

"That's right, sir."

"Do you drive like that in Dellville?"

"I . . . I guess not," Ricky said.

"What makes you think you can come here and get away with it?"

"Everybody else does," Ricky said.

"This street look like a race track to you?"

"No, sir."

"It did a minute ago, didn't it?"

"I suppose I was speeding," Ricky said. "I didn't look at my speedometer . . ."

"Don't be a fool, boy! And don't think I'm one."

Ricky gave the policeman the most honest look he could muster. "You're right, sir. I was racing. I know it was wrong, and I'm sorry."

Ricky had a lot of faith in that meek, honest approach. It had often worked for him.

"Yeah, I know how sorry you are," the policeman said. "You're sorry, all right. Sorry I caught you."

"That other guy started it," Ricky said. "I wasn't doing anything until he started crowding me. There were a couple of guys in the car. I thought maybe they were trying to pick a fight, and I was just trying to get out of trouble."

"You're all alone, are you?"

"Yes, sir."

"What happened to the four boys who drove into town with you?"

Ricky looked startled.

"We saw you a long time ago, son."

"I don't know where they are," Ricky said. "I lost them."

183

"Look behind you," the policeman said. "They're all east of Twelfth Street, watching us. All alone, were you?"

"But that other guy . . ."

"Let me give you some advice, boy. You stop worrying about how the other guys are driving, and take care of your own conduct. You let us worry about those other guys. That's what we're paid for."

"Yes, sir," Ricky said contritely. "I will."

"Yeah," the policeman said, "I know how long that will last. Until you're out of sight."

The policeman looked at Ricky's thin brown face, still wearing its meek expression. He could give the boy a ticket, and the boy would be fined, but that wouldn't stop him. He wrote his book out of tickets every night with these kids, but they were always back for more. There were a lot of small towns in central Iowa, and they seemed to have a constant supply of new young drivers who thought Des Moines was built to be their drag strip. Yet, if he let the boy go, the boy would just think he'd put something over on the police.

"Tell me something, son."

"Yes, sir?"

"Do you have any business in Des Moines?"

"I might buy a Coke or something," Ricky said. "And see what else I need."

The policeman put away his summons book. "I want to tell you something, and I want you to listen. You go get your Coke, and whatever else you need, and then you head for home." He looked at his watch. "I want

184

you and your friends on your way out of town by nine. If I catch you in town after that, you'll spend the night in the city jail. And the next time I catch you breaking any laws in this town, you'll wind up in that jail first and do your talking later. You understand?"

"Yes, sir," Ricky said in a low voice.

"We're sick and tired of having you birds prowling around this city causing trouble and endangering lives. If your parents can't keep you at home and out of trouble, we'll find a place for you here. And you know where I mean. Understand?"

"Yes, sir."

"Remember. You be on the road home at nine, and leave at the speed you're supposed to travel. Or we'll be talking again."

"Yes, sir," Ricky said, boiling inside. "I understand."

The policeman went back to the prowl car. Ricky waited while it drove away. Seconds later his friends drove across the intersection, parked, and gathered around his car.

"Get a ticket?" Jerry asked.

"Naw. Just a jawin'."

"You got off easy," Chub said. "The way you peeled up the street."

"You have to know how to handle these cops," Ricky said. "He almost apologized for stopping me."

"What'd he say?" Link wanted details.

Ricky's answer was heavy with indignation. "He said we have to be out of town by nine or he'll put us in jail."

"*We?*" Link demanded. "What'd you do? Rat on all of us?"

"Nobody ratted. They saw us come in town together. You guys were sittin' on our necks."

"That's pretty high-handed if you ask me," Jerry said. "Giving us orders to leave town. We're no riff-raff. I'm not used to being treated like that."

"They got no right to run us out of town," Chub added. "It's a public town, and we've got a right to be in it."

"Build a wall around the lousy place if they don't want nobody in it," Link said viciously.

"Butt me," Ricky said to Link. He took the cigarette and lighted it. For a few seconds they were silent, glowering from the indignity heaped upon them.

"It's just because we're young," Ricky said, tapping his finger on the rim of his steering wheel. "They wouldn't talk that way to anybody over twenty-one."

"Wouldn't dare," Chub said. "They're scared of voters."

"Oh, we *could* rat-race without being bothered," Ricky said sarcastically. "If we had the good manners to own new Cadillacs."

Sherm looked from one to the other as they talked. Talking bored him. "You guys gonna sit and jabber until nine? Let's go get those Cokes while we got time."

"No cop can make me buy a Coke if I don't want one," Ricky said. "I'll do what I please."

"You'll burp too, if you get enough to eat," Sherm said.

186

"We can't fool around downtown," Chub said. "They'll be layin' for us. We might as well park somewhere and get something to eat and go home."

"Don't get yourself in such a sweat," Ricky said. "Just because I got stopped is no reason you guys have to stampede." He didn't want to call it quits. This was his night to lead the pack, and if they followed the policeman's advice, that leadership would slip from him. He had to maintain control, to show the guys that he didn't give up.

"Look," Ricky said. "That prowl car will probably be downtown. Why don't we go out in the residential section and see what we can stir up? They won't be out there."

"They can get there fast enough," Sherm said. "Let's eat, like Chub said."

"We've got the firecrackers," Ricky said. "You gonna chicken out because of a lousy cop?"

"Well, *do* something, then," Sherm said. "Don't spend all night talking about what you're gonna do. Do it."

"All right," Ricky said, drawing deep on his cigarette, then throwing it away. "Here's the pitch. We'll go out to the west end, where all the rich guys live. We ought to find some action out there. Show these cops we don't scare easy, too."

"All right," Link said, nodding with satisfaction. "Now you're talking. Let's peel out of here."

The others went back to their cars. Ricky smiled. He still had his leadership, and he meant to keep it,

187

cop or no cop. He'd show them what it meant to push Ricky Madison around!

Ricky started his car and put it in gear. The guys behind him had their lights on. They were ready. Ricky let out his clutch and cracked the gas pedal hard, taking off in a burst of speed and noise. It was his way of showing the guys that he wasn't chicken, and a challenge to them to keep up with him.

They went west on Grand Avenue to Polk Boulevard, north on Polk to University, east on University to Forty-second, south on Forty-second to Grand again, and west on Grand to Polk. This time Ricky turned south, and into Greenwood Park, looking for parked cars.

He drove deep in the heart of the park, turning when he reached the dead end at the swimming pool. It was either too early or too late for many people to be in the park, he wasn't sure which. There were some families, the parents resting while the little children played in the semi-darkness, all of them finding the park cooler than their houses, but Ricky wasn't hunting for families.

He led his pack out of the park and onto the streets again, and he spotted game. A kid driving a brand new Buick Roadmaster, and with a girl. Prey made to order. Seeing the girl angered Ricky. Other guys could take their girls riding, but he couldn't take Sharon. He'd show 'em.

Ricky slid up behind the Buick, moved over to the right, and inched up on the wrong side. When they were traveling side by side, Ricky held his speed to the

Buick's. He looked over and saw the boy and girl watching him apprehensively. It angered him further. Seeing their fear, he wanted to be cruel.

At one and the same time he wanted to be the other boy in the big car with the girl and to terrorize him.

Snotty-looking kid, Ricky decided. Probably lived in a fancy house, had all the money he wanted and took his girl to dances at the Country Club. Probably get a new Merc for a birthday present. Ricky hated him.

Ricky pulled ahead of the Buick, inviting a drag. The big car didn't follow. Ricky sneered. Probably under strict orders to drive slow or Papa wouldn't let him have the car for a week. The chicken! Ricky slowed until his open window was even with the open window on the girl's side of the Buick.

"Come on!" Ricky yelled. "What can it do?"

The kid driving—he looked about sixteen or seventeen—shook his head and grinned. The girl beside him laughed. Like they were too good to be hurried, Ricky felt.

"What's the matter, junior?" Ricky cried mockingly. "Papa say thirty miles an hour or he spank?"

The kid's face lost its grin. Ricky could see that he was itching to kick the Buick in the rump.

"Hey, sister," Ricky yelled at the girl. "Why don't you ditch that chicken and ride in something hot. Don't you have any pride?"

The girl looked away.

"You can move out of that class, honey," Ricky called to her. "Or are you his baby-sitter?"

189

Ricky grinned as he noticed the Buick picking up a little speed. "Hey, junior!" he bellowed. "Papa spank if you go fast!"

His answer was a roar as the kid booted the Buick. It took off fast, but Ricky knew the kid would back off long before he was near peak rpm. He stayed with it, still on the right side, and the burst of speed was a signal for the others to go into action. Link sailed by, his yellow convertible taking off like a jet, and pulled over until he was directly in front of the Roadmaster. Then Jerry moved up until he was inches away on the left side. Chub moved up from the rear, until his front bumper was within a foot or two of the Buick's rear. Sherm trailed, keeping an eye open for cops.

It was a wide street, and they had the kid boxed the way they wanted him. He couldn't slow, speed or turn. All he could do was keep moving, a prisoner, worried stiff that he would dent or scratch the new car. He was scared. Ricky could tell that by the way the kid was hanging on to the wheel. The girl was scared too, looking from car to car with big frightened eyes.

Perfect! He didn't know who they were, but he hated them, and he liked watching their fright. He'd teach them to ride around in a new Buick. He'd show the girl what a squirt her boy friend was. The stuck-up rats. Too good to live in a dead little town like Dellville. They'd find out what it meant to be too good to live in Dellville!

Link sounded the signal on his goose horn, alerting the others. Ricky grinned, knowing what was coming.

A moment later Link hit his brakes. The kid in the Buick slammed the brakes, the back end of his car threatening to leap-frog over the front end. Then Chub let him have a blast of the horn from behind, and the kid thought Chub was going to ram him. With all their horns blasting at him from every side, he gunned to escape Chub. That was Link's signal to hit his brakes for a fleeting moment, enough to make the kid brake again in panic. Just as it looked as though he would ram Link, sly old Link cracked his gas and jumped ahead, out of danger. At the same moment Ricky dropped back, and with Jerry pressing from the left, the kid went over the curb and bounced to a stop on the parking.

They circled and came back to him. Link stopped where his lights shone on the Buick. The kid was really scared, and the girl looked about ready to scream. It was time for Jerry to go into his act. He got out of his car and strolled toward the Buick, his handsome, frank face showing deep concern.

"Say, I'm sorry we ran you off the road," Jerry said in a friendly tone. "We didn't mean to give you such a rough time."

The kid looked at him cautiously. They had him surrounded, and he wasn't sure what they were going to do. "That's all right," the boy said, trying to sound casual. "I was afraid I was going to smack into that rag-top." He nodded toward Link's convertible.

"Cigarette?" Jerry asked, holding out the pack.

"Thanks." The boy took one and accepted a light. He was beginning to feel more secure now. Evidently

191

these fellows weren't hoodlums. They had given him a bad time, but shucks, he wished he had a rod of his own so he could drive around and do what he wanted to. Not have to creep around in his father's stocker.

"Say," Jerry exclaimed. "Isn't this the new Buick, with the V engine?"

"Sure is," the boy said proudly.

"Mind if I have a look at it? I haven't seen one yet."

The boy slipped the hood catch from inside the car. Jerry raised the hood. He looked for several moments, praising everything he saw. Then he straightened up. "Let's see what she sounds like." Ricky put his hand over his mouth and laughed.

The boy tried the starter but the engine didn't catch. Jerry stood by while the boy tried to get some results from his efforts. "I don't know what's wrong," the boy said, looking helpless. "It always started before."

"Say, that's too bad," Jerry said sympathetically. "Sorry to hear that. Well, next time, maybe." He turned his back on the Buick and walked to Ricky's car.

"What'd you do?" Ricky asked quietly.

"Nothing. Nothing that a couple of factory-trained mechanics can't fix. Those new carbs are awful tricky. Just touch 'em and they are out of whack. At least that's what I hear."

"Good deal," Ricky said. "Give him a good-night kiss."

"I dig you," Jerry said. He got back in his car and

drove it next to the Buick. "Sit tight, kid. We'll stop by a garage and have 'em send somebody out."

"Thanks a lot, guy," the boy said. "Thanks a lot."

"You're welcome," Jerry said gravely. He bent down and lit the fuse of a small firecracker on his cigarette. "So long, junior." Jerry tossed the firecracker into the open window of the Buick and took off, the others after him. The firecracker went off with a loud bang. The boy yelled and the girl screamed.

"Don't stay out too late!" Ricky yelled as he drove past the Buick. He caught a glimpse of the boy and girl looking at him with expressions of shock and pain. "Too good for Dellville, are you?" Ricky screeched. He stuck out his tongue and sped on, followed by the others, feeling he had struck a hard blow in a good cause. There was a sweet taste of revenge in his mouth as he drove away. Revenge for what or against what he didn't know. Only that it was there, and it was good, and he wanted more.

The Dellville boys whooped with laughter as they drove off. That poor nut. He didn't know whether to spit or go blind. They stopped at the first service station. "Hey!" Ricky yelled at the attendant. "There's a kid in a Buick stuck about eight blocks west. He wants you to come get him."

The boy in the Buick was looking at the girl's eye, to see if it had been burned, when the tow truck stopped. "You need help?" the truck driver asked.

"Yes . . . how'd you know?"

"Bunch of kids in rods stopped and told me."

193

"*They* stopped. . . ." The boy looked at the girl's face and at his disabled car. "I don't get it," he said to himself. "I don't get it at all!"

The Dellville boys drove around the residential section a while longer, avoiding the main streets while they threw firecrackers at houses. Twice on narrow streets where they had to squeeze past parked cars, Link and Chub took turns snapping the radio antennas on those cars they could reach by sticking out an arm.

After fifteen or twenty minutes of this Ricky decided it was time to clear out. There was a chance the kid in the Buick had called the cops, or some homeowner who'd been presented with a firecracker. He led the guys back into Greenwood Park where they threw the last of their firecrackers at neckers in parked cars, and then headed downtown, to leave quietly and peacefully in the time set by the police.

A couple of blocks on, Ricky heard one long and two short blasts of a horn that signaled trouble. He looked in his rear-vision mirror and saw Sherm coasting toward the curb. Ricky stopped and jumped out.

"She just up and died," Sherm was saying to the others as Ricky came up.

"What did it sound like?"

"Didn't sound like anything," Sherm said. "Engine never does when it's dead."

"Try to turn her over," Link said, taking a small flashlight from his pocket.

They lifted the hood of Sherm's car and peered inside while he tried to start. When it wouldn't catch Sherm stuck his head out of the window. "You be

194

careful what you do to my pa's engine," he said in a shrill voice. "You naughty boys!"

They laughed at that, and began talking over what they'd done.

"That was a pretty good-looking girl in that Buick," Link said, his dark face and hawk nose down close to the engine, his eyes looking expertly from part to part. "We could have had some fun with her."

Ricky hadn't intended to say the words out loud, but they just popped out. "I felt like I did."

The sudden quiet that followed his words made Ricky feel like a fool. He expected some kidding, but his friends were silent, and didn't look at him. Then Jerry gave him a curious, searching glance, and Ricky knew why they were silent. They'd felt the same way, and they, like him, were uneasy and a little afraid that it had been so.

"I've got a hunch," Link said. "Trouble's in the ig . . ."

"*Listen!*"

They heard it for only a second, then the sound was gone.

"Prowl car," Chub said uneasily.

"Heading this way," Jerry added.

"We'd better make tracks," Link said quickly, pulling down the hood of Sherm's car. "Let's peel out."

"Hey," Sherm protested. "What about me?"

"Ride with me," Link ordered. "Come on."

"Aw, I don't want to leave my rod . . ."

"We'll come back for it. Come on!"

"Wait."

195

Ricky stood by trying to look cool and relaxed and daring, his thumbs hooked in his belt. He wasn't going to let Link take the lead away from him. "We'll take you *and* your car, Sherm. I'll nerf you."

"You'll be caught," Link said.

"Maybe. You other guys get gone. Meet you at the north city limits. We'll go west now, and circle. See you!"

He sprinted for his car and peeled it around in a tight circle, coming in behind Sherm. The others were already on their way. With Ricky pushing, Sherm turned west, and then Ricky opened up as they fled for the city limits.

Ricky didn't take any chances—on being caught by the cops. He pushed fast, and before many blocks he was shoving Sherm ahead at better than sixty. He was slightly to the left of center behind Sherm, so he could see around him, and that tended to twist Sherm, but Ricky knew Sherm would handle the car, and he bore down.

They flew across the city line with the sound of the police siren behind them. Sherm's hand went up in the air, to signal for a right turn. Ricky backed off, giving Sherm a chance to slow down and make the turn. He followed, feeling his wheels leave paving and hit dirt. Then Sherm signaled him up again, and he made contact and pushed Sherm again.

He knew why Sherm had chosen the dirt road. As the two cars sped swaying over the rough surface, they raised a thick cloud of dust, a choking, blinding screen that would shield them from the eyes of the police if the prowl car was close.

Ricky himself was almost blinded, but he kept his eyes glued to Sherm's taillights. Sherm would give the brakes a warning feather touch if he had to, but there were always emergencies. A bad break and they'd have to dig him out of the back of Sherm's neck with a nut-pick.

The dust billowed behind them. Ricky chanced a glance to the rear, but there was no sign of other auto lights. He slowed his rate of speed, and in a little while Sherm signaled for another turn. Again Ricky backed off and followed Sherm into a long, tree-lined drive that ended at a farm house. They turned off their lights and parked in the shadows, where the dark cars melted into the night. Ricky turned off his engine.

The two boys got out of their cars, stretching, wiping dust from their eyes, chuckling softly. The night was still. There were no sounds of pursuit.

"Well, we done her," Sherm said, his big frame shaking with pleased laughter. "A couple of times I thought you were gonna get my head for a new hood ornament."

"I didn't see anything," Ricky said.

"I know. If you had seen what I saw, you'd have turned back to meet those cops."

"Let's see if we can get you started," Ricky said. "Link was saying something about the ignition when he heard the cops."

They raised the hood of the car and looked at the

197

engine with the aid of a flashlight. "Here it is, Sherm," Ricky said. "Your coil got disconnected. No wonder we couldn't get you started. As simple as that."

"I ain't complaining," Sherm said. He tried his car again and the engine caught at once. "We'd better shove," Sherm said. "The guys will be waiting.

"Follow me," Ricky said. "We won't keep 'em long."

The five cars met at the north city limits, and with Ricky in the lead they headed south, down Second Street, long Des Moines' unofficial drag strip at dusk. They drove steadily and slowly, just at the legal limit.

The prowl car picked them up as they were entering the downtown area. Again it was the same policeman who had talked to Ricky before.

"Hello, Officer," Ricky said cheerfully. "We're leaving right on time . . . the way you said we had to."

The policeman looked at him coldly. "Where have you been since I saw you last?"

"North," Ricky said. "We thought we'd go up to Ankeny for our Cokes. It's easier to find a parking place in a small town, you know."

"I don't suppose you could *possibly* be the people who were making trouble in the west end of town, could you?"

"Trouble?" Ricky asked innocently. "What kind of trouble?"

"Maybe throwing firecrackers. Maybe breaking radio antennas on parked cars."

198

Ricky was surprised. The kid with the Buick hadn't ratted. Good for him.

"Couldn't have been us," Ricky said. "We've been in Ankeny drinking Cokes. Now we're going home, just like you told me."

"The descriptions we got fit you . . ." the policeman began.

"All rods look alike at night," Ricky said. "Must be a hundred just like the one I'm driving."

"All right," the policeman said suddenly. "Keep going the way you're headed. But if there's any trouble in town next time you boys are here . . ."

"We're not trouble-makers," Ricky said. "We're just out for a little ride."

"Go home," the policeman said tiredly. He was certain this was the guilty outfit, but the kid had been right. Most rods did look alike at night, and without license numbers, or other positive information, there was little he could do.

On impulse the policeman walked back to Link's car. "Where have you fellows been tonight?" he asked Link.

"No place," Link answered, staring straight ahead.

"You . . . wouldn't by chance be the group that was in Ankeny tonight? . . ."

"Ankeny?" Link echoed, scratching his chin. "Honest, Officer, we weren't as close as ten miles to Ankeny!"

The policeman stood back while the five cars drove

away at a discreet crawl. His lips were tight, his expression one of extreme exasperation. "Next time, the book!" he shouted after the departing rods. "The whole book!"

11

Ricky was leading the pack home when the feeling of defeat began to come over him. He was moving very fast, and the guys were bunched right behind him, almost bumper to bumper. When he passed a car they all passed with him, risking death every time they swung out blindly in his wake rather than lose him.

Ricky's passing technique was designed to provide a maximum amount of show and a minimum amount of safety. Coming upon a car he would crowd it, almost touching, as though he meant to drive through it. At the first moment he thought the road was clear, he stepped hard on the gas and spun his wheel, whipping around the car ahead in a burst of swaying, rocking speed.

Once he started around nothing stopped him. If he saw the lights of another car appproaching he ignored them. It was the other driver's duty to get out of the way. For one thing, Ricky wasn't going to be chicken when he was leading. For another, the guys were following him so closely he didn't dare slow down. For yet another, there was a constant competition among them to see which one could bring them home in the best time. Ricky's car wasn't the fastest, but he tried to make up in daring for the seconds he would lose on the open stretches.

So he led them home, grinning recklessly as he pulled the string of cars through tight passing situations that would curl his friends' hair.

And yet the sense of defeat was there, because he knew what would happen.

About three miles from Dellville the road followed the ridge line of some old glacial hills, curving back and forth in a series of S-turns. Coming out of the last turn, the road straightened as it dipped down a long straight hill. At the bottom there was a long steel bridge, and from the bridge on, the road ran straight as a string to Dellville.

That last turn meant the end of the leader's stint. From there on he held the lead—if he could. And no matter who had been in command until that turn, it was every man for himself as there was a free-for-all scramble to see who would be first in Dellville.

Ricky took them around the S-turns as fast as they had ever made them, their tires screeching as their rear wheels fought to tear loose. Coming out of the last turn he forced his coupe wide open as he went down the long hill to the bridge. He didn't know how fast he was going. He didn't dare look.

202

He hung on as he booted his car down the hill and hoped it would hold together. He flashed across the bridge and onto the flat, gas pedal jammed to the floor.

But he didn't have it. Once they were off the bridge Link's car moved to the left, Link turned on his brights, and the yellow convertible moved past and pulled away. As always, Link would be the first one home.

It was hopeless, but Ricky hung on, flying along wide open, but forced to watch Link's red taillights widening the gap between them. He would be second into town, but there was no solace in that. There would have to be a time when he was first. When he led all the way home. If he could just beat Link *once*, fair and square, he'd be satisfied.

Someday he'd have the power to do it, and then Link would chew his dust. He wouldn't give up until Link followed his lights into Dellville.

Nine forty-five. Arnie VanZuuk stood outside the police station waiting hopefully for a little breeze to make the night more bearable. A huge mass of sweat and discomfort, he closed his eyes as he laboriously breathed in the heavy air and listened.

He opened his eyes at the sound of footsteps. A moment later Ricky's father joined him. Madison was wearing a pair of striped wash pants and a short-sleeved sport shirt.

"Evening, Arnie."

"Evening, Mr. Madison."

"It's a hot night."

"Ya. You can hear the corn grow tonight, I bet."

"Yes, looks like another bumper crop for Iowa."

They stood quietly for a moment. Arnie was sure Madison hadn't come out to talk about the corn crop. The slender bank cashier seemed troubled. He looked pale and uncertain in the light that streamed from the jail window and reflected on his long balding head and rimless glasses.

"Have you seen the boys tonight, Arnie?"

"Earlier. They drove toward Des Moines."

"I don't like it," Madison said, looking in the direction the boys had driven. "I don't like their spending all their time on the road and in strange towns."

"They been pretty mad since the council turned them down," Arnie said. "And not having girls."

"I know. And when they're angry it's no time for them to be on the road—taking it out on others."

They listened for a moment, uneasy and apprehensive.

"I . . . I wonder . . ." Madison began uncertainly, ". . . if you might have any ideas, Arnie."

"About the boys?"

"I was thinking of Ricky in particular. They've been getting in a lot of trouble, haven't they?"

"I got a lot of complaints and reports," Arnie answered.

"If it keeps up, someone is going to get . . . hurt."

"They're overdue for an accident now," Arnie said. "You can't cheat the percentages."

Madison shook his head. "I wish I knew what to do about Ricky. I said when he got his car that I'd take it

204

away if he abused the privilege of driving it. I could do it, and he'd be safe, I suppose. But it's not the answer. The kids tried to meet us halfway and were turned down. I suppose it's up to us to find some constructive way to handle this situation. That's the only right way. Don't you think?"

"I don't know," Arnie said. "I don't know if we ever find a magic answer for everybody. It's like with the doctor. You get a shot of penicillin it makes you well. I take one and it makes me more sick. We just gotta try 'em all, I guess. The bad thing is when we don't try nothin'."

"Now Ricky . . ."

Arnie held up his big hand for silence. They listened. From far away they heard the rods coming around the last S-turn, opening up as they headed down the last long hill onto the flat.

Arnie's head jerked slightly as he counted each new motor. "Five," he said, his voice sounded tired with relief.

"Listen to them come," Madison said, shaking his head. "It's crazy . . . crazy. . . . When I think of Ricky being in the middle of that with that coupe of his . . . Arnie . . . don't they *want* to live?"

"They want to," Arnie said.

"Then why on earth . . ."

"You and me," Arnie said, "we know how many years we got if we're lucky. But them young ones . . . each one thinks he's gonna live forever, no matter what happens to anybody else. It ain't they don't want to live. They don't believe they can die."

205

"Even when they see it happen?"

"That's somebody else," Arnie said. "Anything can happen to somebody else."

"I have to do *something*," Madison said almost desperately. "But it has to be right."

"That's for sure," Arnie said.

In Dellville the five rods parked in front of the drug store, even though it was closed. The boys got out and gathered on the sidewalk in front of the cars, talking, smoking, going over the details of the night's adventure. Then they broke up.

Ricky drove home slowly, turned in at the drive and cut his engine. He got out of the car and stood by it for a moment. It was good to be home again, in back of the familiar white house, in the friendly yard. There was a light in the living room where his father probably was reading. And a light in the kitchen. As he looked, his mother passed in front of the kitchen window. He watched her, loving her for everything, thankful for the darkness that allowed him to look his feelings without being seen. It made him feel like a little child again, hungry for attention and protection.

Then he thought about the Des Moines trip. It just came to him—the wondering if the boy in the Buick might live in a home like this, might have a father in the living room, a mother working alone in the kitchen. Waiting for him to come home. Not knowing what he had run into.

How would his own folks feel if when he was out a gang of guys ran him off the road and fouled-up the engine? Maybe hurt him and Sharon, if she was with him. Pushed him around.

It didn't seem real. Did he really go to Des Moines and do that? Gee . . . he'd never thought of himself as a bully, or a guy that went out picking on other people. It was all like a dream, or something he'd seen in a movie. But knowing it had been he, he felt sick and ashamed. The fun and adventure were gone. A feeling like one of defeat came over him. He was sick of ratting around. Sick of it.

He went in the house with his feet dragging. It was all Link's fault. Whenever Link was along they always wound up doing something mean. One of these nights he'd whip Link right down to the ground. Run him down to dust.

He stood in the kitchen, blinking in the light. " 'Lo, Mom."

"Hello, dear. Are you hungry?"

"Kinda." He grinned.

"I baked a cake today. How about some cake and a glass of milk?"

"Sounds good." He sat down at the kitchen table, watching her. "Is Dad around? Maybe he'd like some too."

She looked at him curiously. There was something subdued and little-boy-like about him. She wondered if he was in any trouble. "Why don't you ask him? I think he'd like that."

Ricky went to the living room door. His father was sitting in an easy chair, his head back and eyes closed. "Dad . . ."

Madison opened his eyes. "What?"

"I'm having some milk and cake. You want some too?"

"Sounds like a good idea, Ricky. I'm glad you asked me to join you."

It had been so long since they had done anything together they didn't have to, that they were awkward about it. Ricky and his father sat at the table, and Mrs. Madison joined them. They were all glad to use the cake as an excuse for conversation.

"Very good cake," Ricky's father said. "Don't you think so, Ricky?"

"Tops," Ricky said. "You sure can bake good cakes, Mom."

"I'd bake more if you were around more to eat them," she said. "The last one went stale."

"I guess I have been pretty busy," Ricky said. "Can I have another piece?"

When he was eating the second piece his father said casually, "How's the coupe running?"

"Like a top," Ricky answered.

"You've put a lot of miles on it in the last couple of weeks."

"I have at that," Ricky agreed.

"Were you out of town again tonight?" his mother asked.

"Yeah," Ricky said carelessly. But he tensed. Had there been a report from Des Moines? He'd deny everything.

"I heard you coming home," Mr. Madison said. "You were coming pretty fast."

"We always speed up a little on the flat," Ricky said. "Everybody does." He was afraid they were going to question him. He forced a yawn. "Gotta get up early and go to work," he mumbled. "Mind if I go to bed?"

They knew he was trying to evade them, and that made them determined to pursue. A few minutes after Ricky went up, his father followed. When he went into Ricky's room, Ricky was sitting on the bed with his shirt off, reading an article about carburetion.

"Rick . . . I'd like to talk to you for a moment."

"Sure, Dad. What about?" He kept looking at his magazine.

"I'll come to the point, Ricky. Are you going to make me treat you like a child and take the car away?"

Ricky didn't look up, but the stubborn, set look came over his face.

"I know what you've been doing, Ricky. I think I know why. But there isn't any reason good enough for me to sit back and let you kill yourself. I want you to know that."

Ricky remained statue-like.

"Tell me something, Ricky. Was that Timing Association idea on the level?"

Ricky looked up, his eyes resentful. "It sure was. And you see how far it got us, too!"

"Did you believe all the things you read to the council about safety, and safe driving? Do you think accidents can be cut down if teen-agers try?"

"Sure they can. It's been proved!"

"Then what made you go chicken on the idea?"

Ricky's jaw dropped. "B-but the council . . ."

"The council turned you down—the first time. And because you didn't get what you wanted when you asked for it, you chickened out on a good idea."

"Nobody wanted to stick," Ricky said. "Not after what happened."

"So you're all going to prove that the council was right. Is that it?"

"What can we do now?" Ricky asked, turning up his palms helplessly.

"In your own language—you can show that you've got guts!"

Ricky shrank back, astounded at his father's vehemence.

"You had a good idea and you wanted official backing for it. Sure. But good ideas are a dime a dozen. What did you have to prove to the council that you could keep your end of the bargain? Nothing but your word and your record. And your record is awful. The way you fellows are acting now, the council was right in thinking you were trying to blackmail them. You're proving it."

"I'm not the only one," Ricky muttered.

"You were the leader. You read the petition. It was your idea. It never occurred to you and your cry-baby friends that you might get results if you proved your responsibility *before* asking for favors, did it?"

"You told me to see the council," Ricky said. "I did it your way."

"I know. And I thought they'd agree. But I didn't think you and your friends would turn yellow and quit

210

the moment you had to fight for what you wanted. No, you couldn't stand up and fight back. You had to be the bullies of the highway because you didn't get what you wanted as soon as you asked for it."

"What do you want me to do?" Ricky cried. "What? What?"

"I want you to act like the man you think you are. Look, Ricky, the Timing Association idea is good, isn't it?"

"Sure."

"And if you fellows get the drag strip, it will help cut down reckless driving and accidents, won't it?"

"Of course. You read about those other clubs."

"Then isn't it worth working for? Isn't it worth having your organization, obeying the rules, and showing that you can be safe, responsible drivers? Don't you think you'd have something to back up your claims to the council if that happened? If your idea is sound, it's sound whether the council likes it right away or not. But it takes guts to do it that way. It's the long way, but after all, it is up to you to prove that you're worthy of the favor you ask. Don't you see?"

"I see," Ricky said slowly, thinking hard. "But I don't know how many guys would join this way."

"Nothing in it for them, is that it?"

"A lot of them would feel that way."

"All right. Start it with the ones who have sense enough to see it's the only way to do it. Alone, if you have to. If you really believe in the aims and objectives of your club, you'll stick by it alone."

"I think Jerry would join," Ricky said. "And maybe

Chub and Sherm. I don't know about Link. And I know some other guys who might try it. How long would we have to . . . be okay before we could get the drag strip?"

Mr. Madison shrugged. "I don't know. Months . . . years. . . . But if you believe in your organization, and follow its rules whether it brings you favors or not, I think you'll find you've earned the respect and trust you need to get that drag strip. What do you say, Ricky? Do you have the stuff to do it? What are you made of?"

Ricky looked down at his magazine and grinned. Then he looked up at his father. "You know something, Dad?"

"What, Ricky?"

"This is the first time you let me have it like . . . like another man. Not like a little kid."

"And? . . ."

"I'm starting up the club again." Ricky's face was serious. "There's something else, too. If I want to have that custom shop, I've got to help prove that guys aren't outlaws just because they want their cars different. Rods have to be made respectable if there's going to be any future in building them."

"Are . . . you and Merle still planning to go into business together?" Ricky's father asked cautiously.

"I don't know about Merle. Do you think we could get a loan from the bank to start the business?"

"That depends. I make crop loans to farmers who I think have the ability to bring in that crop. And I make cattle loans to farmers whose background and

212

experience in the business make them a good risk. Whether or not the bank can lend you money will also depend on how good a risk you appear to be. Just like getting the drag strip, Ricky. Ideas and wishes are necessary for any enterprise, but when you need the help of others, you have to show a reasonable chance for success."

"I've never tried anything and Merle's never succeeded," Ricky said wryly. "Guess that doesn't make for much of a start."

"Merle's a good practical mechanic," Mr. Madison said. "But your business needs someone who can create designs, and manage the financial end of it. Someone to manage the business. And that takes . . ."

"College?" Ricky interrupted.

"It would help."

"I know," Ricky admitted. "Sometimes when I'm up here trying to figure out new designs I get stuck. It's not just a question of what lines I'd like to draw, but what can be done with different materials and what can't. I think there's a big future in new kinds of plastic bodies, but I don't know enough about the materials. If I could experiment . . ."

"Iowa State's close . . . and good," Mr. Madison said. "We could work something out, Ricky. All we have to do is try."

"I'll try, Dad. And I'll prove it by starting up the Dellville Timing Association again. We might get the horse laugh from a lot of guys, but what we want is important. Too important to let anybody kid us out of it."

Mr. Madison paused at Ricky's door. Ricky's brown eyes were glowing with excitement and wonderful plans for the future. "You know something Ricky. . . ."

"What, Dad?"

"I'm going to be sleeping better from now on."

Ricky laughed, the excitement he felt making it a long, loud laugh. "I don't think I'll get any sleep at all!"

"Night, Son."

"Night, Dad. And thanks."

Ricky undressed and lay down on his bed, but he was too excited to sleep. A tremendous, thrilling plan was forming in his mind. First the DTA would get started, and he'd really work to keep it going. With luck, maybe they would get the drag strip, and that would help get clubs started all over the state.

At the same time, he'd have to begin thinking pretty seriously about learning the custom business. He could read a lot, and fool with his car to experiment, and plan on college too. Iowa State wasn't far away, and maybe he could help work his way through school by customizing cars for other students.

Sure! Then summers, he'd work at it in Dellville. Once he'd sold a few designs, he bet he could get a loan from the bank, and he could hire Merle to work with him. By the time he got out of college he'd be a real engineer and he'd have his own business well under way. And the Timing Associations would help create that respectable market he needed. Boy, it was working out! It was working out! He felt the need to tell someone about it, to talk endlessly about his plan. Someone who would be interested. Someone like . . . He laughed to himself. Why kid himself? There was Sharon's face in his mind all the time. And his dad. His dad had sure turned out to be a regular guy. His dad knew an awful lot about things, and he was a real good guy, too. He'd be a good guy to have as a partner. He really knew how to run things. Yes, sir! Dad would be a real partner. Funny how his dad had kind of unbent all of a sudden and become a buddy. Good, too.

12

The new Dellville Timing Association was three weeks old, and as far as Ricky was concerned it had produced only one tangible result—Sharon was allowed to drive with him again. They decided to celebrate by going to a drive-in movie in Des Moines.

The little coupe was washed and polished to a spotless finish when Ricky parked it in front of Sharon's house. In the right-hand corner of his windshield he carried the sticker of the DTA, a blue wheel with the letters DTA in the center in gold.

So far the sticker was producing everything but the desired effect. Designed to inform police and other authorities that the driver was careful, helpful and competent, it had been ignored by all authorities other than Arnie. He said it looked fine. Most adults scowled at it as the symbol of bad driving, and the other teen-age drivers went out of their way trying to tease him into

216

drag races and other violations of the DTA code. It hadn't been an easy three weeks.

Ricky went to the front door and knocked. In contrast to the careless dress he had affected earlier in the summer, he wore gray slacks, a white short-sleeved sport shirt with a collar, and white buck shoes. His brown hair was carefully combed to bring out the small wave near the front.

Mr. Bruce opened the door, pipe in mouth. "She'll be down in a minute, Ricky," he said, leading Ricky to the living room. "Acts as though she'd never seen you before, and is afraid to meet you."

"I guess women think it's fashionable to be late," Ricky said, glancing at his wrist watch.

Mr. Bruce snorted. "That's what they *say*, my boy. The truth is, they're born without any sense of time at all."

"Dad says Mom thinks time stands still when she's on the telephone."

"Don't mention that instrument to me," Mr. Bruce said, shuddering. "If you ever have any teen-age daughters of your own, you'll know what I mean."

Ricky blushed. "I guess some of that's my fault."

"Well. I'd hope she isn't talking to herself. By the way, how's the DTA coming?"

"Pretty slow," Ricky said glumly. "We have seven members. "Jerry, Sherm, me and four kids who don't even own cars. They drive the family cars—when they can get them."

"What's your program now?"

"That's what we can't figure out. We don't have

enough members to do much of anything but sit around and talk shop."

"You're in the same boat as all the other organizations," Mr. Bruce said. "What to do that will create a little interest and build membership."

"The drag strip would do it," Ricky said. "But the way we're going, it will be a thousand years before we get that."

"You'll have to work toward it. You'll make it. Just don't be discouraged."

"Oh, I'm not," Ricky said. But he was.

"You need something that will focus attention on your group. A driving team might do it."

"We don't have any place to practice."

"It would be easier to get than a drag strip. And a step in the right direction. I . . . Ah, here comes Sharon."

Ricky stood up as Sharon came into the room. He'd expected her to be in a skirt and blouse or slacks. His eyes widened when he saw her in a print dress with a wide belt and full skirt. And she was wearing white sandals with a fairly high heel. She had combed her hair back and up, to be cool, and Ricky, who had been expecting an informal girl, was suddenly struck numb at the sight of the beautiful girl who was to be his date.

"Approve?" Sharon asked Ricky, her smile teasing a little.

"I guess I do," he answered awkwardly. "You look real nice."

"Well, kids," Mr. Bruce said, "I won't insult you by

sending you off telling you to be careful. Have a good time."

"Thanks," Ricky said. "We will. And no drags."

"You can drive in high," Mr. Bruce said dryly.

The late-afternoon sun bathed the fields in slanting golden light as Ricky drove out of town. The countryside was peaceful and productive-looking. Birds taking flight swooped by the car, trailed by the echoes of their whistling. A pheasant, startled by the coupe, broke from cover and ran across the road in front of the car. Ricky braked and turned to avoid it. Once, he knew, he would have made a pass at the bird.

He wondered how fast he ought to drive. There was no speed limit in Iowa. Reasonable and proper was the rule for the open highway. It was for the motorist to decide what was reasonable and proper. Ricky decided that sixty would be a good compromise, since it was light and the road was clear and dry.

For the first time he discovered how pleasant it was to drive across the open country at sixty. There were few turns he had to slow for, and he could relax. It was easy driving. And it was surprising how fast a steady sixty ate up the miles.

"Sharon . . ."

"What?"

Ricky kept his eyes on the road ahead. "What do you think about college?"

"Do you mean am I going?"

He hadn't thought about that. "Well, yes."

"I'd like to. Even if you just get married, the things you learn in college help you."

219

"Do you think a fellow should go?"

"If he can."

"Would you think less of a fellow because he didn't go to college?"

Sharon bit her underlip thoughtfully. "Well, if I liked a fellow I wouldn't think less of him if he couldn't go to college. But I do think a boy has to go to college these days if he wants to get anywhere in the world."

"Suppose," Ricky said, "he could get where he wanted to get without college? Do you think he ought to go anyway?"

She nodded. "I think college does something for you. It makes you a more intelligent person, no matter what you do."

"I suppose it does," Ricky agreed.

"Which college are you going to?" Sharon asked.

"Which . . . Oh, I don't know. I've been thinking about Iowa State. For the engineering courses."

"I've been thinking about Iowa City," Sharon said. "The State University offers more courses for girls."

"I hear they have a pretty good engineering school too," Ricky said. "But I don't know if they teach anything about automobile designing and engineering."

"Is that what you want to do?"

Ricky nodded. "I still want to build custom cars. I could probably start my own business without college, if I wanted to. There's a real future in design. You can buy engines that have been modified any way you want them, but the individual design—there's a real field."

"I think you'd need college for that," Sharon said. "To be real good."

"I intend to be the best," Ricky said, and he wasn't bragging.

"I think you ought to go."

"I guess I will, then."

"Because I said so?"

"That's one reason."

"I'm glad you value my opinion."

Ricky grinned. "I'm glad you've got one for me."

He held to sixty all the way to Des Moines, obediently slowing down when he went through the little towns. From time to time a car would come up from behind and sweep past, and when he was passed by cars that he knew were slower than his, it was hard to keep from chasing them. There was just something about being passed and left that irritated him. He couldn't help it. He didn't think he'd ever get over it. It was like a glove across the face.

In Des Moines Ricky drove carefully. He had hardly entered the city limits when another street rod appeared alongside him and gave him the challenge. It took will power, but Ricky ignored the challenge. He maintained his speed and kept to the right as the other rod jumped ahead and dropped back time after time, trying to tempt him to drag. By the time the other driver left with a blast of straight pipes, Ricky was sweating.

Because he was being so good and so careful, he ignored the police siren when it sounded behind him, and kept on driving. It wasn't until the prowl car cut

221

in front of him that he realized the siren was for him. He pulled to the side, feeling anger smoldering within him.

The cop who walked back to his window was the same big guy he'd had the run-in with before. "Didn't you hear the siren?" he demanded as he approached.

"Yeah," Ricky said. "But I didn't think it was for me."

"Oh, you didn't think it was for you," the cop said sarcastically. "Who did you think it was for?"

"I wasn't doing anything wrong," Ricky said, bold because he knew he had the right on his side. It was a good feeling, too.

"Oh, no. You're the lad who never does anything wrong. No speeding, no firecrackers, no nothing. A little angel."

Ricky reddened angrily. He didn't like to be made fun of in front of Sharon. It made him seem like a child. He looked the cop in the face, determined to have it out like a man. "I think I have a right to know why you stopped me," Ricky said.

"You have a right . . . Well, I'll tell you, youngster. I want to warn you that if there's any trouble in the city tonight, I'll know where to look. I . . ."

The policeman broke off as he saw the DTA sticker. He walked around to the right side of the car, examined it, and returned to Ricky's window. "What's the DTA?" he demanded.

"The Dellville Timing Association," Ricky said. "Here's my membership card.

He handed his card to the policeman, who studied it. "Ricky Madison, President . . . Dedicated to sportsmanlike driving, courtesy, cooperation with the police, observance of all laws . . ."

The policeman leaned on Ricky's window, his manner suddenly friendly. "So you've got one too, eh? How many members?"

"Only seven," Ricky said. "But we're hoping for more."

"You didn't have this the last time I saw you. . . ."

"We just started," Ricky said. "We're trying to get a supervised drag strip. And maybe start a driving team."

"Son," the policeman said, "I know about these clubs and I'm all for them. I was ready to give you a lecture, but I don't think you need it. As far as I'm concerned, I'll honor that sticker, and until it's proved otherwise, in my book you're a good, careful, reliable driver. Have a good time in the city, kids."

"Thanks," Ricky said, his throat tight with emotion. "Gee, I . . . Thanks."

"Thank *you*," the cop said. "The more of you there are, the easier my job is. Say, I just thought of something."

Ricky looked interested. It was pleasant having a big city cop talking to him like a friend. Darn pleasant.

The policeman stepped back and looked at Ricky's coupe with a critical eye. "Not fancy, but not too bad," he said. "It has possibilities."

Ricky watched the policeman carefully, wondering what he was talking about.

"It hasn't been in the papers yet," the policeman said, standing by Ricky's window, "but around Thanksgiving the Allied Auto Council is going to sponsor a hot-rod auto show here. There are going to be some mighty fine prizes, too. The idea is to build up the constructive side of the interest you kids have in hopping up cars. There'll be prizes for the best engines, the best design and all that. Interested?"

"Sounds right down my alley," Ricky said, moving about restlessly as the idea began to burn inside him.

"We want to get kids from all over the state to enter," the policeman added. "And from the people who come, we might have the beginning of a state hot-rod organization that would keep the sports angle and get rid of the recklessness that goes with driving rods now."

"You can count me in," Ricky said. "Where do I sign up?"

The policeman laughed. "I'll take your name and see that you get on the list. One thing, though. In order to qualify for the show, you've got to have a clean record. Any moving violations between the time you sign and the show, and you're out."

"Don't worry about that," Ricky said earnestly. "If you knew what a big chance . . . You see, I'm going to go into business doing . . . I'll keep my nose clean. And how!"

"Okay," the policeman said, reaching in to give Ricky a friendly pat on the shoulder. "We'll look for you."

Ricky caught a flash of moving yellow behind the policeman. It was Link's convertible, moving past slowly as Link looked toward Ricky with a mocking grin on his face. After Link came Chub . . . and Sherm! With his DTA sticker on the windshield.

Ricky sat back with his shoulders sagging as the policeman walked away. Suddenly he hit the steering wheel with his fist. "That dumb Sherm!"

"What's the matter, Ricky?" Sharon hadn't noticed the other Dellville cars.

"Just as we're getting somewhere. . . . Sherm's up ahead with Link and Chub, and he's got a DTA sticker on his car. If he gets in any trouble, what will that make us look like?"

"Sherm doesn't mean any harm. He probably doesn't even realize what he's doing."

"I'd like to warn him," Ricky said. "But I don't know where they're going, and I don't dare try to catch them. And I won't tell the cops. . . . That would be like ratting."

"He'll be all right, Ricky."

"I don't know. I wouldn't put it past Link to figure out something, just so the DTA would get a bad name. He's got Sherm along for a purpose."

Ricky started his car and drove slowly toward the drive-in movie, looking for his friends. He didn't have to look long. Several blocks on they came out of a side street, and fell in behind him. Ricky laughed, relieved.

"Look behind us," he said to Sharon.

"They're following us. . . ."

"Yeah. I know Link's idea. He thinks he'll stick with us and spoil our date. But this is one time I'm glad to see him try."

When Ricky turned in at the drive-in, his friends were right behind him. He purposely picked an open row, so they could come up on both sides of him. By the time they stopped, he was out of his car, walking toward Sherm.

Sherm looked shame-faced as Ricky opened the door of his car and slid in beside him. "Hi, Rick. We thought we'd keep you company."

"That's all right with me," Ricky said. He moved closer to Sherm, grabbing his big friend by the arm. "I just want to tell you one thing, Sherm. You're carrying the DTA sticker. The cops know about it. They're beginning to respect it, too. If you get in any trouble while you're carrying that sticker, I'll wring your big neck. It would mean the end of our club."

"I wouldn't do anything to hurt the club," Sherm protested.

"Don't let Link suck you into anything. Understand?"

"I gotta follow him if I'm with him, Ricky. You know that."

"Then don't be with him. Be with me. Follow me."

"Aw . . ." Sherm looked uncomfortable. "You've got a date."

"You bet I have," Ricky said. "Right around Thanksgiving. And I aim to keep it. Now look . . ."

"The movie's starting," Sherm said. "I can't talk."

"Sherm . . ."

"It's the cartoon. Shut up."

Sherm was staring intently at the huge screen. Ricky slid his hand cautiously along the dash until his fingers closed around Sherm's keys. He pulled the ignition key and withdrew his hand.

"See you later, Sherm."

"Quiet, Ricky."

Ricky walked back to his car, slipping Sherm's keys in his pocket. There was more than one way to protect the good name of the DTA.

"I thought you were never coming back," Sharon said.

"I had to straighten Sherm out."

Ricky looked from left to right. Chub was parked close on his left, Link to the right. Instead of watching the screen they were staring into the coupe.

"Picture's up ahead," Ricky said to Chub.

Chub grinned. "Might be a better show in your coupe."

Ricky slumped behind his wheel. "I'm getting tired of those guys. For two cents I'd . . ."

"Don't let them get your goat," Sharon said. "They'll get tired of being pests if we ignore them."

"Next thing I put on this coupe will be Venetian blinds," Ricky said savagely.

"Watch the movie," Sharon said soothingly. "That's what we came for."

They sat close together, shoulders touching. It was pleasant, quietly thrilling. Ricky looked at the screen, but he wasn't following the movie. His mind was whirling with ideas and plans for the auto show, and his senses—those he could spare from that dream—were aware only of the softness and the fresh scent of the girl at his side.

Link leaned far out of his convertible, until his face was almost inside Ricky's coupe on Sharon's side. "Yo, Chub!" he yelled.

Chub slid over and leaned out of his car until his face was inches away from Ricky. "Did you call me, Link?"

"Pretty dull movie," Link said. "I feel like talking."

"Me too. What shall we talk about?"

Ricky tried to ignore the two grinning faces at his windows, talking to each other through his car. It was an old trick. Usually he'd been one of the guys to do it. Now he knew what it was like to be the victim.

"Say," Link yelled, pushing his head in a little more. "I found a girl who ain't doing nothing. She must be alone. You find anything?"

"Nope," Chub said. "Nobody here but us chickens."

Ricky turned his head slightly, his whisper covered by the loudspeaker in the car. "Lock your door and get ready to roll up the window."

When the doors were locked, Ricky waited his chance, until Chub and Link had their heads stuck way in the car, trying to block the view while they yelled at each other.

"Now," Ricky said.

With his left hand he rolled his window as fast as he could. It wasn't a big window, and in a moment he had

Chub caught by the neck. A yell from Link indicated Sharon had caught him.

"Roll down the window, you big lug!" Link yelled. "Or I'll break every bone in your body!"

"Watch your language in front of me," Sharon said indignantly. "Or I'll roll this window all the way to the top!"

Ricky blew his horn.

"Aw, Ricky, don't be a louse," Chub pleaded.

"I'm not. You know who's been lousing up the evening." He blew the horn again and again, until two ushers with flashlights ran up to see what was going on. Ricky and Sharon rolled down their windows, freeing their prisoners.

"These boys were annoying us," Sharon told the ushers. "Can't you make them move?"

"Outside, you two," one of the ushers said to Link and Chub. "You'll get your money back."

They climbed into their cars, disgusted and angry, starting them up with a roar calculated to annoy as many people as it could reach.

"Come on, Sherm!" Chub bellowed. "We're leaving!"

Sherm's distraught face showed at his window. "I lost my key. Wait till I find it."

"We can't wait!" Chub yelled. "We're being kicked out! Meet us outside, and we'll have some fun!"

The two rods flanking Ricky pulled ahead and roared toward the exit, churning gravel as they tried to spray it against the parked cars along the ramp. Sherm was on his knees in the darkness, trying to feel for his key.

"Sherm!" Ricky called. "I know where your key is. Watch the movie and I'll give it to you later."

"But the guys . . ."

"Never mind the guys," Ricky said. "From now on you're staying part of this date if I have to take you home in my trunk."

Sherm got up and dusted off his knees. "All right, Ricky, if you say so." Sherm's good-natured face lit up with a wide smile. "I didn't think you cared."

"I care," Ricky said grimly. "I care about the DTA. Now watch the movie, will you? And give me a chance. I don't even know what's playing."

Ricky scowled at the screen, trying to make some sense out of the action.

"Ricky . . ." Sharon sounded worried.

"What?"

"What do you think Link will do when you get home?"

"Do about what?"

"About what we did. He was mad."

"Let him be mad. What can he do?"

"He might beat you up."

Ricky reddened. Sharon didn't know it, but this particular concern about his welfare was more insulting than complimentary. It made him feel that in her eyes he was inferior to Link.

"He can try, for all the good it will do him," Ricky muttered. "Just because he got in a lucky punch last time . . . I can take care of myself and Link too."

"But he's bigger than you are."

"Watch the picture, will you? Let me worry about Link."

"I'm sorry. I didn't mean to hurt your feelings." There was frost in her voice.

"That guy," Ricky said angrily. "He's spoiling our date even though he's not around!"

"Then let's forget him. Let's have a good time."

"Right," Ricky said, relaxing.

When the show was over, Ricky gave Sherm his key. He waited until the impatient drivers had raced out before starting. Sherm followed.

Ricky drove out of town and onto the highway toward home. He drove at fifty. It was a safe speed—and he wasn't in any hurry to get home. Sherm stuck right behind him.

They'd gone about ten miles when Ricky growled and looked irritated.

"What's wrong?" Sharon asked.

"Sherm. He's right on my bumper. What's wrong with that guy?"

A moment later Ricky and Sharon were jarred as the car behind them bumped them slightly.

"The crazy fool!" Ricky exclaimed. "Nerfing me!"

Sharon looked back. "Ricky . . . it isn't Sherm."

"Huh?"

"It's Link."

"He must have been waiting for us and sneaked in," Ricky muttered. His speed increased slightly.

"Don't try to race with him, Ricky."

"I've got to keep ahead of him." Ricky swore as Link bumped him again.

"Ricky, please. Can't you see he's trying to make you mad enough to race? Then he can laugh in your face. He's trying to wreck the DTA."

"I know," Ricky gritted as Link bumped him again. "But what can I do? He won't pass. I have to keep ahead."

"Stop."

"Stop?"

"It's better than risking everything. Your chance to enter the auto show . . . the DTA . . ."

"He'll stop with us."

"Let him. We can outwait him."

"I have to get you home. Your folks . . ."

"They'll understand. The way Link acts, I think he wants us to go fast so he can wreck us."

"I knew that," Ricky said. "But I hate to give in . . ."

"You're giving in if you let him tease you into trouble. Show him you dare stop."

"Okay. I'll stop."

Ricky signaled with his hand, slowed, and pulled off the road, coming to a stop. Link followed, then Sherm and finally Chub.

"Now what?" Ricky asked Sharon.

"We don't move until he's gone on ahead."

"He'll think I'm scared."

"What do you care what he thinks? His opinion doesn't mean anything."

"I'm not yellow," Ricky grumbled. He took a deep breath, snorting his annoyance.

They waited about ten minutes. Ricky was impatient, turning constantly to look at the cars behind them.

"They're not going to leave as long as we're here," Ricky said, peering out the back window.

"You know what will happen if you start. He'll bump you again."

"I feel like I could outrun him tonight," Ricky said. "But I've got too much at stake to let him make me lose it."

"The trouble with him, he's jealous of you," Sharon said.

"You weren't ever his girl."

"Not over me. He's jealous because you're taking over the leadership in Dellville. Until you came along everybody followed him. He's mad because you thought up the DTA."

"I don't like this!" Ricky turned and twisted behind the wheel. "I'm not going to let Link decide when I can drive or not."

"You said you wouldn't race."

"I won't," Ricky said, opening his door. "I'm going back there to see him."

Sharon took hold of his arm. "Don't fight, Ricky." Her wide eyes pleaded with him.

"I gotta do something!"

"Wait. We've only been here a few minutes."

Ricky shook his head stubbornly. "I'm tired of waiting. Tired of having that guy ride me. It's a good time to settle this thing for once and for all."

"Ricky . . . you'll be hurt."

"I can take care of myself. Wait here."

Ricky got out of his car and walked back to Link's yellow convertible. When he did, Chub and Sherm got out of their cars and walked to the same place, but standing a little apart. Link stayed where he was.

Ricky had spoken bravely to Sharon, but his legs were trembling as he stood beside Link's car. He'd started to make his play, and the guys were waiting to see how he finished it. Link's insulting, arrogant smirk was clearly visible as he lounged behind the steering wheel. Ricky looked tall and slight in his dark slacks and crisp white shirt.

"What's the idea?" Ricky demanded, his voice uncontrollably shrill.

"Idea of what?"

"Nerfing me."

"Don't you like it?"

"No, I don't. I'm telling you to quit."

"You and who else?"

"I don't need anybody else."

"Big talk from a small boy."

"Big enough to back it up."

"Yeah?"

"Yeah!"

Chub and Sherm stood by quietly, neutral, and curious.

Link studied Ricky's angry face, and it helped him work up the anger he needed for the occasion.

234

"I got a good mind to whip your tail," Link said.

"I'm waiting," Ricky said, the words almost sticking in his throat. "Come on, if you're not yellow."

"Don't you call *me* yellow!" Link opened his door.

"Yellow! . . . Yellow!" Ricky taunted, his voice rising to a half-scream of anger and fear.

"You! . . ." Link scrambled out of the convertible, a look of hatred on his face.

There were no preliminaries, no squaring-off, no feeling-out with jabs and footwork. As Link came out of his car Ricky hurled himself at his enemy, striking blindly and wildly, with only one thought in mind— to kill!

Ricky struck with a punch, grappled, and clawed at Link, trying to pull him down. Link was carried back against his car, grunting with pain as Ricky's fingers raked across his face. He used the white shirt as a target and hit out as hard as he could. He felt Ricky's body sag as his hard fists connected, and then felt numbing jolts as Ricky struck back.

They came together, grunting, panting, striking out, the sickening sound of knuckles against flesh followed by gasps and curses.

Ricky staggered as Link's fists came out of the darkness and smashed against his nose and mouth. He fell forward, trying to hit, and felt his knuckles punish Link's ear. They grappled again, and as they twisted away, Ricky's torn white shirt was sprayed with blood from his nose.

He was crying now. Sobbing and making threats as he ran into the barrage of fists and sought to destroy the dark shape that eluded and punished him. A blow on the jaw stopped Ricky in his tracks. He tried to swing, but took a hard blow to the body. He stumbled to his knees, reaching out to grab Link's legs. Link went down, and Ricky went after him, trying to scream his hatred through the blood and tears that choked him. He clawed, struck, tried to bite, fought like a maddened child, bawling as he stumbled forward for more.

At close quarters Link had the weight advantage. He used fists, feet and elbows to batter down Ricky's attack and strike short, vicious blows that cut when they landed and brought new blood streaming down Ricky's face.

They were both mad beyond reason as they rolled over and over on the ground, kicking and clawing. Link butted Ricky with his head, followed with a knee, and got Ricky under him, pounding at the smeared, helpless face that looked up from the ground.

It was then that Sherm and Chub moved forward and pulled him off roughly.

"Lemme go," Link shouted hoarsely. "Lemme finish him!"

"He's got enough," Sherm said calmly. "You git back or I'll bash your head in." He picked Link up in his arms and carried him to the convertible, pushing him inside. Then he went back to Chub, who was bending over Ricky. Ricky lay on his back, his shirt ripped to ribbons, his face smeared with dirt and blood. His gasping breath bubbled through his bloody nose and mouth.

"You all right, Rick?" Chub demanded loudly.

"Help him up," Sherm said, dropping to his knees. He lifted Ricky and held him in a sitting position. Ricky put his hands on his temples. "My head . . . my head . . ." he moaned.

"You'll be all right," Sherm said. "Get in your car. Come on, I'll help you." He and Chub helped Ricky to the coupe.

They passed Link, who sat in his car wiping his face with a handkerchief. He gave a short, triumphant laugh, choked with nervous tension. "I showed the guy. . . . Fight me . . . huh!"

"Shut up," Sherm said. "Or I'll finish what he started."

Sharon watched in horror as they eased Ricky under the wheel. She had her hands clenched around a handkerchief that she held to her mouth. It was soaked with tears. All through the fight she had crouched in the car crying, trying to shut out the animal noises. Wanting to run out and stop them, tear them apart, and knowing that she shouldn't.

Ricky sat up straight for a moment, then leaned forward, lying against the steering wheel, his breathing noisy and sobbing.

"You're a mess, Rick," Chub said awkwardly, his round face looking as remorseful as though he were responsible for Ricky's condition. "You better clean up before you get home."

"You gonna be all right?" Sherm asked, peering anxiously at Ricky.

"You . . . you're fine friends, you are!" Sharon

shouted tearfully. "Why didn't you stop them? Why?"

"Ricky started it," Chub said. "He chose Link."

"Go ahead, stand up for Link," Sharon said scornfully. "Who started the trouble, bumping into us?"

"Ricky wanted to fight," Chub said. "It's been a long time coming. You all right, Rick?"

Ricky was able to sit up now. "I'm all ri . . ." His mouth and lips were cut and hurt.

"Guess we'd better shove," Chub mumbled. "You . . . put up a good scrap, Rick."

Ricky's head went erect for a moment. Then he remembered how it had ended, in a blur of knuckles pounding on his face, and his crying for help . . . for mercy. . . . He didn't know the words hadn't come out. He thought they knew how he had finished, crying for help like a baby.

Sherm and Chub backed away. A moment later Link's car pulled out on the road with Chub and Sherm following. They disappeared around a turn, and the coupe was alone.

Ricky tried to start the car, but his hands were trembling so badly he couldn't manage the key. Sharon dried her eyes with the damp handkerchief. "Let me, Ricky."

He looked at her dumbly, his face a mess of drying blood and dirt. "You . . . all right. . . ." he said tiredly. "All right."

Sharon got out and walked around the car. She got into the driver's seat as Ricky dragged himself to the right side, trying to lie down on the seat.

Sharon started the car and drove out on the road.

The little coupe purred along steadily at forty-five. Ricky stirred and groaned. It was coming back to him. The fight, the beating, the humiliation in front of Sharon and the others. He was hurt, beaten, his clothes a mess. Big talk . . . big talk . . .

"Ricky . . ." Sharon's voice was anxious, full of concern.

She even had to drive him home. *Oh, God!*

He sat up a little, trying to hold back his groans. "I . . . I guess I won a . . . moral victory. . . . We . . . I didn't break any club . . . laws. . . ." He tried to laugh, and the movement started the blood flowing inside his mouth.

It hurt. He hurt where he had been hit, but the worst hurt of all was inside. Twice she'd seen him choose Link, and twice he had been beaten for his pains. He couldn't look her in the eyes again until he'd whipped Link at something! Until then it would always be inside him—that she had seen him whipped by another guy. Whipped bad. By Link. . . . Always by Link . . . car . . . fists . . . always by Link. . . .

"You shouldn't have tried to fight him," Sharon said. "He doesn't mean anything to you . . . or me. . . . He's just a big bully who likes to pick on . . . on people."

She meant to be kind, but it was the worst thing she could have said. It was like another blow to Ricky. One that went in like a blade, and twisted.

He turned so he could sit with his head back. It was easier to breathe that way. He closed his eyes, hurting with every bump and jolt. Some day he'd get Link.

239

Get him good. Whip him in front of Sharon. Show her he *was* Link's equal. He *was!*

The little coupe rolled across the bridge and the flat, and entered Dellville. Sharon drove to her house first. "Let's clean you up here," she said. "You'll frighten your parents the way you look now."

She had to help him out and up to the house. The big evening, the big date, was over.

13

Ricky Madison sat alone in the Dellville Drug. He sat at the soda fountain, leaning on folded arms as he read a magazine he had borrowed from the rack. It was an outdoor magazine, and he was reading about bear hunting.

He heard the front door open but he didn't look up. He didn't care who it was. But the steps that came toward him were familiar, and even though he looked at the magazine, the words blurred.

"Ricky . . ."

He looked up reluctantly, self-conscious because he knew his right eye was still discolored and his lips were still puffy. And there was a scab on his forehead where a scrape was healing.

She stood close, looking at him with her wide, serious, gray-green eyes, as though trying to look behind his eyes and read what was in his mind.

"Oh . . . hi . . ." he said awkwardly, dropping his gaze.

"Where have you been?"

"Oh . . . around."

"I thought you'd call me."

He blushed. "I didn't think you'd want to see me until I . . . looked a little better."

"As though that mattered. How are you coming with your plans for the auto show?"

"Oh, that?" He avoided her look. "I've decided not to enter this year."

"Oh, Ricky. . . . Why not?"

He looked at her shamefacedly. There was an expression of disappointment on her pretty face.

"I thought it over. I wouldn't have a chance, Sharon. Not a chance. Gosh, there'll be guys there with dream jobs. I'd look foolish with what I've got."

She looked at him searchingly, noticing his hesitancy and lack of confidence. "Is that the only reason you're quitting? Because you're afraid you won't win?"

"I don't have the money . . . or the time. . . . I'd be foolish to try."

"What about the DTA?" Sharon asked. "What's going to happen to that idea? Have you given that up too?"

"It gave me up," Ricky said. "I'm the only guy with a sticker now. I might as well give it up too."

"Then what?"

Ricky shrugged and looked outside. There was only one answer. He didn't want to be a lone wolf. He'd just take his old place with the guys again. Following

Link. A guy had to have friends, and do what they did. Even if they did have a fight once in a while. That didn't mean anything. And he'd lead Link home some night. It might take a Merc engine to do it, but he'd get it done.

"Don't give up, Ricky. Please." She was pleading. He didn't want to look at her. Gray-green eyes, a sprinkle of freckles across a small nose and a full, soft lower lip could make a guy forget how to keep up with the guys. Make him forget there was a guy he had to lead home some night.

"It's hopeless, Sharon. Why try to kid myself?"

"Ricky." She sounded almost severe.

"Yeah?"

"For a long time, Ricky, you've been telling everybody about your wonderful ideas for custom bodies, and the business you were going to start. Isn't it time you either put up or shut up?"

"Huh?" He was startled.

"This is your chance. You *say* you have good ideas, but the first chance you get to show what you can do, you turn chicken. You're afraid. Afraid someone might have a better idea."

Ricky looked at her for a moment. "Let me show you something," he said quietly. "Wait here." He went out to his car and came back with a portfolio in his hand. "Let me show you some of my designs."

He opened the portfolio to the first, a long, low sports car with sweeping lines. "Like it?"

"It's beautiful!"

"Yeah. I could make my coupe look like that—for

about five thousand dollars. And look at this design. Like it?"

"Even better than the first."

"I thought I'd find out if it could be built. Looks good on paper, but the way I have it drawn, the body won't fit the frame. If I alter the frame, I can't fit the engine. If I change to give the engine its room, the drive-shaft won't fit. Look at this plan. Nice?"

Sharon nodded.

"Nice. But I forgot the state has laws about the minimum height of headlights and minimum road clearance. If I change to obey the laws, my design won't work at all. Even if these designs were good, I couldn't afford to have them built."

"So?"

"So," Ricky said. "So what's the use of trying to enter the auto show? I can't build anything anyone would want to buy, or have me build."

"Wait a minute," Sharon said. "Wait a minute. Come outside, Ricky. Please."

He followed her out. They stood in front of his coupe.

"Ricky, have you seen any other coupes that look like yours?"

"Only about a million. Every other rod in Iowa looks like this. Black, shaved, rear end lowered."

"How many of those drivers do you think would like their cars to look—well, a *little* different from the others?"

"All of 'em, I suppose."

"How many could afford to buy those fancy sports-car designs you showed me?"

"None of 'em."

"Don't you see what I'm getting at, Ricky? Don't you see?"

He scratched his head thoughtfully. "Yeah . . . yeah, I do see. Suppose I modified my coupe just enough so it was something different. Nothing else like it. The average guy could see his way clear to afford that much work."

"Make the best of what you have, Ricky," Sharon urged. "This is a show for street rods. Make yours the most attractive one at the show. Show them what can be done with an old car for a reasonable amount. You'll give everyone who sees it a real feeling of hope that they can afford a nice-looking car too."

"It would advertise my business," Ricky said, beginning to get excited. "I might even get orders at the show."

"I'm sure you will. And I might help you design . . ."

"You?" Ricky asked incredulously.

"Yes, me," Sharon said, almost defiantly. "Have you ever made a dress, Ricky?"

"Of course not!"

"Well, you'll be surprised how much help I can give you. Anyone can draw a pretty dress, Ricky, but one that looks good on paper and one that looks good on people—they're sometimes two different dresses. And I know it's the same with cars. You'll see."

"I could do it," Ricky said, looking thoughtfully at his coupe. "What I want, I want to get away from that humpbacked look most rods have. And that dragging rear end. I want something that looks graceful, that expresses motion, even while at rest."

He went to the coupe and drew lines with his finger to show her what he had in mind.

"I'd like to start fairly high in front, see, and make a long line that sweeps back and down. Then, about three-quarters of the way back, I want to start my second line, a little higher than the end of the first, and sweep that back and down. No boxy look, no lightning zig-zags or that kind of chrome-plated stuff. Just something simple, almost severe, but graceful. Only, the more simple you make it, the harder it is to do. You can't cover up design faults with hunks of chrome and gadgets."

"Just like a dress," Sharon said. "A cheap dress can hide bad lines under a lot of ruffles and sashes. But the hardest thing in the world to make is a simple black dress. It has to be good, or it shows."

"That's what I want," Ricky said. "Something simple, that shows good."

He looked up at the sound of a goose horn in the street. Link was there in his convertible, followed by Chub, Jerry and Sherm. "You coming?" Link yelled. It was a command.

Ricky hesitated. He'd made a fool out of himself so many times with his big talk. He looked at Sharon. She looked away. It was his decision.

246

"We're making a run to Des Moines," Link said. "Ought to find a little fun up there. Come on."

Ricky looked at him. The rods were purring, the sound of their mellow exhausts a siren song of invitation to forget everything in the sound of their singing on the open road. There would be drags, car against car, driver against driver, and the long run home, and the race for town. Link was watching him, with the bold look of a leader.

"You . . . you go on without me," Ricky said.

"Come on, Rick!" Jerry yelled. "We need you!"

"Gotta work!" Ricky yelled back. "Gotta get my coupe in shape for the show!"

"Aw . . . come on. . . ."

Link didn't wait to argue. He cracked his throttle and was off with a squeal of tires and a roar of power. The others jumped after him. They circled the square and headed out of town, engines straining toward peak.

Ricky stared at the DTA sticker on his windshield. He laughed bitterly. "The only member," he said, pointing to the sticker. "Big deal."

"It will be," Sharon said. "If you stick you'll find others to follow. If the fellows see that you won't quit, they'll come back. And if you win a prize, they'll all want to be in for next year."

Ricky nodded, but not very enthusiastically. "Looks like I'm left with you for a helper. Still want in?"

"Yes."

He grinned. "Got any coveralls?"

"Why?"

"Because the first thing we have to do is get down under that car and begin studying how it's put together, so we'll know how to take it apart. And we've got to get all the measurements of everything. You game?"

"It sounds like fun.'

"You'll think so when the dirt and grime starts falling in your face."

She wrinkled her nose at him. "It will still look better than yours."

Mr. Madison sat at his living room desk and listened to Ricky's story.

"I like your idea, Ricky," he said. "I think it worthwhile. But I don't see how the bank can lend you any money on it."

"But Dad, it's not just for me," Ricky said earnestly. "If I do good at the show, other guys will want in next year. That means they'll drive carefully, because they can't enter if they have any moving violations against them. That means we'll get a lot of guys in the DTA again, and that ought to mean *something*. We might get the drag strip, but the main thing, we'd have all good drivers here."

Mr. Madison rubbed his temple and adjusted his glasses. "I agree, Ricky. It's a wonderful idea. It will show you whether you have talent in this field, and it will have a social value. But banks don't lend money on good deeds."

"Then I have to give it up," Ricky said mournfully.

"Why?"

"If the bank won't . . ."

"The bank cashier might."

"Dad!"

"Doggone you, Ricky," his father said fondly, "do I have to beg you to let me in as a partner? I want to see what you can do, and I want to work alongside of you, if I can."

Ricky's eyes were suddenly moist. "Gee, Dad, I didn't think you . . . I don't know . . . I guess I *didn't* think."

"I ought to be as good with a hammer as Sharon Bruce," his father grumbled. "Even if I don't look as good in coveralls."

"Gee, Dad, what this means . . ."

His father looked at him seriously. "It's nothing you haven't earned, boy. I've been watching you from the first day you bought your car. I saw you go through that wild, reckless stage, and I almost took it away. Then I saw you fight for your organization, and I saw you're really serious about car design. And I've watched you drive according to your DTA rules when all the others gave up. I know it wasn't easy, but you did it, and alone. Now I'd like to help you win the reward you've earned."

"I guess you know I'll go to college before I start in business," Ricky said solemnly. "Boy, do I have a lot to learn before I dare work on anybody's car."

"You're coming along fine, Son," Madison said. "I know you have good sense, and now you have good goals. Stick by both."

"You bet I will!"

"And you'll be surprised, I think," Madison continued, "at just how much support you'll get from this town once it's convinced you are worth backing. It's a better town than you might think."

"I'm willing to give it the benefit of any doubt," Ricky said grandiloquently, and they laughed together, enjoying to the utmost their comradeship.

Because he was proud of his son's project, Madison talked about it to the editor and publisher of the Dellville *Recorder*. The following week Ricky was on the front page. There was a picture of him with his coupe and a story.

LOCAL BOY TO COMPETE
IN AUTO DESIGN SHOW

Under the headline there was a long story that told not only about Ricky and his plans, but that also mentioned him as a member of the Dellville Timing Association, the sponsoring group. And it told something about the DTA.

The results Ricky garnered from the story were quick and amazing.

The first phone call to him was from the local body shop, offering him use of their facilities, advice, and some labor.

The next caller was from one of the service stations. He offered Ricky free gas and oil in return for Ricky's endorsement.

The third call was from the big garage in Dellville, also offering space, tools and parts at dealer's prices.

A few days later the Booster Club collected fifty dollars to help costs, and Ricky's biggest thrill came when Sherm dropped around to offer him five dollars he had collected from former members of the DTA—who wanted to know when the next meeting would be held! And they offered to give him any parts they had which he needed.

Ricky was overwhelmed, and at first it seemed everything had been done. All he needed now was to attend the show and walk off with his prize. It was sobering and almost disheartening to realize that the work now had to be done. The real work.

Spare time ceased to exist in Ricky's life. He lived in the garage and the body shop.

First he had made the rounds with his plans, getting expert opinion, and he'd been forced to revise again and again as possibilities clashed with design again and again. And when at last he had a good, workable design, the physical work began. The stripping and cleaning, the pounding, shaping, lifting, hammering, filing, leading and sanding. Dull, laborious, dirty work that took hour after hour after hour.

The men at the body shop were interested, but they had their own work to do, and although they helped when they could, and did the most delicate work, the bulk of it fell to Ricky. They showed him where to hammer or file, and hammer and file he did, carefully, steadily, hour after hour after hour.

251

Sometimes his friends dropped in to help, but most of their help came in the form of advice or wishful talking. Sharon was working on plans for the interior. Once she had the measurements, they would decide on the colors and materials to be used.

Little by little the coupe assumed a new shape. Obedient to the torch it became lower and a little shorter. The shape of the nose changed to a simple curve with just the right amount of bend. The fenders changed too, sweeping back, dipping gently, fading into the body. And the rear fenders began, picking up at just the right point, and going back gracefully, in the right curve.

He had decided to keep it a coupe, but the lines were smoothed. It was combed back, so to speak, given a curved windshield, a graceful slope and a flowing rear deck. And when it was assembled and sanded to the bone, all joints leaded and smoothed, he was ready to paint. He wanted at least seven coats when the color had been decided upon.

He was sanding on it the night Sharon came in to ask about upholstery materials. He had been working hard for months and looked it. He was thinner, and pale, and his eyes were red-rimmed and tired. Now school had started again, and his working time had been cut way down.

Sharon looked at the unpainted body of the new coupe. Then she looked at Ricky. "You did it."

"Did what?"

"The lines you wanted. Even now it has a look of

252

lightness, of flight, almost. As though it would be as light and graceful as a bird. It's terrific."

"I see it jet black," Ricky said, sitting down tiredly. "Jet, glossy black. Like a panther."

"Black?" Sharon wrinkled her nose.

"Sure. With white leather upholstery."

"Like nine out of ten others will be."

Ricky's thin face sagged. "What else? That's where I'm weak, on colors."

"I have an idea," Sharon said. "If it works, you'll have a crowd around your coupe all the time. And that's what you want, attention."

"What's your idea?"

"I saw an interesting color combination for home decoration in a magazine. It combined pink, brown, and copper. It was . . ."

"Pink!" Ricky yelled. "Pink! Not *my* coupe, lady. Oh, no."

"But Ricky . . ."

"Pink!"

"I thought you'd react like that," Sharon said. "So I bought a little model car and painted it that way. Soft pink, brown and copper. Like this."

She unwrapped the little car she had brought and Ricky's eyes bulged. It was something!

The body of the car was a soft, glowing pink. The wheels and other metal trim had been tinted a coppery color instead of the usual chrome. The interior was the brown of good leather. The wheel was white, the dash a natural-wood tone. All metal parts were also coppery.

253

"Well?" Sharon asked.

Ricky looked from the little model to his coupe, seeing it done in the same way. Talk about something special. . . . It was terrific. It would steal the show.

"You've got it," Ricky said. "You've got it. You're a terrific partner. I . . . I could kiss you for that."

"Do you need *other* reasons?" Sharon teased.

The coupe's fate was decided. It would be pink, brown and copper.

"You know what?" Ricky said when they were walking home. "I'm going to keep that color scheme secret. I don't want anybody duplicating it. It's between you, me, the body shop, Dad . . ."

"Big secret." Sharon laughed.

"It will be. And we won't even let Dellville see it until the morning I drive to the show."

"You sound like a Hollywood publicity man," Sharon said. "But it's a good idea."

They walked along without talking for a few minutes. "Golly," Ricky suddenly said in an amazed tone. "I forgot how good it was!"

"What?" Her mouth was ready.

"Walking," Ricky said, striding on. "It's not half bad when you get used to it."

14

The secrecy did it. Had he worked openly, Dellville would have been bored and critical. But when Ricky's rod was put under wraps, Dellville became curious, and interested. Ricky wouldn't talk, nor Sharon, nor his father, nor the body-shop men who were helping. And because everyone working on the coupe kept the secret, Dellville wondered if it really had something big coming up.

Asked about his rod at school, Ricky would just grin and shake his head. Asked about it at the bank, his father would say it was "something," and change the subject. Queried at the cafe, the body-shop men would laugh and say that Dellville was going to be surprised, and that was all.

The way interest piled up, the day of the unveiling was looked forward to like a holiday, and the town made plans to send its boy off in style.

And the day came.

It was during the Thanksgiving holiday, and although school was out, the school band had assembled on the square, where Ricky's car would be shown for the first time. A few speeches were scheduled, and the Mayor was going to give him the town's blessing. They were proud of him, and they wanted him to know that Dellville was behind him all the way.

He didn't drive to the square. Rather than risk getting the coupe dirty, or in an accident, a car dealer had offered him the use of a truck to deliver the coupe to the show. It was on the truck, covered, and it would be shown to the town before they drove away.

Ricky sat beside the driver as the truck drove away from the body shop to the square. He was nervous, and scared. What if they were disappointed? What if they thought it stank? What if they booed?

As the truck went around the square toward its parking place in front of the city hall, the school band struck up the school song. Kids on bikes trailed the truck, and it sounded as if a million people were yelling.

As soon as the truck parked, the crowd closed in. Ricky climbed up the back and stood by the coupe, nervously fingering a corner of its canvas cover. The Mayor came up a small ladder and walked to Ricky, shaking his hand.

"Quite a day," Mayor Travis puffed, beaming at the crowd.

"I hope they like the coupe," Ricky said. "All these people . . ."

256

The Mayor signaled for quiet, and after the crowd had yelled a little louder in response, he said a few words. He said he guessed that both young folks and old cars were here to stay, and it was his opinion in this respect that if you couldn't beat 'em you jined 'em. He said the town was proud of the way Ricky had worked, and that if this was an example of the serious purpose behind the young folks' interest in cars, the town would be glad to cooperate. He said he had noticed certain young drivers with a certain sticker on their cars, with the initials of a certain club, and he had been impressed by their courtesy. He imagined, he said, that the council would be glad to listen to any plans they might have about auto-sports events.

When the cheers subsided the Mayor said he guessed he'd talked enough, and he was just as curious as the next fellow to see what their local young Henry Ford had turned out to take to the big city show. And that was the signal for the unveiling.

The canvas was rolled back and the little coupe was revealed to every eye in the brittle light of the November morning. For a moment the crowd was quiet, curiously quiet, and Ricky thought he had failed. And then the yell went up as the crowd surged forward for a closer look, and the little kids tried to swarm over the truck.

It was beautiful. The pink body shone with the soft depth of the inside of a sea shell, the copper trim and copper-wire wheels added a subdued richness. And the inside! Completely lined with a dark brown leather-like fabric, the instrument panel finished in antique

257

pine, the instruments ringed with a thin line of copper, and the steering wheel a circle of gleaming white.

Ricky stood by proudly while the crowd pressed in close around the truck, looking in the open doors of the coupe, exclaiming, amazed, impressed.

Arnie VanZuuk climbed the ladder at the back of the truck and walked toward Ricky, every ounce of his bulk exuding pleasure and pride.

"How do you like it, Arnie?" Ricky asked the big policeman.

"A beauty . . . ya, a beauty." Arnie chuckled. "Who would guess this is the same one you bought six months ago from Merle?"

"It has changed a little," Ricky admitted, ready to burst with pride. "Think I'll win any prizes?"

"I think you win them all," Arnie said. "But the big one you win is here."

"Here?"

"I think maybe you fellers get a drag strip. I been listening to the Mayor. You'd think it was his idea."

"The DTA guys have been pretty good," Ricky said. "And they all want to exhibit next year. I guess things are really going to work out."

"You have come a long way since that day you bought the car," Arnie said. "A long, good way. Ya, maybe we found the answer for you and some others now."

It was almost time to go, and time for Ricky to say something.

"I want to thank everybody who's been so kind to me," Ricky said as loudly as he could, his voice seeming to him thin and weak. "I couldn't have done what I did . . . did what I did . . . done . . . couldn't have built the coupe without an awful lot of help, and I'm thankful for it. If I win any prizes, they belong as much to everybody who helped as to me."

Ricky was able to pick out individual faces now. They looked friendly. He waved to a couple of his friends and grinned. Then he saw Link standing at the far edge of the crowd, leaning against a tree, looking superior and scornful. Ricky ignored the dark figure and moved his gaze to more cheerful faces.

"Before I leave," Ricky continued, "I want you to see how this coupe will be exhibited."

He unwrapped a long cylindrical object he had been carrying, and held it up, letting it unroll in front of him. The crowd let out a terrific yell. On gold letters, against a blue background (Sharon's idea and work), they read:

STREET ROD

Shown by

Ricky Madison

DELLVILLE TIMING ASSOCIATION

Ricky turned the sign from side to side, giving everyone a good look. Then he rolled it up and tossed it on the seat of the coupe. It was time to go. With several willing hands to help, the tarp was spread over the coupe again and tied down.

There were a few last farewells as he stood beside the cab of the truck before getting in beside the driver.

259

Handshakes and good wishes from the DTA guys, from his parents, from Arnie, the Mayor, and finally Sharon.

"I'm coming up on the bus tomorrow," she said, looking at him proudly. "And I'll ride back with you tomorrow evening—if you want me to."

"It's a date," Ricky said. "Wish me luck."

He climbed in the truck and looked out, smiling. His father and mother stood below him. They looked proud and happy. And he was proud of them. Proud of the way his father had worked beside him for weeks, and had the confidence to invest money in the project. Proud that his mother had understood, and hadn't minded their crazy schedule that upset the house.

He lifted his hand. " 'By, Mom . . . Dad . . ."

They waved back. "Good-bye, Ricky. Be good."

"I will."

The truck moved ahead slowly, the farewells echoed in his ears. This was it. He turned to say something to the driver and blinked. He hadn't noticed before. It was Merle.

Merle was grinning cautiously as Ricky looked at him. "Hi, sprout."

"Gee . . . hello, Merle. I didn't notice it was you."

"You were pretty excited. Nice rod you built."

"Yeah. It's all right, I guess." He didn't want Merle to feel bad, after their failure together.

"You still planning to have your own shop someday?"

"You bet I am. But I guess I'll go to college first. There's a lot I have to learn."

"Uh-huh. Well, if you ever need somebody to run the place for you, and you ain't got anybody else in mind . . ."

"I thought about that," Ricky said. "If I started in a small way while I was still in college, I thought you might be interested."

"I sure am," Merle said, wheeling the truck around a turn. "It could be big. Mighty big."

"Merle . . ."

"Sprout?"

"Did you see the nameplate on the coupe?"

"No. What'd you use?"

"Nothing outside," Ricky said, a half-ashamed smile on his face. "But inside there's a little monogram that reads C-M."

"Well, I'll be doggoned," Merle said. "Does it mean what I think?"

"I didn't forget the help you gave me, or the plans we made," Ricky said. "Merle, the Connor-Madison is on its way to its first public showing."

"Well," Merle repeated, pleased to the heels. "I'll be doggoned."

"There he goes," Ricky's mother said as the truck moved away.

"Our boy," Ricky's father said. "And what a boy."

"All grown up, and so suddenly. I . . . I missed him when he made the change . . ."

"It wasn't an easy time," Madison said, squinting at the retreating truck. "But he made it. He'll be all right now."

261

Arnie came up, grunting and puffing. "Good send-off, eh, Mr. Madison? He won't forget it soon."

"He really accomplished something, Arnie. We've been looking for the magic something. I guess this is it."

"Ya," Arnie said, his blue eyes twinkling deep in his big face. "A good boy, Ricky. A good boy."

Mayor Travis joined them, his red face friendly. "I hope you're proud of your boy, Madison."

"We sure are, Mayor."

"He's doing a great deal for himself," the Mayor lectured, "and a great deal for the town. The boys in that driving club have certainly made things easier and safer for us all. I do think they deserve a reward. I'd like to see Dellville turn up with the champion teen-age driving team in the state. And I think we can do it. We'll certainly try."

"Ricky will like that," Madison said.

"Well," the Mayor grumbled, "it's like I said—or maybe you didn't hear—if you can't beat 'em, jine 'em. And I think we have to admit—as I also said—that young boys and old cars are with us to stay. Yes sir, I would like to see this town lead the way in finding an answer to dangerous driving, and I believe we will, providing . . ."

The Mayor broke off. "There I go," he said petulantly, "making another speech. A fellow gets used to it, I tell you. Yes, he does. But I do believe, and I am not saying this to make a speech or curry favor . . . I do believe . . ."

Ricky's father nodded gravely at the Mayor's words, and turned to look at his wife, hoping to share the amusement he felt with her. But she wasn't listening to the Mayor. She stared after the departing truck, a tense, worried expression on her face.

Madison touched her arm lightly. "He's all right. Nothing to worry about now."

Ricky's mother sighed and smiled tiredly. "It's watching him go off with such high hopes and with everyone cheering," she said. "Suppose after all this is over he doesn't win anything? How do you think he'll feel if he has to return without any prize?"

"Oh, he'll win something," Madison said. "Don't worry."

"They should have waited until he did. It isn't fair to him. Just think of the letdown, the sense of failure he'll have if he doesn't win anything."

"He won't be the only one who doesn't win a prize —if he doesn't. And the other boys probably worked just as hard on their cars. He'll have to learn that hard work isn't always rewarded the moment it's done."

"I hope he wins something," Ricky's mother said as the truck disappeared. "Even if it's only a little pin, or a ribbon. But something! He needs to win something."

"We'll see," Ricky's father said. "We'll know to-morrow night."

15

Sharon arrived in Des Moines the following afternoon. She took a trolley-bus to the state fairgrounds, where the show was being held in one of the huge buildings.

The floor space was crowded with cars of every description. There were rods for show and rods that were built strictly for competition. There was everything from cars that sagged under the weight of chrome gadgets to stripped models that boasted little more than wheels, a seat, a steering wheel to go with the tremendous and beautiful power plant. There were rods of every size, shape, color and breed.

But it was easy to find Ricky. She headed toward the largest crowd, and sure enough, when she worked her way through, they were looking at the coupe.

The little car, like the others in the show, had been roped off to protect it from the over-curious and the souvenir hunters. Ricky stood just inside the roped

264

area, talking to another boy and writing in a little pad he carried.

Sharon moved toward him, waiting until he was through talking to the other boy before she moved into his line of vision. The moment he saw her, Ricky's eyes shone.

"You made it," he said in a pleased tone, putting away the notebook.

"I said I would. Your coupe certainly is popular."

"You don't know the half of it. Let's get something to eat and I'll tell you all about it."

Ricky called to a boy near him who was showing a compact little '34 Ford roadster that had been stripped of fenders, channeled, and sported a heavily-chromed Mercury engine with three carburetors. "Hey Swede . . . keep an eye on the coupe for me, will you? I'm going for chow."

The boy raised his hand and touched two fingers to his brow. "Will do, Ricky."

"Thanks."

Ricky took Sharon by the arm and steered her toward a lunch counter that had been set up. "What a time I've had here," Ricky said. "I'm dizzy."

"What from?"

Ricky took the notebook from his pocket as they sat at the counter. "Know what's in there?"

"How could I?"

"Names," Ricky said, his voice heavy with excitement. "Names. Names of at least a dozen guys who want to buy the coupe. All I have to do is name a price. And of all the guys who've asked me to make designs

265

for them! Honey . . . I mean Sharon . . . I'm in business!"

"Oh, Ricky . . . that's *wonderful!*"

"Wonderful . . . it's everything. It's . . . I can't believe it. Honest. I'm afraid I'll wake up and find out I'm dreaming."

"I was sure it would be this way," Sharon said loyally.

"It was your color scheme that did it," Ricky said. "The guys wander around and the first thing they look at are the rods with the top engines. You know. Full house Mercs, and GMC 270s with Hilburn fuel injectors. When they see enough engines, they start looking at bodies, and when they do that, they get around to me. And you ought to see their faces! After all, you can install any engine you want in anything you've got, almost, and the engine's only half of a sharp street rod. The guys want something different. So when they go by you know who it is. Something out of this world. Like the coupe."

"Eat your hamburger," Sharon ordered when Ricky stopped for breath. "You look half-starved."

"I haven't been able to eat." His gaze went back to the floor, toward the coupe. "You know, I've had people who aren't hot rodders ask me about the coupe too. One guy who wanted to know how much it would take for me to design him a new body for a Cadillac. You know what that means, Sharon? Do you know what that means? I'm on my way!"

Ricky took a couple of quick bites from his ham-

266

burger and pushed it away. "I can't eat," he said, getting to his feet. "Let's go back to the coupe. I might get a few more customers."

The show was over. The crowd was gone. All around the floor contestants were readying their rods to be driven or trucked home. Exhibitors were tearing down their displays and booths.

Sharon sat in the coupe, with the door open. Ricky sat on the floor, his back against a coppery wire front wheel. The gold cup was beside him. First prize, street-rod division. He was tired, sick to his stomach, feeling ready to cry.

Everything had worked out. Impossible everything. It was like a dream. He thought of the help Sharon had given him, and his parents, and the guys, and Merle, and Arnie. . . . They had been so good to him he wanted to shed tears of gratitude. And at the same time he felt sick. It was over. The work, the tension, the worry, it was all over. And now he felt an awful letdown, almost a feeling of despair. And tired . . . tired. . . .

A shrill whistle brought his head up, his eyes open. He scrambled to his feet as he saw them strolling toward him in their boots, Levis and black jackets. Jerry, Chub, Sherm . . . and Link.

"I see you fooled them," Jerry said, his handsome face showing his pleasure. "We heard about it on the radio, so we thought we'd be your honor guard home."

"Those judges must have been blind!" Chub exclaimed. "I saw fifty cars better than this broken-down heap. How much did you pay to win?" He grinned broadly, proud and pleased.

"Does everybody down home know I won?" Ricky asked.

"A couple of cats and dogs might not," Jerry said. "Well, you ready to go?"

"I'm waiting for Merle. We have to load the coupe on his truck."

"Awwww . . ." Chub's lip curled with disappointment. "Ain't you gonna drive home? We want a real parade."

Link spat. "Maybe it won't run under its own power," he said sarcastically.

"It might run better than you think," Ricky said grimly.

"No fights, you two," Jerry said.

"I ain't fighting," Link said. He cast a contemptuous glance at the coupe. "But I got a right to say what I think. I think it's a gook wagon. All show and no guts."

Ricky smiled. Link didn't know what was under the hood. He didn't know. He thought it was the same old engine. It was, mainly, but it had a three-pot manifold, Edelbrock high-compression heads, a 3/4-race cam, Kong ignition and a high-speed rear end.

"I know what you're driving, Link," Ricky said insolently. "But you don't know what I'm driving. You just take my word for it now—my coupe's got more guts in the paint than yours has under the hood."

268

"Talk is cheap," Link said, his lips curling. He looked hard and mean.

"Wait until we have that drag strip in Dellville," Ricky said. "You'll see."

"I think we're gonna get it too," Sherm said. "Everybody wants to join the DTA now, and the Mayor said if we can all keep out of trouble this winter, he'll see about the strip next spring. Boy, are we gonna have a slow-moving town!"

Ricky looked at Link's narrow, dark face. "You joined yet?"

"I'm no lousy kid. I drive the way I want to."

"You won't drag on our strip, then."

"If I don't, you won't have to run that gook wagon against me. Nice way to chicken out." He turned and walked away, spitting disdainfully. Ricky wanted to go after him and beat his brains out, but he kept his place. Link *would* try to spoil everything.

"Don't let him get your goat," Jerry said. "He's just mad because the guys are all following your lead. Let's go home."

"I need gas," Ricky said, his eyes still following Link.

Sharon looked troubled. "I thought Merle was coming with the truck."

Ricky shook his head, his eyes shining. "Naw. Not the truck. I'd like to drive back with the guys. You know something? I've never driven the coupe since it was re-designed. Maybe Link was right. Maybe it won't run."

"Roll it outside," Chub said. "We'll give you enough gas to get to a station. Got oil and water?"

"Yeah. But I didn't want gas while we were carrying it."

"Let's go, then."

"Grab on," Ricky said, tossing his gold cup on the front seat.

"Ricky . . ." Sharon was still troubled. "Let's wait for the truck."

He laughed and patted her cheek. "You're still worried about Link. He won't be anywhere near any parade I lead. And we won't race, will we, guys?"

"Race?" Jerry repeated, trying to look shocked. "We're DTA members." Still grinning he added seriously, "We won't do anything to gum up the works, Sharon. Don't worry."

The boys laid hands on the little coupe and rolled it toward one of the big doors. Sharon followed, actually pleased that they would drive back. She hadn't ridden in the coupe, and she wanted to know what it was like too.

Ricky drove out of Des Moines very slowly, with Jerry, Chub and Sherm following. They blew their horns, but not to make him hurry. They wanted everyone to see that they belonged with the prize-winning little car.

"Runs like a top," Ricky said to Sharon. "Handles like a dream. It's a feather. Oh, baby, but I bet it can drag! Some time I'll have to find a place where I can find out what it will really do."

270

"Not tonight," Sharon cautioned.

"Still worrying? I won't be careless. I've got everything to be careful for now. Why, I'm in business. I really am. I can probably get a bank loan now if I need money. Kid, I've got it made!"

They drove out of Des Moines on to the open highway. The night was bright and clear, the road was dry, there was little traffic.

Ricky pressed down on the gas pedal with just a little pressure. The coupe picked up like a bird. It rolled smoothly, easily, without effort, the twin pipes crooning. He glanced at his speedometer. Sixty! It didn't seem possible. He'd thought he was doing forty-five, at the most. There was that much difference between the new coupe and the old. Maybe that's what new shocks did for it—plus everything else.

He sailed down the smooth white highway behind his lights. It was so easy, so effortless. What a feeling, driving a rod that did everything right. Look at that . . . seventy, and he wasn't even trying. It was like something alive. It wanted to go. He couldn't hold it back.

He glanced at Sharon. She looked peaceful, happy and pretty. The ride was so smooth she didn't even know he was hitting seventy. If it was that smooth, it couldn't be considered speeding. He looked in his rearvision mirror. The guys were giving him plenty of room as they trailed him. Nobody was risking a sudden stop and a bump. Good guys! Ricky began to hum.

Sharon looked at him and smiled. "Happy?" she asked.

"So happy I could loop the loop with this baby."

"You sound happy."

"I've got plenty to be happy for . . ." He sang it. "Mainly you."

"Me?"

"You talked me into entering the show after I'd given up."

"I knew you would do a good job, I guess. And it was important not to give up the DTA ideals. That won a lot of respect for you."

"You did it, though. I was ready to give up and go back to ratting around."

"But you didn't."

"I won't, ever. I'm through with that crazy stuff. When I think of the crazy things I used to do. . . . I was stupid."

Sharon sighed and leaned back. She looked tired. Ricky smiled and began to sing quietly. He kept glancing at her sweet, relaxed face. Her eyes closed, the long lashes lying darkly against her cheeks. There was a faint smile on her full red mouth. He wanted to lean over and . . .

The lights were moving up on him. He knew . . . he knew. . . . The lights coming fast, like an arrow aimed at the back of his head. . . .

So this was Link's way. He wanted another of the same . . . the bumping, the bullying, and a fight, so he could use his fists. . . .

It was Link all right, and he was riding inches away from Ricky's back bumper.

Ricky glanced at Sharon. She was asleep. Tired as

she was, car motion wouldn't wake her. And once, just once. . . . It would be better than beating Link in a fight. Better than anything. It was the only thing that would cut Link down to size. Ricky knew now what was missing in his life. He had accomplished everything, reached every goal but the one he had striven for the longest without progress. Once to beat Link at something!

And this was it. This was the way. The night or day that he ran Link's convertible into the ground, the fight would be won. His life would be complete. It was all he needed to make everything perfect. Just once, and Link would never dare bother him again. He'd have Link where it hurt, and he could squeeze. Just once. . . . Now. . . .

He hit the gas pedal, but not too hard. He didn't want to jump the coupe and wake Sharon. She'd know about it later, but it would be over then. If she woke she'd stop him, and after all, if he'd won anything with all his hard work, he'd won the right to beat Link home on this particular night. And he would!

Ricky licked his lips and took a fresh grip on the steering wheel. He could feel the muscles in his face grow taut as he made his decision. He had more power and speed than ever before, and Link was asking for it. The one thing that stood between him and happiness, and tonight he would chase that shadow too. It had to be. It was fated. Everything was going his way now. All the omens were good. It was the night, with the guys there to see it, to run the wheels off Link for once and for all. He'd never have to do it again.

Seventy to eighty. Pink lightning on the road, smooth as cream. Link stuck with him doggedly.

Eighty-five. A tight grin thinned Ricky's lips. He bent over his wheel slightly, every sense alert. "You won't lead *this* parade home," Ricky muttered under his breath as though Link were with him. "Not *this* parade."

He knew Link's plan. To let Ricky stay ahead, breaking the path through the night until they were around the last S-turn. And then, with victory in sight, to let Ricky lead down the hill and across the bridge —and pass him.

Ninety. Sharon stirred slightly. Ricky cast a quick, anxious look in her direction. If she woke now . . . But she sighed and turned her head and slept again, more deeply. He relaxed. If she only knew. . . . But it had to be. Just once he had to humiliate Link. Just once.

He stopped looking at his speedometer or tach as his speed increased. He was going too fast to do anything but watch the road every second. How good it felt to split the night like the point of a knife, pipes blasting against the road! Speed . . . speed . . . Good speed. . . .

He was pulling away. He wanted to shout and whoop as he saw Link's lights slowly fall back. Link was eating his smoke now. And it was bitter. He could just see Link's face looking sour as a lemon, his black hair falling forward over his forehead as he saw the pink rod move away. Boy, would Link be sore.

Ricky's heart seemed to be flying as lightly and quickly as the coupe. He had Link whipped! Link couldn't stay with him! Now to pour it on!

He could have slacked off, staying just ahead, teasing with his lights, but he was going to give it to Link good. The fever was on Ricky. He was on his way, and he couldn't stop. His foot was down. It had to stay there.

He went into the first of the S-turns fifteen miles an hour faster than he'd ever dared before. And the little coupe stuck like glue. No pull, no drift, no wheel fight, no sway. Just the torque he needed to send him around with just a faint squeal from the tires. But the coupe snuggled down to the road and held on, and he knew he was pulling away from Link with every turn of the wheel.

Ricky came out of the last turn as fast as he dared push the coupe. Now the long hill dipped before him, and the concrete bridge, and then the long, straight flat. Tonight he'd find out what his horses could do!

On the way out of the turn Ricky pushed his foot to the floor. He made it around with rubber screaming. There were the lights of town, three miles away. Here was his victorious return. Tonight no one would lead him home!

Down the hill with the engine screaming like a dive bomber, the tach bouncing like mad. Down, down, down . . . all the way!

Sharon wakened suddenly as they lurched out of the turn. She heard the shrill roar of the engine, felt the terrific speed. Half-awake she looked at Ricky, beginning to understand the noise, the vibration, the tense, wild look on his face.

She meant to speak his name, but it came out a sleepy moan. He sensed she was moving, and turned to look at her. Halfway down the hill, moving faster than he had ever traveled before, steering a rod that looked like a kitten and drove like a bomb. Hurtling forward into the last few straight miles to home.

Halfway down the hill, a meteor of speed and noise, winding all the way up as it bettered a hundred . . . and five . . . and ten. . . .

Halfway down the hill, wide open, drifting toward the center of the road. Ricky eased the wheel back to the right. The drift to the left continued.

The tense smile became a look of horror. He wanted to scream, but there was no time for the sound to rise from his throat. He was still pulling the wheel to the right, his foot on the gas, when the coupe left the road.

The rough shoulder tossed the front end high. The pink coupe roared into the air, twisting in agony. That first surge tore Ricky from the wheel. His head met Sharon's with a bone-splintering crunch.

They were unconscious when the coupe hit on its nose, bounced high, cleared the low end of the bridge and dropped into the black water top first. Before the splash was over the little car sank out of sight, its copper-colored wire wheels turning slowly as they sank, like little waterwheels.

The coupe was still sinking when Link roared

around the last S-turn in his convertible, hurling his car forward with a raging foot. As he started down the hill with the engine wide open he looked for Ricky's taillights ahead. There were no lights.

Link couldn't believe that Ricky was across the flat. It couldn't be . . . unless Ricky had a full-race Merc under his hood. Even so . . .

Link roared across the bridge, his echo rolling over the muddy water that swirled over the little coupe. He didn't know where Ricky was, but he wouldn't give up. Gas pedal to the floor he raced on as fast as his convertible would travel. He didn't care what Rick had. He'd catch up with him yet!